ACKNOWLEDGEMENTS

I am very grateful to Victoria Blake, Daryl Arambhan, Bruce Winslow, Jonathan Dyson, and my editor, Andrew Hinkinson for making invaluable suggestions for the improvement of this novel. I am also greatly indebted to Jean Drèze and Amartya Sen for the socio-economic information in their book, *An Uncertain Glory: India and its Contradictions*.

For Brian and Audrey

with love

The Assassins

The Assassins

JEREMY TRAFFORD

SPELLBINDING
MEDIA

LONDON

Published by Spellbinding Media 2014

Copyright © Jeremy Trafford 2014

First published in Great Britain in 2014 by
by Spellbinding Media.

www.spellbindingmedia.co.uk

Spellbinding Media Ltd Reg. No. 08482364
A CIP catalogue record for this book is available from the British Library

ISBN 9781909964099

Typeset in Adobe Garamond by ForDesign, London
Printed and bound by TJ International Ltd, Padstow, Cornwall

Chapter One

Clare and Max left the temple through the gateway of a soaring tower that was carved with a hundred gods and goddesses. They walked towards the main square, where an election meeting was taking place. A crowd was being fervently addressed through an amplifier. Clare watched Max as he threaded his way through the crowd towards the speaker. Huge silken flags rippled in the breeze. The orator's voice, passionate and strong, reverberated and crackled around the square. Max got in closer, so he could take some photos of the man. The flags and glossy banners, and the enormous posters of politicians would all make for an effective and dramatic background, he thought as he took his shots, with the ancient temple tower brooding over this tense, animated, modern scene.

Two young men followed Max as he worked his way back to Clare. They thrust their way through the crowd. Clare, watching through the glare of a spotlight as her husband approached, could see the faces of his pursuers clearly. One of them was somewhat fat, with a thick moustache. The other was younger, hardly more than a boy. They seemed very determined to catch up with Max. He reached her side completely unaware of them.

The spotlight moved on over the crowd. Clare shouted out, seeing the boy trying to snatch Max's camera. In response, Max seized him in a judo hold, twisting his arm up behind him until he shouted in pain, and the camera fell from his grip. As Max picked it up, the man with the moustache flicked open a knife and made a feint lunge; the steel glinted in the light. Max let go of the boy, who sprang to his feet and moved out of reach. Clare was struck by his tearful, flashing eyes, with their look of injury and anger. He stared at Max for an instant before darting away with his companion, who threw a threatening look behind him.

The crowd swayed and jostled. There were shouts and startled faces, and a growing murmur of excited sympathy. An old man with a huge, untidy turban yelled in indignation. A cow ambled forward, waving its heavy head as if it disapproved. The voice of the orator angrily rattled on, enunciating endless grievous facts, while, high above, a rushing explosion shook the air. Fireworks. They burst into a hundred glittering threads of light that illuminated a tall, bearded figure lurching heavily on his crutches towards Max and Clare. Upon reaching them, he opened his mouth and pointed into it, holding out his begging bowl with a solemn look of dignity upon his face. He was middle-aged, his beard flecked with grey. As Max gave the man some money he leant forward to peer into his face, then Clare's, before touching his head in a gentle salutation and swinging away.

Clare saw the two youths dart out of the crowd to join the cripple in a tense debate. She noticed that the fat one seemed frustrated as he looked at Max, as if there was more to the attack than the theft of an expensive camera. But this was mere conjecture on her part. It worried her more to think that they were somehow connected with the cripple, that he might not have been as harmless as he'd appeared.

'Max,' she whispered urgently, 'I think they might be planning to have another try.'

'Let's go,' he replied.

As they walked away, Clare noticed with dismay that the youths were in pursuit, appearing and disappearing from view among the people milling about in the street. Sometimes they were silhouetted by exploding fireworks; sometimes they were hidden in the shadows. She could hear them calling out menacingly. One of the youths came near, as if about to lunge at Max again to seize his camera. The other shook his fist in the smoky air.

Eventually Clare and Max put some distance between themselves and the youths and managed to lose them. At least they could relax now, although Clare kept looking behind, just in case. As they walked, Max started talking about something else. He referred to the corruption that had recently become a major issue in Indian politics, and the courage of Venkataraman, the speaker in the square, in apparently confronting it so strongly.

'But Westerners are not so spotlessly corrupt that they can condescend to India on the matter,' Max added. 'Not after some of our recent Congressional and Parliamentary financial scandals.'

Trying to dismiss the attempted mugging from her mind, Clare began to worry about her marriage instead, as she had for a while now. Who or what was taking her husband's interest away from her? She imagined it might be Vijaya, a vivacious and humorous woman they'd got to know while staying with

Vijaya's brother, Narayan, in Chennai. As Clare thought about Vijaya's luxuriant black hair, she considered her own, very English, looks: her pale, thirty-year-old face, blue eyes and auburn hair made her appear so conspicuous out here in Southern India. Max could conceivably have developed an attraction to Narayan's sister because of his close friendship with Narayan, who occasionally seemed to subtly flirt with Clare. Or did she flatter herself in suspecting this? He'd surely never risk the comradeship with Max that had led to Max and Clare's visit in the first place. However, Narayan had said Vijaya was very much in love with her cousin, Tamilazhagam, whose name they shortened to Tammy.

Tammy was an odd puzzle of a man, really. He'd come with them on this expedition but was waiting back at the hotel. He'd refused to join them at the temple, although he'd looked curiously torn when Clare had pressed him to do so.

As they reached the hotel, Clare watched a few streamers sail across the temple's silhouette. They sputtered in the air, their delicate embers floating slowly down. She could make out the temple's tower in the moonlight, looming above the crowded streets. She heard the resonant clanging of its bell. But then the brutal memory came back: the boy seizing the camera and then shouting in agony; the older one with his flick-knife; the glint of sharp steel. She imagined that knife ripping into Max's muscular smooth body, and a sudden warmth of tenderness spread through her. Fearful, thinking Max could have been killed in that terrible moment, Clare decided to summon up the courage to discuss their marriage with him.

Tammy had been waiting on the veranda of the hotel. A meal was ordered and he listened, intrigued, as Max told him about the attempted theft of the camera.

'They could've been ordinary thieves,' Tammy said. 'There are enough of those. Or they could, conceivably, have had political loyalties that your photography might've offended.' He paused, looking at Max. 'You can seem a touch intrusive with that telescopic lens of yours. They may not like their leaders being snapped without consent, especially by someone standing out as much as you do. They might think you a nosey foreign journalist, or a shady CIA agent.'

'I try not to be too intrusive with my photos,' Max said.

Tammy grinned broadly, as if wanting to emphasise that he'd been joking. He led Max and Clare upstairs, where he produced a bottle of whisky. While he poured the drinks, he talked about being an economist in India.

'I'm driven round the bend by the country's problems,' he said. 'This is the sorry fate of many economists out here.'

The meal arrived.

'Some vegetarian mess wrapped in a banana leaf,' Tammy said with joke disparagement.

Max had come to like the spicy food.

'Chilli hunger,' Narayan had called it when telling Max and Clare back in Los Angeles how much he craved the pungent, vegetarian dishes of his homeland.

'It keeps my Indian soul intact, even after a year of insidious Americanisation,' he'd said laughingly. If only Narayan had come with them, Max thought for the hundredth time. He longed for Narayan's lively curiosity and the way he talked about his background with the exuberant affection that characterised his general attitude. Still, he wasn't there. Max turned his thoughts back to Tammy as they began to eat. He couldn't understand why Tammy had been so keen to come to this distant town of Madurai, given that he hadn't wanted to visit its famous temple.

A fan rotated sluggishly on the ceiling, squeaking in complaint as if every revolution was going to be its very last. Max ate using his fingers, Indian style, as Narayan had taught him. Clare, who was less ambitious, relied upon a spoon. Outside, the noise of the electioneering was getting louder. A parade was going around the town, heading in their direction. Tammy was telling them about a regional political figure who, after years of spectacular misrule, recently had the good grace to die.

'He was a hammy film star earlier in his life, and his flashy ostentation commanded huge loyalty from the sheep-like masses. In truth, he was appallingly corrupt. He appointed sycophantic lackeys to overpaid positions. He handed out dodgy contracts to his backhanding cronies and ruthlessly suppressed any rivals. Now they've decided he was a monster and they clamour for change.'

Max listened sceptically to Tammy, whose political information seemed to be so luridly exaggerated. Max and Clare were working on a book together on India, Max taking the photographs collaborating with Clare on the text. Their aim was to provide a balanced portrait of modern India, avoiding too much cynicism and doom as well as excessive optimism. It was through getting to know Narayan in Los Angeles that the ambition to produce the book had been born. Narayan had been flattered by Max's interest in India. When he learned that Max had written a book on Mexico and had studied comparative religion, he suggested that Max write a book about India. Max had been flattered but wondered if he and Clare were really up to it. He still did at times, despite Narayan's enthusiastic help, and Tammy's. The insights provided by this economics lecturer were especially beneficial.

'Of course,' Tammy went on, 'the chemical works and nuclear reactors have done wonders for India's morale, regardless, that is, of the dire environmental side effects or the fact that we could've put the money to much better use by spreading it around more.'

'Spending it on what in particular?' asked Max. 'What are the priorities in your view?'

'We need drains and tractors, and mobile medical units, and drilling equipment to combat increasing water shortages. The trouble is, we're far too keen on national prestige and less concerned with popular well-being. So we make these gestures of false affluence and ignore our real problems: poverty, disease and massive social inequality. There's inadequate spending on health and education and on the feeding of our undernourished children.'

Tammy's voice drifted away, or seemed to as far as Clare was concerned. She was thinking about her marriage again. She remembered the figure of Vishnu tenderly holding Lakshmi in the temple. It brought to mind an awareness of how open Hinduism was to amorous relationships, and how it celebrated sexual, married love such as she and Max had known for two years now. She and Max had met in a hilltop castle, eighty miles from Rome. They'd been on a study course that covered Italian language and civilisation. The castle had been reluctantly converted into a hostel, but it retained its leaking roof, reverberating plumbing and elderly, spasmodic electricity.

Max had shyly invited Clare up to his room, which overlooked a narrow valley that corkscrewed through the hills. She stood beside him at the window while he talked about his father, whose affection he'd always craved but whose political views he had abhorred. This came to a head with Bush's invasion of Iraq, which his father had strenuously supported and Max had angrily opposed. He spoke of their bitter arguments, his father's illness and their partial, uneasy reconciliation. He seemed so stressed about it that Clare felt the need to say he shouldn't hand his father such power over him by caring so painfully about what he thought.

Max had kissed her then, on the lips, for the very first time. It had been diffident at first but it deepened as Clare responded. She'd sensed he would make no further moves unless invited, which she found both challenging and reassuring. As she said goodnight to him, she knew she wanted to go on seeing this troubled man who had been so open with her.

'Look, I'd better join the crowds outside,' Max said all of a sudden, breaking into Clare's reverie. 'There's the potential for some really good pictures. Clare, don't bother to come. It's been a long day. You're pretty whacked.'

Max got to his feet and reached for his camera. Tammy rose too, apologising to Max and hoping he hadn't hogged the conversation.

'Was I being too sweeping and dogmatic?' he asked.

'Oh don't worry,' Max said. 'I like your critical spirit. It's just my photographer's neurosis coming into play. I'm terrified of missing out on some great photos.'

'Sit down, Tammy,' said Clare as Max departed. 'Have more whisky.'

Tammy smiled at her, a little awkwardly. She liked his face but no one could convincingly call him good looking. He had a beaky nose and irregular features, and his skin was paler than Narayan's. Clare thought Narayan more handsome, although he seemed genuinely oblivious to the fact. Vijaya was paler still. Her disarming little jokes and delicate gestures contrasted with the anger she expressed about the inferior status of most women in India. Clare wondered once more about Vijaya and Max, but her suspicion seemed far-fetched. Then she thought about Tammy's feelings for Vijaya. He seldom mentioned her; when he did, he did so casually. He often assumed an air of cool indifference, as if he thought this made him seem self-possessed.

Clare decided she must press him gently on the subject – but not now.

'Have you read the Bhagavad Gita?' she asked him instead. 'Or perhaps you're so involved with the problems of modern India that your ancient classics seem irrelevant.'

'You know, the trouble you India freaks cause us poor Indians,' said Tammy, smiling. 'I was shamed into reading it at

Cambridge.'

'In Sanskrit?'

'You must be joking! Our classic language is Greek to me because of all that foreign education my Anglophile father insisted on. He sentenced me to a frigid English public school, in thrall to muscular Christianity, football and the sacred cricket pitch. I suffered from English insularity and just a touch of politely hidden racism. When I first returned to India, I felt like a sort of rootless and out-of-place expatriate.'

'Did you do anything about that?' Clare asked.

'Yes. I travelled around India to find my roots. It's an incredibly beautiful country, with its temples and mosques, great rivers, palaces and forts. Even the simple villages have a quiet beauty, with peacocks perching in banyan trees, and goats and monkeys and cattle ambling down the streets. The people are so friendly and smiling. And the vibrant colours of the clothing… the saris and turbans… I'd almost forgotten how gorgeous they could be. For the first time I fell in love with my own country, in spite of all its problems and basic poverty. One forgets the primitive sanitation!'

'Did you do all this travelling alone?'

'No. I went with an Indian Muslim friend, Shahpur. We met at Cambridge, where we both read economics and became close friends. There are 180 million Muslims in India, and he opened my mind to their religion. I tried to give him some vague idea of mine, although he's a practising Muslim and I'm a rather lapsed Hindu.'

'How did he open your mind about Islam?'

'Well, about jihad for instance. The non-Islamic world thinks this means only holy war, but it principally means our inner war, in the cause of God. It's about the fight between good and evil in one's own self, despite what a tiny minority of hotheads might assume. God is closer to us than our own jugular veins. There's nothing between God and ourselves. It's a fine religion. The Koran exalts compassion, brotherhood and social justice. It stresses the moral and spiritual equality of the sexes, giving women the legal rights of inheritance and divorce.'

'I didn't know all of that,' Clare said. 'Getting back to feeling like an expatriate, I'm one too, I suppose. An Englishwoman living in Los Angeles, married to an American. But does having a country really matter? Belonging to one exclusively, I mean.'

'Your case is different. I've got my over-extended family here, and this is where I'm expected to settle down and marry. You've met Vijaya. She's a nice, high caste, traditional Indian girl, although she deplores the caste system as much as I do. She's very sweet and has quite a sense of humour. I just can't see us making a success of being married.'

'That depends on whether you find her anything more than sweet and nice. You speak of her very condescendingly. It's very unappealing.'

'I'm sorry, but she's so limited. She's hardly left her wondrous South India. Okay, she once went to stay with some old relatives in Kolkata, where they're sacrilegious enough to actually eat meat. As much as she hates me pouring fiendish booze down my throat, she's far more shocked if I gorge myself on the flesh of animals. She's full of feminist outrage, and I sympathise. But beneath the surface sophistication, surely you can see how naive she is. How can I talk to her about the real India, about the blood and guts of the poor country?'

'And where is this real India, in your opinion?'

'Out there,' he said, gesturing through the window at the packed and sweltering town. 'The reality of India is open drains and undernourished children, of which I've made a recent study. Over forty per cent of children here are underweight or stunted. Half of all living accommodation lacks flush toilets, so there's open defecation, which breeds disease, something Vijaya is too refined and sheltered to discuss. There's hideous overcrowding in the cities and the shantytowns are proliferating. It's no wonder there's growing frustration, communal prejudice and strife. I lecture and write about these things in the hope of pressuring government to try and make them better.'

'Has there been all that much strife in recent years?'

'There's always the underlying possibility. It erupted at Ayodha ten years ago, when there were riots across Northern India. Shahpur came from near there. Thousands of Muslims were killed, and his terrified family had to flee. Hindu fundamentalists demolished an ancient mosque they claimed had been built above an even more ancient Hindu holy place. A few extremist Hindu nationalists urged them on, but it was deeply regretted by the Hindu moderate majority. Such rabid fanaticism! Such senseless rage and violence! The real enemies aren't other people's races and religions but hunger and the lack of plumbing and clean water, with the typhus and cholera that inevitably follow.'

Although Clare was impressed by the range and eloquence of

Tammy's opinions, she wanted a breath of air, and she suggested they move onto the terrace. The breeze had dropped. The moon seemed icy and remote. A moth trembled past on soft wings. A bat hurtled down, shuddered in mid-flight, then vanished like the shadow of a moment. A burst of cheering rent the air, briefly drowning out a pop song, all throbbing beat and quivering melody. An amplified political speech came echoing raucously over the rooftops. A large and brightly lit open-top bus was moving slowly along the street below.

Eventually, Clare spoke.

'Surely you can discuss all of that with Vijaya?'

'Vijaya? Cocooned as she is within her privileged, cushy background?'

'Who isn't cocooned a bit? We all need a cocoon to some extent.'

'You've managed to escape from yours. You're so adventurous, Clare. Coming out here, wanting to know about all things Indian… the grim as well as the good. I want to help with your book. I admire you so much.'

'That's nice of you. But, without being boringly full of wifely pride, there's more to admire in Max. Not that either of us are all that wonderful.'

'You are very wonderful to me,' Tammy said.

As Clare looked into Tammy's eyes, she saw bewilderment and much anxiety. She turned away, wanting to discourage the feelings she feared she was sensing but not to snub him. She gazed down at the bus, with Venkataraman up aloft. People waving flags and banners followed the exuberant procession. Clare looked across at the now-distant temple tower, seeing in her mind those gods and goddesses, carved on its sides, gazing serenely down at what went on in the hectic world below: all the excitement and frustration, conflict and confusion of the human heart.

'I've been feeling this for a while,' Tammy said. 'It's why I came with you on this trip.'

'You'd no right to come because of that.'

'I know. It's wrong of me. I suppose it was the way we talked together. Vijaya's so backward looking. She's got a whole collection of ancient carvings. Her room is like a shrine… a shrine to a past age. She has so little involvement in the present, living world, apart from her fervent feminism.'

'Then why not help her to become more involved?'

'I don't want to marry her, Clare,' Tammy said bluntly. 'That's the truth of it.'

'You're surely a free agent. Do you feel bound by your dead parents' wishes?'

'It's not just that. It's the expectations of both our families. It's Narayan, who's been like a brother to me since our childhood. Vijaya is like a kid sister. I can't bear the thought of hurting her in what would be a cruelly public manner. She'd be totally humiliated. All this makes me feel so claustrophobic.'

'I'm sorry, Tammy. I see your problem.'

He looked at her. What he said came out so softly Clare thought she had misheard him.

'I'm afraid I've fallen in love with you.'

Time stopped for Clare for a few awkward, heavy seconds. Tammy's words were absurd. She felt he had had no right to be embarrassing her like this.

'That's mad,' she said. 'I don't believe you.'

'Please believe me.'

'You shouldn't say things like that, Tammy. I love Max more than I can say. I think I'd better go. I'm sorry.'

Clare left, feeling an urgent need to be with her husband. What Tammy had said was both annoying and unreal. She didn't believe he loved her, although, frustrated as he was over his engagement, he might indulge himself with such a fanciful idea. She thought she might find Max following the electioneering bus and so she went downstairs, trying to wipe Tammy's words from her mind. Out on the street, she turned a corner and found herself in a throng of people pushing along and cheering. Between the whoops and shouts, she could hear Venkataraman's continuing oratory and the whooshes and bangs of the fireworks. Over the noise, she heard Tammy call her name, doubtless anxious about her venturing alone into this seething mass of people. She really disliked him saying he loved her. It was just a transient infatuation, and one she had to tactfully discourage.

There came a burst of applause as the bus – draped with strings of marigolds – turned a corner. Its sides were painted with scenes of a glowing heaven-upon-earth. There was a hero, glaring with romantic fierceness, a plump heroine, lustrous-eyed and smiling beatifically, and a flight of crimson parrots. A multicoloured elephant and a cow with golden horns also formed part of this touching vision of paradise.

The drums beat on. Some boys were jogging along and

dancing. A man on crutches dipped with a convulsive movement of his shoulders. The bus was crawling past, and Clare found herself being pushed with sudden violence. On top of the bus, Venkataraman was energetically waving at the crowd. Someone threw a flower up at him, which he caught with surprising skill. Two small, excited boys sat on the bumpers beneath ropes of wilting flowers and dusty paper streamers. Joss sticks sent up smoky threads of incense that mingled with the smells of sweat and diesel fumes.

Tammy caught up with Clare. He was smiling hesitantly, as if about to apologise for declaring his love. Clare couldn't see Max anywhere, but she suddenly found herself next to the thin boy who'd tried to snatch Max's camera. She'd clearly seen his face before the incident, but Max hadn't because it had been dark. The boy was pushing forward now, and she was struck by his expression of fear and by his smooth, good looks; they were extraordinary, even for India, where beauty and ugliness were starkly contrasted. The boy was trembling slightly, as if nervous, his mouth slightly open and his eyes a little tearful. In front of him was his overweight accomplice. He put his hand on the boy's shoulder in a gesture of affectionate encouragement.

Then he noticed Clare and seemed to recognise her.

Clare caught her breath and tried to hang back, but the crowd was irresistibly carrying her along. On her left hobbled a man with crinkly hair dangling down to his shoulders and parallel white lines painted on his forehead. On her right strode a tall, middle-aged woman with fiercely made-up eyes and a distinctly imperious air. She seemed to be the leader of a group of women, whose brilliant saris in red, vermilion and icy green contrasted with the stark whiteness of the clothing of the men or with their dark, naked upper torsos.

The two youths were conferring with an older, bearded, man. It was the man Clare had seen earlier, whom she now recognised as the cripple who had approached them with his begging bowl. The boy seemed fearful as the cripple and the boy's companion urgently exhorted him. The cripple had a commanding but not unkind expression. The boy at first seemed unwilling to do something. He briefly argued back, stammering in frustration. The plump youth stared at Clare, as if disliking her observation of them, while the boy's nervous glances gave way to a look of steely resolution.

A push from behind carried Clare right to the back of the bus, where she saw a tiny, shivering monkey held by a smiling boy riding on the bumper. He had displaced the boys who had been sitting there, and they were now trudging sulkily along behind. The monkey clung tightly to the boy with wrinkled and leathery black fingers. It twisted its head to stare with enormous, blinking eyes at the people around it.

The bus stopped completely, such was the crush of people in the street. The women had been pushed into a huddle, which the tall woman did not appreciate at all. She glared haughtily around, hands held up in protest at this unceremonious treatment of her flock, which she was bossily trying to protect like a flustered mother hen. Her flock paid her scant attention, though, and carried on smoothing their saris and chewing betel nut. One of them opened her reddened mouth to merrily spit out the juice. They were chattering to each other excitedly.

All attention was diverted. The fat youth bent down and the younger one jumped on his back, vaulted up the side of the vehicle, caught the railing and swung his legs up and over. An astonished cheer rose up at this achievement. The women shrieked out their approval. The boy had been holding a marigold between his teeth, which he now presented to Venkataraman with a theatrical low bow, perhaps something he seen in some romantic Bollywood film full of improbable heroics. Nonetheless, it was rather touching.

Venkataraman smiled and stepped forward to accept the flower. Clare wondered if this was why the boy had been so scared? Had it been the stage fright of an ardent devotee? Was it political devotion that had made him try to seize Max's camera? Maybe he hadn't wanted his hero photographed without consent, as Tammy had suggested. That could explain his look of mild fanaticism. Perhaps he was a shade simple-minded too, bowing so extravagantly low, as if struck with sudden shyness, before moving quickly forward to embrace the speaker.

The women clapped their hands, which sparkled with bright rings. Venkataraman looked surprised as the youth put his arm around his neck. At this, the women raised their arms, bangles jangling, and made further noises of encouragement. Venkataraman smiled again, less certainly this time, and hesitantly accepted the embrace.

But then the boy's arm drove hard forward. His elbow jerked backwards with a plucking motion, and he again thrust forward with a violent twist.

Venkataraman looked astounded and let out a sharp cry. The boy held his body close but as though it were a shield to prevent his face being seen.

The cheering died away to a hush. Then there came a throb of strident music, fast and hectic, vibrating along the narrow streets. A trumpet blared. A drum was beaten. The man and boy seemed to cling to one another, as if in some weird climax of devotion.

But then Venkataraman stumbled backwards.

A knife had been stuck into his chest.

Blood was pulsing from the wound, spreading through Venkataraman's shirt and down his arm.

Clare looked away in horror. She saw the cripple again, with his grizzled beard and furrowed cheeks. He was staring up at Venkataraman with a look of appalling triumph. Seconds later, he noticed Clare. Their eyes met, for just a second, and then his gaze returned to the terrible scene above.

One of the women let out a stifled scream. A heavy collective groan spread among the onlookers. Venkataraman slumped against a horrified colleague. Two of the women clung to each other, shrieking. A guard edged forward, holding a revolver.

The boy suddenly leapt over the side of the bus. He hit the ground right next to Tammy, who seized him around the waist. They faced each other, and the boy began twisting frantically in Tammy's grasp. He stared into his face, whimpering in frustration. He thrashed the air with his arms and shouted out. His mouth was trembling. His shirt was patchy with his victim's blood. The older youth dodged forward and raised a knife, glaring aggressively at Tammy. Before he had time to attack, the tall woman stepped forward. Her mouth gaped open, with its snaggle teeth and bright red gums. Incensed, she spat a gob of betel juice into the moustachioed face.

The young boy broke free of Tammy.

The guard jumped down. The swaying crowd pushed Clare until she was almost off her feet. Although seized by a momentary, claustrophobic panic, she managed to recover her balance and found the older youth standing right in front of her. He looked at her with hostility before he and his accomplice bolted off and vanished down an alley. The guard fired at them but missed. Two astonished colleagues were supporting Venkataraman, a look of utter disbelief on his face.

There was pandemonium. People began running in all directions, wailing and shouting. Clare saw a thin little girl toddling forward, weeping. She looked totally lost and seemed about to be trampled on by people hurtling about in confusion. In terrified bewilderment, the girl fell to the ground, where a man almost stumbled over her in panic. Clare pushed forward and snatched the girl up. She held the child close and could feel the heavy thumping of her heart within her emaciated, trembling body.

The cripple came swinging up, distraught and gasping, accompanied by a woman in a state of hysteria. They'd seen Clare rescuing the child and looked at her with enormous gratitude. Tammy spoke with them in Tamil. He told Clare the cripple was the child's father. His wife had been knocked down in the rush and the crowd had carried off their child. Clare handed the girl over to the cripple. He cradled his daughter in his arms with desperate protectiveness, tears of relief welling in his eyes. The little girl clung tightly to him, while his wife sobbed uncontrollably.

Clare gazed into the cripple's face, realising this was the man she'd seen with that repulsive look of triumph just after Venkataraman had been stabbed. She'd first seen him after the camera incident. Had he approached them at the time only to see their faces better? Had the youths conferred with him? Had the three of them plotted to seize the camera because Max had photographed something they didn't want recorded? Was he their accomplice or the mastermind?

The man handed the child to his wife, who was talking rapidly. She was pleading with the cripple, in ashamed apology for having lost their daughter in the turmoil. The cripple spoke to her forgivingly, and she gazed at him in thankful adoration. He explained to Tammy that they'd been childless for many years; their only child had been born to them late in life, and they felt very blessed because of her. Turning back to Clare, he put his hands together in the gesture of Namaste, and his wife bowed her head and touched her forehead.

Guards rushed past, chasing after the youths. Clare heard the siren of a police car. Venkataraman, who was still on his feet and being supported by two horrified colleagues, seemed mesmerised by the fireworks that had incongruously started up again, exploding in glittering hoops and whirling circles in a mad crescendo of now wholly inappropriate celebration. Amazingly,

Venkataraman still held the flower, now soaked in blood that dripped as if it leaked his life away. The cripple continued to regard Clare with great appreciation, honouring her with another salutation before turning and moving away; the little girl was carried by her weeping mother.

The police and the ambulance arrived. Venkataraman was laid upon a stretcher. He stared at the sputtering fireworks, their descending sparks extinguished one by one, as if he was gazing at some bright yet disappearing vision. As he was lifted into the ambulance, the tall woman placed a red hibiscus flower on his chest. One of her followers, a crystal stud in her nostril and a shimmer of blue beads around her neck, took the coil of flowers from her hair and placed it at Venkataraman's feet.

Tammy offered himself to the police as a witness. Clare wanted to do the same, but he advised her to return to the hotel. He asked a policeman to accompany her there, and they walked past huddled groups of murmuring people. When they reached the hotel, Clare was anxious to find out where Max was. She went up to their bedroom and was relieved to find him already there. He hadn't followed the procession after all but had returned to the temple to take more photos. When she told him about the stabbing, he was appalled. He held her in his arms with that firm protectiveness she loved.

Tammy returned about twenty minutes later, saying that the police wanted to see him again the next day. He said Venkataraman wasn't expected to survive. The police pursuit of the assassin had been in vain, and they regarded Tammy as the best eyewitness. They seemed confident he would be able to describe the young boy. No one else had seen the face of the assassin clearly, that hypocritical low bow having served its purpose.

'I told the policeman who brought me back here about the cripple,' Clare said. 'And I told him I can identify the killer and his accomplice.'

'If it gets round that a European woman saw what happened, you could surely be in danger,' Max said.

'Well I insist on talking to the police again at some point,' Clare declared.

The following morning it was announced on the news that Venkataraman had died in hospital in the early hours.

'I'm really angry,' Clare said over breakfast. 'The savagery of it, disguised in that gesture of false homage! I hope those assassins are caught as soon as possible. I must talk to the police.'

She didn't have to go to see them. Inspector Veerapan, a senior police official, had been quickly flown down from Chennai and put in charge of the case. He came to see Clare and Tammy. The Inspector, a man with meticulously combed hair and a politely mournful manner, told them he'd been involved in the investigation into Rajiv Gandhi's assassination in 1961.

'His murder was unwittingly filmed by an amateur photographer,' he said. 'The photographer died in the explosion but his camera was found at the site. That was an election meeting, too. Rajiv was approached by a suicide terrorist who had an explosive device hidden under her sari. As she touched his feet in pretend respect, she detonated it. I hear

Venkataraman's assassin approached him with similar false devotion, but no one inadvertently filmed this killing. At least not as far as we know.'

'They could be lone fanatics with personal, obsessive grievances,' Tammy suggested.

'I agree it's possible,' said the Inspector. 'I fear, however, that they're hit men hired by some group that felt threatened by Venkataraman's campaign against corruption.'

Max told him about the attempted theft of his camera.

'Do you think there's a connection?'

The Inspector nodded.

'I think it's very likely,' he said. 'I suspect you must have unwittingly photographed more than just Venkataraman speaking.'

'The cripple and the older youth urged on the younger one,' said Clare. 'He seemed nervous at first. He seemed reluctant. The cripple looked… well, he looked triumphant when Venkataraman was stabbed. The killer looked so delicate and innocent, though.'

'That might be why he was chosen,' the Inspector said. 'Anyone looking rough or sinister would hardly have presented a flower without exciting suspicion. The guards would've been alerted. Venkataraman wouldn't have so readily stepped forward. This suggests it was a group operation, and the boy had been carefully selected.'

'He'd probably been chosen because of his slimness and agility,' Tammy added. 'The other youth was far too fat and lumpish to have been able to leap up the side of the bus like that.'

Veerapan pushed long fingers through his impeccably burnished hair before fastidiously polishing his already brilliant spectacles.

'I've studied the psychology of terrorists,' he went on. 'They feel fear, certainly, but they transmute it into angry grievance. They suppress any guilt by feeling outraged instead.'

'Is there a lot of terrorism these days?' Max asked.

'It's much increased of late. Questions have been asked in Parliament about the country's capacity to defend itself against terrorist attacks. Three months ago, a radio journalist was shot in Chennai. We don't yet know who's responsible. He was due to lead a demonstration against corruption and attempts to stop it being investigated.'

The Inspector hesitantly touched his flawless hair again, as if fearful of it getting even mildly out of hand. Clare suspected he was worried because it might have been dislodged; such perfection told her it was probably a wig. He now spoke about an aim to strengthen those in charge of prosecutions, although it was hard to prove how widespread the corruption was.

'It's a worldwide problem, like terrorism. It's a political disease we must do our best to see eradicated.'

He asked for a copy of the photo Max had taken at the election meeting. The photo did include the boy but only in quarter-profile. As Veerapan readied himself to leave, he stressed there was a need for Clare and Tammy to be cautious about where they went alone, since hit men might pursue a couple of prime witnesses. The couple were disturbed by this warning, although Tammy made light of it once the Inspector had gone.

'Being alarmist makes him feel important,' he declared. 'There's no great reason for us to worry. I'm quite sure nobody is coming after us.'

Chapter Two

Clare's respect for Tammy grew after witnessing his struggle with the killer, while the danger somehow aroused and intensified her need for Max. Moments after they went to bed that night, Max fell asleep. As he slept, Clare looked down at his body and wondered again what had come between them. She found herself thinking back to the night they first made love, three years earlier, after they'd looked out from their window in the castle in that twisting valley. A river of cloud had moved slowly above it, investing her with a feeling of both calm and reassurance. The beauty of the moment had been unaffected by the noise made by rats scuffling beneath the floorboards. Clare remembered the suggestion she'd made: the rodents were just having a bit of fun. Max had kissed her then, with greater confidence, as if her humour had lent him this.

He gently caressed her breasts, slowly seducing her. Clare's urgent response took her by surprise, and Max displayed equal passion as he hungrily penetrated her. She loved the feeling of his thrusts inside her, and the tension of his body. He cried her name. The commencement of his spasms filled her with an awed delight. She exulted in his obvious deep attraction to her and in the gasps he made on coming so convulsively.

They rose early the following morning. Together they watched as the night mist evaporated, curling and twisting up and away like bonfire smoke. The air was vibrant as they walked along the riverbank, and the little river quivered in the dazzle of the sun. They stretched out by a river pool while a breeze blew over them. The poplars above them rustled and the autumn grasses shivered. Tiny insects hummed delicately all around them.

They undressed and waded into the water. As they floated in the pool and kissed, holding each other in a loose embrace, Max told Clare that he was falling in love with her. He flushed as he admitted this, and she was touched by his being so tenderly disarming. Although flattered, Clare was puzzled by the suddenness of this disclosure, thinking people didn't fall in love that quickly.

Clare brought her thoughts back to the present and set about waking Max. She kissed his mouth before sliding her hand down his body to caress his cock. He didn't respond with the immediacy she was accustomed to, and this provoked her into saying what was on her mind.

'What's come between us?' she forced herself to ask but felt the question falter on her tongue. 'You're elsewhere. You're with me and not with me.'

The fan swished on. Clare waited for his reply, too long she thought. She became aware of the soft beat of rain upon the roof. Max shifted uncomfortably.

'I can't tell you,' he said at last. 'I'm sorry. I really am.'

He reached out, obviously wanting to protect Clare from something. He pulled her towards him and embraced her tightly. This caring part of him had always impressed her but now she didn't know what to think. She said nothing; she hardly moved.

Max's hold on her loosened and he fell asleep again, lost to her in dreams. Waves of slow fatigue began to wash over her too and she gave in to them.

She dreamt of the figures of Vishnu and his wife, Lakshmi, holding each other in an amorous embrace. But the dream kept changing. A boy appeared; he bore a look of innocence that changed abruptly to one of cold brutality. He had a flower in his hand, which was sweating drops of blood, and a man was staring up in cruel triumph. A little girl had fallen down and Clare was desperate to save her. She picked the child up and gave her to a man who looked at her with melting pity. But then he changed too. His look altered to one of murderous fanaticism as he began swinging towards Clare on his crutches.

Horrified, Clare jolted awake.

Forcing the nightmare from her mind, she resolved to put the whole terrible experience behind her. She deliberately recalled the image of Shiva, his hand raised in a gesture of intrepidity. Then she turned her thoughts back to the castle: the wooded hills visible through high lancet windows, firelight reflected on the frescoed walls and fluttering in the shadows on the coffered ceiling. All the students had been dining there together on their last night, when Max, surrounded by that loud and vivacious company, had whispered in her ear.

'Will you marry me?' he asked.

Clare said yes, thinking she'd never met a man as gentle and solicitous as Max.

∴

Max was scrolling through the photos on his camera. When he came to those of the crowd around the orator, he focused his attention on a face in quarter-profile that might be that of the boy assassin. There was the shadowy suggestion of the cripple but no image of the chunky young man who'd made that feint lunge at him with his flick-knife and had subsequently gone on to threaten Tammy with it.

Max hoped Tammy was right in thinking the two youths were just crazy loners, although he took seriously Inspector Veerapan's theory that the youths belonged to a group of hit men who might want to eliminate the key witnesses to their crime. The youths knew that Tammy and Clare had seen their faces, but it was the mysterious cripple who had paid Clare most attention. It was his child she'd rescued and his gratitude had seemed genuine. Clare thought it was he who'd approached them at the election meeting, and Max recalled being impressed by his quiet dignity.

Max was anxious, however. He was worried for his wife's safety and for Tammy's as well. Their time in Madurai was coming to an end, though, and then they'd be returning to Chennai, with its larger population and greater anonymity. The fact of their imminent departure reassured him, and his thoughts switched to his personal dilemma, which was growing ever more pressing and demanding to be faced. He knew he had to tell Clare, and he'd have to tell her soon. She'd be more hurt than angry, he reasoned. Although he knew he could confront anger well enough, he was far less certain he could face up to hurting her. She wasn't always as tough as she liked people to think. It had been that combination of strength and sensitivity that had first attracted Max to her.

∴

The early days of their lovemaking were still warm in Max's memory. He'd been surprised by Clare's passion, not having encountered strong sexual feelings in women before. His two previous experiences had been disappointing; they had made him feel undesired and intrusive and diminished his passion.

Rick's tanned and animated face, his bold advances, his enviable lack of inhibitions and his impetuous flood of words all stood in sharp contrast to Max's experiences with women. Rick had moved too fast, though, and he'd been too demanding. Their affair came to a head two months before Max met Clare. In the end, Max had rejected the man he'd half-wittingly encouraged, responding to Rick's resentment and indignation with a level of anger he knew was more assumed as a protective measure; it wasn't what he truly felt.

As Max had been determined to push his feelings for Rick away, he met Clare while in a decisively reactive mood. He fell in love with her in Italy, delighting in the quickness of her mind and the quiet irony of her observations. He hadn't minded that she often outshone him. He felt himself to be one of life's admirers, unable to love someone unless he much admired them and the other person displayed obvious reassuring affection.

When Clare returned from Italy to London, she introduced

Max to her mother. Her father had died some years before. It was then Max learned of Clare's younger sister, Violet, who had Down's Syndrome. Their mother had developed a heart complaint, which meant she now had to keep Violet in a care home. Clare confessed how she felt guilty for having ever resented her sister getting so much more of her mother's attention, even though she felt so sorry for her.

'You have to let me help you overcome that,' Max said. 'We should share each other's irrational anxieties.'

They'd made love with a demanding intensity. Max revelled in the soft kisses they shared, although sometimes he would find himself involuntarily recalling Rick's harder, rougher kisses, knowing he'd found them to be equally exciting. He still sometimes thought of Rick and his seemingly endless supply of sexy stories; he recalled how he'd laughed at some of those erotic flights of fantasy. It was as if the more frustrated Rick became, the more bizarre the anecdotes. But then the furious and inevitable row had happened. Max knew how unfair he'd been to Rick, aroused by his ardent declarations yet nervous of the demands they'd seemed to place on him.

Because of that, Max had tried to be more honest with Clare, at least as far as it seemed necessary. He'd told her about Rick's existence but not everything about their relationship; he said they'd been good friends. He didn't talk about the mutual sexual attraction because it seemed a needless risk to take.

Their marriage had worked extremely well until recently. Max took pride in his wife's career. He respected her feelings about having children, which they'd decided to put off till they were in their early thirties. Max could see that Clare needed to have children eventually but was now driven to establish her career. She achieved more than Max had done. Her success as a fundraiser for charity contrasted with his occasional photographic commissions, and the one book he'd had published had attracted very mixed reviews, the worst of them having depressed him enormously. He hadn't felt competitive, though. He was proud of Clare's abilities. He suspected, however, that she nurtured a covert anxiety about being seen to so obviously outshine him. Was this why she took time off from her career to accompany him on this shared enterprise? Had she already had a premonition that their marriage was threatened? Or was there a blind spot in her vision, some unconscious determination not to see? Was this similar to what had affected Max when he'd first met Narayan?

Max often thought back to those first encounters in Los Angeles a year ago, those demonstrations of Narayan's vitality and sometimes rather disconcerting humour. Max's first sight of him had been in a gym, where he was lifting weights from his chest. Max had been struck by his handsome face, high cheekbones, responsive eyes and finely delineated lips. He loved his cheerfulness when he'd later asked Narayan where he came from.

'Southeast India,' Narayan had replied. 'Tamil Nadu. Perhaps you've heard of Madras, which is now called Chennai, or the Coromandel Coast, with its tropical palms and thousand temples? Most foreigners visit Northern India, though, knowing nothing of Tamil Nadu and its ancient culture.'

'It sounds fascinating,' Max said. 'So what are you doing in

Los Angeles?'

'I'm a physicist... a university lecturer. I've just qualified and I'm on an exchange scheme with the university here: UCLA. I'm feeling a little cast adrift. So, what do you do?'

'I'm a writer and photographer. So far I've published only one book. It's on Mexico.'

'You must let me read it some time. Have you always lived in LA?'

'Yes,' Max confirmed. 'I went to UCLA, too. I majored in political economy. I also studied comparative religion, which has always fascinated me. My father didn't approve of either. He was a three R father: rich, reactionary and Republican. He was also a fundamentalist Christian who hated gays, illegal immigrants and single motherhood.'

'He doesn't sound much fun.'

'He wasn't. But I wish I'd got to him more before he died last year.' He paused. 'So why've you taken up weight training?'

'Because I don't want to become all fat and flabby,' Narayan said with a smile. 'With too much wobbling stomach and too little breath.'

'There doesn't seem to be much risk of that!'

'You don't know what might happen in a few years' time. You see, I'm really greedy, which makes life difficult in this land of the hot dog and the hamburger. All this horrible meat you Americans wolf down, which I can never touch, being a respectable vegetarian. You know, back home in Tamil Nadu, beef and pork are quite unheard of, save among a few benighted Europeans.'

'Cattle for you being sacred animals?'

'Yes. But to eat meat of any kind is pretty horrific. We Tamils think of vegetables as the food of the god Shiva, who's especially venerated in the South. But you Americans do have some vegetarians, fortunately for me. Not all of you are shameless carnivores.'

Narayan laughed then, amusing Max with his slightly aggressive humour.

'I do the weight training,' Narayan went on, 'only partly because I fear to become as fat as my two almost elephantine uncles, whose examples I'm not at all keen to follow. It's also because of the physical release it gives me when I feel anxious and self-doubtful.'

Max had felt much the same after his father's death. Narayan's openness impressed and disarmed him. He invited Narayan home the following week, as Clare was away. Max showed Narayan around and then offered him a drink. Narayan made clear that he found the house and garden beautiful. His spontaneous reactions and the fact he didn't affect a lack of interest became his endearing characteristics for Max.

'I'm afraid I'm going to be boring,' Narayan said. 'I just don't drink alcohol at all.'

'That's not against your religion, is it?'

'Not really. Some of my friends back home are virtual slaves to alcohol, although Hinduism is against us being slaves to anything material. We're allowed to seek artha, a reasonable level of prosperity, but must be free from the prison of our physical desires. Our souls should not be captive to our bodies. Well, that's the distant ideal that most of us never reach: moksha, spiritual enlightenment.'

'Do the joys of sex also represent the captivity of the soul by the body?'

'Well, it is captivity of a sort,' Narayan answered. 'Some Hindus believe in brahmacharya, the sacred joys of chastity.'

When Max asked if he believed in that, Narayan ruefully joked that unfortunately he'd experienced those joys far more than he'd wished to. He laughed then, curiously embarrassed, and Max found his amused confusion disconcertingly appealing.

As Max talked Narayan about those differences in customs and culture, he became aware that he found him attractive but thought he could deal with this without getting at all frustrated. He liked Narayan's weirdly humorous charm but he'd been able to resist masculine charm before; at least he had with the shamelessly appealing Rick. So Max had concluded that the situation between him and Narayan would go no further than he wished, and he felt sure that it would be no threat to his marriage with Clare. What he hadn't anticipated was how, in time, thoughts of Narayan would fill his mind by day and agitate his dreams at night. He couldn't have predicted how far he would travel on this unintended, much resisted, journey.

Chapter Three

Tammy had hesitantly asked Clare to come for a mid-afternoon walk, and she'd been much torn as to whether she should go. This was partly because she thought Max wouldn't like it, not out of jealousy (which wasn't normally one of his failings) but because he'd be anxious about her safety. On radio and television there had been endless talk of the assassination, and newspaper accounts were packed with overblown dramatic details. Clare recalled the Inspector's warning about the precautions they should take. Tammy, however, had been quite insistent, arguing that Veerapan was a scaremonger. He pointed out that they would be driving several miles away from the town, so it was fairly unlikely they'd be followed. Clare was not entirely convinced and so had sent a text to Max, letting him know what they were going to do. Max had gone back to the temple to take more photos.

Clare sat with Tammy on a riverbank in the shade of a banyan tree; they were half-enclosed by a curtain of gnarled roots, which hung down from the massive branches overhead, as if thirstily reaching for the ground. The river stretched flatly away into the distance. They watched some buffaloes being washed by a young man, who was scooping up silty water in a can and then pouring it over their fat, waddling bodies. This action, repeated over and over, solicited the occasional plaintive bellow from the animals.

Clare knew her attitude towards Tammy was much affected by what had happened the previous night. Her initial annoyance about hearing his absurd confession of love had dissipated, partly because of his concern for her in the crowd and partly because of his display of courage when struggling with the assassin. Tammy, however, claimed he'd have fled at once if he'd actually known the youth had knifed someone. He'd been too close to the vehicle to see what was happening above his head. Clare wasn't inclined to believe him. His valour impressed her even more by virtue of his having made this amusing, self-deprecating effort to deny it.

Despite Tammy's cynicism about the police, he'd cooperated with them, although he wouldn't bring himself to admit there either he or Clare were in any need of their protection. Sometimes he talked about who might have been behind the crime, his own ideas now chiming with those of Veerapan's: dispossessed peasants recruited as hit men, who were angry and rebellious because of the injustices they suffered. A radio commentator suggested the assassination was the work of Maoist revolutionaries seeking to establish a classless society through armed struggle. However, Venkataraman, with his campaign against political corruption, wasn't part of any system of class oppression but rather a vocal critic of such, and so Tammy discounted that theory along with several others being bandied about in the media.

Leaving the banyan tree behind, Tammy and Clare walked along the riverbank. Tammy had said nothing more about his feelings for her, and she was impressed by his restraint. Instead, he spoke at length about the political and economic problems of India, presumably out of a desire to help with her and Max's research.

'We spend forty per cent of the budget on defence,' he said. 'Far more on tanks and missiles than on factories to make mechanical diggers, drains and ambulances. Without a doubt, we'll use these arms when it comes to the next slugging match with Pakistan.'

'Over Kashmir?' Clare asked.

'Yes. Three wars have already been fought over Kashmir,' Tammy pointed out. 'Fifty thousand people have been killed. It's full of militant groups, and there's always tension on the unofficial borders. It's the main reason India and Pakistan spend their relatively scarce resources on weapons of mass destruction. In a moment of panic misunderstanding, these nuclear bombs could so easily be launched.' He paused. 'Remember Shahpur, the Indian Muslim friend I told you about? He thinks the Partition of India in the first place was unfortunate.'

'Why?' Clare asked. 'Surely there was no alternative?'

'Who can really say?' Tammy countered. 'A million people were massacred and eleven million more – Muslims, Sikhs and Hindus – fled for their lives across the new frontiers. Shahpur loves his religion, its fervent monotheism and egalitarian spirit, but he can't see why these different religions couldn't have coexisted in the same undivided country. The Koran is not exclusivist. It doesn't regard other religions as wrong. It says Muslims must acknowledge their kinship with other faiths, as the Muslim Emperor Akbar did when he showed great interest in Hinduism. That was something you imperial British failed to do, far preferring to divide and rule instead.'

'Did we British do nothing right in your opinion?' asked Clare, irked. 'We built railways and bridges. We introduced democracy and freedom of opposition, however limited.'

'Yes, very limited. Democracy didn't arrive soon enough. You imprisoned Gandhi and Nehru, for instance. Of course, you gave us the unifying English language. You also outlawed widow burning, without which the widowed Indira Gandhi might never have come to power. Some of her critics think that was a big mistake.' He paused, just for a second. 'I'm joking.'

'In poor taste,' said Clare. 'A woman prime minister must've been a real inspiration to the women of India. Are you sure you're not a closet misogynist, Tammy? It's disgraceful that the majority of women are seen as inferior to men. Vijaya's right to think this must be strenuously fought.'

'She's very right, of course. Pregnant women are often made to have ultrasound scans to determine the sex of foetuses. Female ones sometimes get aborted. It's against the law but it happens.'

'It's monstrous. Why is it thought so terrible to have a female child?'

'It's partly economic. Boy children earn money when they grow up. Girls can become expensive because of the wretched dowry system. Brides are expected to bring valuable goods with them, which their parents can't always afford. Husbands and in-laws can put terrifying pressure on the wives.'

Tammy seemed to like Clare critically asserting her opinions, prompting him to make plainer his feminist convictions.

'Incidentally, Shahpur is deeply in love with a Hindu girl, Kalyani. They met at Cambridge but now live in Kolkata. They want to marry but both sets of parents are against it. Kalyani says her father's parents were killed in the Partition riots, in a massacre on a train. He was young enough to be overlooked but he witnessed it and is very bitter as a consequence. That's a personal reason for Shahpur being so against these religious divisions and longing for mutual tolerance.'

Clare liked Tammy confiding in her about his Muslim friend. She was touched by his concern. With nothing to say at that moment, she shifted her focus to the landscape surrounding them. Dotted across the paddy fields were occasional coconut palms, their trunks sometimes bent towards the sun, as if making supplication to it. A vulture, suspended on wide serrated wings, slowly glided by above their heads. A farmer was driving two oxen yoked together, laboriously dragging a plough.

'They shouldn't be using draught animals.' Tammy said. 'The wooden ploughshare doesn't go deep enough. Not that there hasn't been great agricultural improvement on the whole. The Green Revolution was launched after the droughts of the sixties and early seventies. Yields improved by thirty per cent during the eighties.'

'What other general improvements have there been?' Clare asked. 'You seem to have all the facts and figures at your fingertips.'

'I've recently prepared some lectures on the topic,' Tammy said. 'Life expectancy has gone up considerably. The number of children per woman has gone down from six to two point four. The female literacy rate has risen from nine per cent to sixty-five per cent. We've many major problems, of course, especially to do with health care and education for the poor, but we've made impressive progress in many ways since Independence.'

'You're not as much of a gloom merchant as you seemed at first,' Clare said. 'Have we far to go?' she asked anxiously then. 'I'm beginning to feel a bit weird.'

'Oh lord, I've kept you out under this sun for too long,' Tammy replied with concern in his voice.

They walked on towards a village that was blurry from a distance, owing to the heat and dust. As they got closer, some children walked towards them, staring with wondering eyes. It was as if they'd never seen a curious pale creature such as Clare before. A couple of scruffy-looking dogs barked furiously at the strangers, hair bristling and fangs bared, before sulkily retreating to cause a sudden panic among some chickens that flapped off on ruffled wings, squawking in indignation.

'Look, Tammy,' Clare began, her voice urgent, 'can you find me somewhere to lie down? I feel awful. It must be something more than just the heat.'

Soon they came to what must have once been quite an imposing building but was now dilapidated. A faded sign outside indicated it was a hotel. It was set back from the road behind a clump of bedraggled banana plants, as if hiding for shame behind their tattered leaves. A spectacularly fat man was lounging half-naked on a rope bed outside, staring rather haughtily at the visitors.

'Tammy, I'm parched,' Clare said. 'I've got to drink something. And I need somewhere to lie down please!'

Tammy spoke with the man, who announced himself as the proprietor of the hotel. He called back over his shoulder with stately condescension. A youth emerged, with the faintest bloom of a moustache, hands dangling awkwardly by his sides as if he wasn't quite sure they belonged to him. The proprietor motioned him upstairs with a lordly twiddle of his fingers and then glanced at Clare, tapping his massive stomach as though it were a feature of much pride he was quite determined they should notice if not actively admire.

'There's a room with a bed,' Tammy told her. 'The air conditioning's defunct but they're sending for some ice to cool us down.'

They were guided upstairs to a room furnished with a narrow bed. The windows were shuttered, with just a few slits of light leaking in from the glare outside. Clare lay down. The youth returned, carrying an enamel basin that contained a slab of ice scattered with sawdust. The proprietor took it and set it ceremoniously down before brushing off the sawdust to reveal, like a solemn mystery, the gleaming shape beneath. The youth scampered out and in again, bringing bottles of a vividly coloured drink. Clare took one and gulped it down, despite its lurid look and peculiar taste. The youth then produced an antiquated table fan, over which the proprietor waved his hands as if bestowing an optimistic blessing on it. The youth plugged the fan into a disconcertingly loose socket on the wall that, with its cracked plaster and eccentric bulges, seemed well advanced on its inevitable journey to collapse.

Against the odds – or so Clare thought – a spasm of electricity jerked the fan into a frenzy of activity. Tammy positioned it by the basin so that it whirred across the ice; it twisted and shuddered from side to side, delivering a shaft of coolness onto her sweating face.

The youth retreated, touching his forehead with a murmur. The proprietor bowed out, beaming beatifically, sketching a princely little gesture of commiseration in the air with his podgy fingers.

'That's wonderful, Tammy,' Clare said. 'Sorry to be such a bore.'

Tammy's response was to soak a cloth and set it on her forehead.

'I've been talking too much,' he said. 'I wanted to cheer you up. I fear this could be a touch of sunstroke.'

So he'd been able to see she needed cheering up. He was making these moves not out of naïve infatuation but out of real, sensitive regard for her wellbeing. His anxious wiping of her face caused a stir of gratitude within her, which she found surprising.

She wasn't physically attracted to him at all, though. He was so plain, the poor soul, and good looks in a man had always been important to her. She never liked admitting this to people, for fear they would think her shallow. But Tammy had kind eyes and she liked his diffident smile. His behaviour was charming but she saw nothing beyond his charm. She was to be surprised again, though, when he shyly kissed her open palm; she felt herself warm to him, albeit only slightly.

But then Tammy whispered something.

'I've never loved anyone like this before.'

Clare felt embarrassed but not annoyed this time. She wondered if she had been unfair in deciding to come on this walk in the first place.

'I respect what you've told me, but as I've said, I'm very much in love with my husband.'

'But he…' Tammy's voice trailed off, just for a moment, before he summoned the courage to go on. 'He just doesn't seem to be in love with you.'

'Why do you say that?' Clare asked, horrified.

'How can he be?' Tammy blurted out, looking almost frightened. 'He can't be in love with more than one person, surely?'

'What the hell do you mean?'

'I'm sorry. I shouldn't have said that.'

'Certainly you shouldn't, even if it were true, which it bloody well isn't!' she shouted. She felt sick again, suddenly hating him.

'I never meant to tell you,' Tammy said. 'But you don't know what I'm going through. I wouldn't allow myself to feel this way if I thought he really loved you.'

For a moment Clare wanted to ask what had been said to him, and by whom. She had a huge and painful need to know. She felt her anger grow; she was furious that he should have been so base as to tell her this, and that he should be expressing her own insidious doubts. This much she recognised. Frustrated and appalled, she stared at the fan, which was rasping as if outraged; it seemed to be turning ever faster and at risk of falling over in the now so claustrophobic room.

Of course, Clare knew there was this gap in what she knew about Max, and her anger drained away. Vijaya? The idea came back but now seemed totally implausible. Vijaya was Narayan's sister. A memory of Narayan flashed upon her suddenly: joking at a barbecue party in Los Angeles as she helped to turn the sizzling meat he'd said was so barbaric, pouring her wine he'd never drink himself, charming her with his wish to please and his provocative yet disarming humour. Clare had suspected he might've had a crush on her, one that would never be declared because she was Max's wife and Narayan was Max's friend.

She got up from the bed, telling Tammy she wanted to be alone. She went downstairs and passed the youth with the barely detectable moustache. With the proprietor not around, the boy had assumed a mimicking grandeur of his own and was talking a bit snootily to a bearded man who peered at Clare as she came near. She was used to being stared at by now, being seen as an exotic oddity in these remoter parts of the country. It was only when she reached the door, where the light dazzled her eyes, that she began to wonder why his attention had disturbed her so.

She turned back. The hallway was so dark in contrast to the blinding light and she couldn't see the man's face clearly. He stood motionless at first, but then swivelled and twisted and began swinging towards her. His shoulders jerked. His crutches clicked across the tiled floor. He stopped a couple of metres from Clare.

He gazed at her, smiling awkwardly. He made a gesture, friendly but cautionary, as if expressing some grave solicitude.

It was surely the same cripple.

Clare recalled him lit up by the sparkling fireworks, holding out his begging bowl, urging on the boy assassin, watching Venkataraman being stabbed, staring up in revolting grim delight at the bloody scene. But then she recalled him tenderly holding his little girl, showing gratitude to Clare, comforting his desolated wife when he might've chided her instead.

This was a man of glaring contradictions. What was he doing here? Why approach her? Had he followed them from the town to express his gratitude again, unable to forget how Clare had saved his child? Or had he come to warn her? Was it even the same man, or was her imagination playing tricks, fuelled by her lingering anxieties?

Clare looked at his grave face, his forehead puckered in concern. Was he really the mastermind behind a cold-blooded murder? He gestured to Clare with the back of his hand, as if urging her to leave, to go far away, before turning and swinging off on his crutches.

Clare remained in the hallway, utterly bewildered. Tammy came downstairs, too late to see the cripple. The youth was still there, but his confidence began fizzling out when he heard the proprietor imperiously demanding his attendance, and Clare got the full glory of his monumental belly a moment later as he graciously wobbled into view. After an indulgent smile and a courtly wave of his hand, the proprietor wobbled off again, with the youth reluctantly in tow, bearing a browbeaten air.

Clare told Tammy about the cripple. He said the chances of this man being the same as the one in Madurai were unlikely.

'It was a nasty experience for you,' he reasoned. 'You mustn't imagine that pursuers are lurking around every corner. Resist getting needlessly alarmed.'

She was glad of the reassurance but noted that Tammy took her alarm seriously enough to look around in hope of seeing the man. Her mobile phone buzzed, and she looked at the screen. Max had texted her to say he'd got back to the hotel and was worrying about where they she was.

A minute later, Clare and Tammy saw a car drive away from the hotel. A bearded man was in the driving seat; beside him was a woman with a child on her lap. The woman saw Clare and her face broke into a diffident, soft smile. She bowed her head and touched her forehead with her right palm.

'It must be the same cripple,' Clare told Tammy.

'A crippled beggar wouldn't possess a car, let alone be able to drive one,' he replied.

Slightly irked by Tammy's dismissal of her suppositions, Clare started to think about the man's warning gesture. It was as if he had warned her to go far away, even to leave the country. Was he fearful of what might happen to her if she did not?

Chapter Four

While Max was waiting for Clare to get back, he scrolled through the photos on his camera again, looking for one in particular: the possible quarter-profile of the boy assassin, staring upwards as Venkataraman orated, the enigmatic cripple standing near him. Max scrutinised it but he wasn't sure. He kept thinking of the Inspector's warning that the assassins might follow Clare and Tammy, a warning they weren't paying much attention to.

He decided to put it to the back of his mind for now and scrolled on in search of photos he might want to use in the book: a holy man with corded tentacles of ash-streaked hair, an emaciated child in a backstreet slum, the patched and ragged hovels of a shanty town. In contrast was a village wedding procession with the garlanded bridegroom on a horse, sleek and gaily caparisoned, and a beautiful woman sweeper in an embroidered sari, determined to dignify her labour with her dress. He continued scrolling until he came to a photo of Narayan in Los Angeles, snapped the year before. An even older one of Rick was next.

Thinking of Narayan often brought back memories of Rick.

Max had kept his friendship with Rick alive. He even asked him to be best man at his wedding, and that had somehow helped to heal the hurt between them. Rick had amused Clare and Max at the reception, standing unsteadily on a table, pretending to be even drunker than he was. He crooned a romantic song from the 1930s, but with salacious variations of his own invention. He clutched the microphone greedily to his mouth and quivered with simulated rapture.

Clare was pleased that Max had such a colourful and outrageous friend, for whom she also felt a humorous concern. Rick's accounts of adventures with various women, about which he boasted with exuberant untruthfulness, never put a strain on their sympathetic friendship. Max still sometimes worried that he hadn't told Clare anything about his brief sexual relationship with Rick, but he justified the omission by resolving to commit himself to his wife exclusively. Because of that, he hadn't been concerned by Narayan's immediate appeal when he met him in Los Angeles. It was something he could contain; it would not threaten his marriage. Clare had gone away on a month's visit to London, to see her mother, who'd fallen ill. The next time he invited Narayan home, Max stated clearly how happy he was in his marriage.

'When will you be getting married yourself?' Max asked.

'Oh, some day,' Narayan replied. 'It's inevitable. Pretty well everyone gets married in India. Not to want to have children would be thought of as being really freakish, although we're supposed to ration them these days.'

'What about the family you come from?'

'There's just the two of us. Our parents died in a car accident when we were teenagers.'

'That must've been traumatic,' Max said.

'I mustn't be self-pitying. I live with my sister, Vijayalakshmi, which we shorten to Vijaya. She's quite a livewire, rebelling against what she sees as her repressive, conventional female upbringing. We live in our parents' old house, but she's soon to marry Tammy, a cousin of ours. She's very much in love with him, although she'd sooner cut out her tongue than admit it. Tammy, being far more English than Indian because of his English public school education, thinks romantic love a bit embarrassing. We're a very small family in the immediate sense, but our extended family is alarmingly big.'

'You mentioned some elephantine uncles. I remember.'

'So huge and heavy they're difficult to ignore. There are some nosey aunts as well; they don't exactly make life any easier. Vijaya has secret names for them that aren't too complimentary. One she calls The Battleaxe, because she's sharp and lethal. The other is The Sergeant Majorette because she's got a bit of a moustache and expects us to do her instant bidding. She's loud too, with a voice like a mad screech owl. The two are deadly rivals. Well, I exaggerate, but you've no idea what the pressure of family life in India is like. Even at one remove away, you can seldom escape its strangling influence.'

'Families in America can sometimes be strangling too, you know.'

Narayan laughed.

'I often thought I'd like to live in America. I love what I've seen of Americans so far. I've experienced extraordinary friendliness and hospitality. As I have with you, and as I have with a guy who took me to a restaurant in Venice Beach. It specialises in vegetarian food. He jokes about the cult of the cowboy in America.'

'Who is this guy?' Max asked. 'And what's the cult of the cowboy?'

'José,' Narayan replied. 'He's a Hispanic immigrant. He lives in a house very unlike this one. It has a view of a gas station and a lot of concrete jungle. The cult of the cowboy means steak eating and hard drinking and being forever on the move; it's the cult of masculinity, toughness and hitting back. And now you have a cowboy president, he claims.'

'Yes, we do. To be fair, though, he gave up the hard drinking a long time back.'

'But he hasn't given up attacking the wretched Indians, by which he means Afghans and Iraqis. I too think that's pretty crazy.'

'So do I. My father was fanatically supportive of the Iraq invasion, but I demonstrated against it in a candlelit procession. He was mad at me for doing that. We had some very bad arguments.'

'I also argued with my father. He was not all that affectionate. My mother influenced me far more. She was a devoted strict Hindu, and I'm a rather lax one. Still, my religion is important to me, as is being a Tamil. I'm extremely proud of being Tamil. My cousin Tammy thinks I'm being too regionalist on this account. But we Tamils produced music, dance and poetry, and our bronze sculptures are among the finest in the world! I'm boasting, Max, and I must be off now.'

'So soon?' Max was aware of the disappointment in his voice. 'Where are you going?

'José has invited me for a meal to meet his family. I must introduce you to him some time, although he's always going on about top-dog WASPS, with their high salaries, guarded condominiums and gilded private medical insurance. But you're a conscientious liberal, Max. I'm sure you'll get on. Look, it's really kind of you to ask me home and let me prattle on. I hope to meet Clare soon, when I'll try and be rather less of a chatterbox. I'm afraid it's a family failing. Vijaya's even worse than I, if that's possible.'

Narayan laughed and, being on the point of leaving, held Max's hand in a very prolonged handshake. Max didn't infer anything from this because he'd heard that Indians were demonstrative. Despite that, the action stirred him.

A week later he invited Narayan to his home again, suggesting they swim together in his pool. He'd always been uncritically proud of having this, although he now felt a touch less confident about it. The two of them undressed and dived into the pool. Narayan swam well, and Max thought his body looked beautiful as he moved through the water. He loved the hard curves of Narayan's body, of his thighs and pectoral muscles especially. He liked the fact they were not overdeveloped. Later, Max stood on the poolside and watched Narayan swimming underwater in a sheath of whirling bubbles. He felt a thrill as he emerged from the pool; drops of water glistened on his skin and formed tiny rivulets that coursed down his body.

Afterwards Narayan did some yoga exercises. Max quipped that his contortions must be so uncomfortable, and wondered if he inflicted them on himself for the sake of his poor soul. Narayan was sitting cross-legged, his fingers resting lightly on his knees. He was so still and calm that Max was startled when he spoke.

'Tell me, do you believe in immortal souls, Max?'

'I'd give anything to do so, but I find it difficult.'

'Why? Because you think the soul is just the brain, and the physical brain dies when the body dies?' Narayan paused. 'Oh well, I admit that's quite a question. And here am I, a physicist knowing a fair amount about the physical world, yet still believing there's a spiritual one that is far more significant. You know, the more I examine the physical world, the more it seems to have been designed somehow.'

'Rank heresy in the eyes of many modern scientists,' Max observed.

'I know, but it seems so beautifully and intricately designed. How could life have just happened from the chance vagaries of evolution? Although it's not always for human benefit, as it seems to us. Then there's the mystery of it all. The world of physics seems almost wilfully enigmatic, and science doesn't explain it all away. It only makes it seem more impressive.'

Whatever his doubts about the physical world, Max was certainly finding Narayan impressive. There was a tranquil air about him as he practised yoga on the lawn or lay sprawled and happy among cushions on the floor. He enjoyed listening to a CD of classical Indian music – an evening raga played by Ravi Shankar – that Max had bought to impress and please him. Narayan fell asleep one evening without intending to, his body so clearly at peace that Max almost envied him.

Max hadn't touched Narayan's body yet and thought he didn't wish to. He tried to convince himself he only wanted his affectionate warm comradeship. But he found him increasingly appealing and his very innocence was one of the main causes of his appeal, that and his intellectual earnestness, his curious humour and the fact he came from this remote exotic culture. Max certainly didn't want to make a physical pass at him, feeling this would be cheating on Clare. But he wanted to be physically close as well as mentally intimate. He wanted to share so many things with him, believing he wouldn't need anything more than this.

Eventually he suggested Narayan should stay late to watch a DVD. Max had borrowed Satyajit Ray's Pather Panchali from a friend who was a film buff. They watched it till half past one at night. The beautifully shot scenes of village life in India greatly moved Narayan, such was his nostalgia for his country.

When it was over, Max said it was too late to drive him back and invited him to sleep on the sofa in the living room. The night was hot and muggy, and Max suggested they have a shower to cool down. They went into the bedroom and undressed. Max again put on the CD of Ravi Shankar and went into the bathroom, exhilarated by the music. As he stepped into the shower, he nonchalantly invited Narayan to join him. He offered to wash his back, joking that washing another man's back was part of the new cult of male bonding, which was almost obligatory in America these days. Max hoped that joking about it would make it seem more naturally acceptable. But Narayan delayed joining him, and began speaking of the raga's subtle improvisations and how glad he was that Max had taken to its spontaneous beauty.

When Narayan finally moved under the shower, Max soaped his back, his hands sliding over the muscular wet body. The raga continued its progression, which caught at him with its plangent charm. Max pushed Narayan beneath the shower, the lather pouring down in a froth of bubbles that foamed in a slow ripple down his back.

Max turned the power shower full on, and it pounded on Narayan's head. With an action that seemed almost involuntary, Max put his hand through the cascade to touch Narayan's face.

'I've never felt this much for another guy before,' Max said.

The raga suggested both yearning and frustration, the sitar rising to a climax and the drum beats quickening.

'Please don't say things like that,' Narayan replied. 'You go too far.'

'I'm sorry,' Max said. 'I didn't mean to. Don't be mad at me.'

'I'm not mad at you.'

'Then let's just listen to the music, shall we?'

The raga had moved on to an echoing of delicately plucked strings, and the singer's voice had descended to a trembling hush. This sense of melancholy connected with Max's mingled tenderness and bafflement. Since he had come this far, if only half-intentionally, he felt he should at least explain.

'Sorry… but I've fallen for you a bit. Idiotic of me, isn't it?'

He searched Narayan's eyes, seeing disquiet and confusion, and then a sudden defensive hardness. Narayan stepped out to go into the bedroom. Max feared he'd now phone for a taxi and go back home, never appearing again in Max's life. When Max went into the bedroom he saw Narayan standing by the window.

'I don't understand you, Max,' Narayan said. 'You're a married man.'

'I deeply love my wife, but it's possible to love two people. We can love in different ways.'

He'd used the word 'love' at last, but it had come out on impulse and he now regretted it. Narayan didn't reply but abruptly left to go and spend the night on the sofa. Sleep eluded Max for a couple of hours. He felt shame at the advance he'd made, however hesitantly, but then relief that he'd not actively pursued it. Early the next morning, Max found Narayan lying on his side in a strangely vulnerable position, one arm outstretched.

Max was still standing there, not wanting to wake him, when the phone rang. It was Clare calling from London. She said her mother had just died. Max felt a sharp stab of guilt over his now undeniable attraction to Narayan. He woke Narayan to tell him of Clare's loss, adding that he had to go to London to support her. Narayan was sympathetic and acted as if last night's incident hadn't happened at all. Max was relieved. He resolved to discipline his feelings, maintaining only a sympathetic friendship with him, whatever its intensity.

Max caught a flight that same evening, and reached Clare's mother's house the next afternoon. There, surrounded by the furniture she'd known through childhood was Clare; she was enormously distressed. Only after much coaxing did she express the guilt she felt about her mother, an emotion that clouded her grief and shock.

'I have such mixed feelings about her because of Violet. I feel guilty that, as a girl, I was slightly jealous of her. I feel that I didn't love either of them enough.'

Max sensed her need of him acutely.

'Don't go in for distant retrospective guilt, for God's sake,' Max said. 'I've had enough of that myself. You've been very good to Violet since. Don't worry about it so. No intense relationship is free of such anguished doubts.'

Her admission of her feelings of guilt intensified his own. His sorrow for her filled him with such tender concern he almost wished to forget Narayan altogether.

'I'll have to spend longer in London,' Clare told Max after the funeral. 'I can't leave Violet until she's more settled. She suffers from severe breathing problems, and this could be aggravated by her bereavement. Darling, I'm sorry, but I'll have to stay on with her for a time.'

Even if he'd wanted to stay with her, Max had to return home for a photographic assignment. He felt frustrated at the idea of further separation from Clare, while admiring her protectiveness towards her sister. He sent Narayan a text message, restrained to the point of blandness, saying he hoped to see him again when Clare was back with him in Los Angeles, to which he received an equally bland reply of equivocal assent. As the plane back to the USA climbed skywards, he watched through scattered cloud the winding of the Thames into the heart of England. He couldn't help wondering about the windings of his own divided heart, and where the half-hidden river of his future could be taking him.

Chapter Five

When Clare returned to the hotel in the middle of Madurai, she saw Max sitting on the veranda, looking as if he'd been waiting quite a while for her return. The sight encouraged her; she loved being missed by him. Nonetheless, she feared what Tammy had implied. She knew she had to find out the truth for herself.

'I'm sorry I'm late,' she said. 'We went down to the river and lost our way.'

'After Veerapan's warning, is it wise to wander around like that?' Max asked, great concern in his voice.

'Oh, come on,' Clare chided, albeit gently. 'We can't be thinking like that for the rest of our time out here. Or we'd never go anywhere at all. Anyhow, Tammy looked after me. He should be back soon. Are you looking at the photos? I'd love to see them again.'

Max handed her the camera and she scrolled through some of the images. She stopped at the one taken at the election meeting, wondering if the face in quarter-profile might be the boy's, and if the blurry figure in the background could possibly be the cripple. There followed several shots of the procession, and the rioting. The photos showed police wielding batons, a man in handcuffs, and an angry crowd.

There were photos Max had taken before the assassination: an old woman in a mobile clinic, being operated on to remove her cataracts; a man having a vasectomy; a village school with posters of Gandhi and Nehru and other political heroes going back to the Emperors Ashoka and Akbar. There was a shot of a modern well and one of irrigated paddy fields. She liked the image of Shiva with his circling arms, his flames of life, one hand outstretched in that gesture of fearlessness Clare found increasingly so inspiring.

'They make for a good balance,' she said. 'The subjects are so diverse.'

'Yes, but the photography itself is so uninspired.'

'That's nonsense. You're so ridiculously hard on yourself.'

Clare felt sorry for Max's loss of confidence but also impatient that he didn't fight it better.

'Why give in to this self-undermining mood of yours?' she asked. 'This loss of heart in all you do that's good?'

'And what have I ever done that's really good?'

'That book on Mexico for one thing.'

'Which got all those bad reviews.'

'From professional rivals,' Clare countered. 'You got three good reviews, which you've typically forgotten. Didn't you get a sense of real achievement from it? Isn't that what ultimately matters? Think of what we're doing together. All the research you've done. History… mythology… religion. You've read much more than I have. You put me to shame.'

'In LA I had more time to research,' said Max. 'Not having a proper full-time job like you had. You know what gets me really badly? I've earned so damn little in my career.'

'What's it really matter about earning money?'

'Only that my father earned it for me. And you make far more than I do, and without my initial advantages. You didn't come from a cushy, moneyed background.'

'You've got such a complex about being over-privileged, but don't start comparing and competing. Haven't we agreed we don't compete? About anything, let alone our earnings. As for your father, he left you money! So what? If it hurts that badly, give it away. You've already donated some to good causes.'

'But I never earned the dough that I donated. I've failed so far in most of my ambitions and, frankly, I'm worried about our book. I can't help wondering if I at least am up to it.' Max paused before blurting out what he'd been working up to admitting for some time. 'There's something else I should've told you a long time back.'

This is it, Clare thought. Whatever it might be.

'I feel bad I've never told you,' Max said. 'It contributes to my feelings of inadequacy.' He ran his hands through his hair, which was thick and dishevelled. Clare felt her impatience with him soften.

'So at last you're going to tell me, darling.'

'I would have done so before but I feared to lose you.'

'Lose me?'

'I've never stopped loving you. That's what makes this difficult.' Max paused a second. 'I feel so guilty.'

'Makes what difficult?' Clare asked, feeling slightly breathless. Max looked acutely unhappy now as well as tongue-tied. 'Makes what difficult?' she repeated, wondering if she really wished to know after all. Did she really want him to clarify her doubts and possibly intensify her pain? But she was no coward.

'Are you in love with someone else?' she asked.

'Yes.'

'Who?'

'Narayan.'

For a moment Clare stared at Max without comprehending what he had just said.

'Oh, Christ!' she exclaimed. 'Not Narayan.'

'Surely you suspected it?' he asked.

'Dammit, Max. I only knew you were intrigued by him… as a good friend.'

Clare pictured Narayan now; she forced herself to concentrate on him. There was a vivid memory of a barbecue party. She recalled how he'd jokingly raised his hands in horror at the sputtering, charred steak upon the grill. They'd been sitting together under the patchy moon shadows of a eucalyptus tree, the pungent scent of which she'd associated with him ever since. Narayan had suddenly gone solemn, looking at her almost with contrition, which she'd found confusing at the time. She'd imagined he was regretting his attraction to her, the tenderness she thought was directed at her and which conflicted with his friendship with her husband.

How blind I was, she thought now. How presumptuous.

'I knew you were fascinated,' she said at last, returning fully to the present. 'I thought it was his being so different. His Indian culture, his way with words, maybe. His wit. I didn't think of you as ever being in love with him. Does he love you back?'

'He's said so, yes. But sometimes it all seems so hopeless.'

'Is that so?' Clare snapped. 'And yet you love me still. How complicated for you!'

She regretted the sarcasm instantly. She was sounding bitter when what she was really feeling was sheer despair.

'I love our life together,' Max protested. 'Everything we've built. I love you. I could never live without you.'

He spoke earnestly. Although Clare believed what he was saying, it seemed so meagre in the context of the admission he'd now made.

'But physically,' she said, choosing her words carefully, 'you're more in love with him?'

Max didn't answer this and so Clare turned away. She felt a fierce anger as she went into their bedroom. He followed her, but she rejected his attempt to touch her. She thought about the despair in his eyes and in his voice before he told her this shattering news. It was one of those crises of confidence that often happened when he was feeling guilty over something. She listened as he spoke about how he was equally attracted to both of them but she felt empty.

'I don't want to talk about it anymore,' she said quietly. 'Not right now.'

Max seemed highly distressed and tried to take her in his arms, but she pushed him away. How dare he assume she'd accept his embrace, imagining her pain so easily alleviated.

'I'm going to bed,' she told him, barely containing her fury. 'Alone.'

Once Clare was away from Max, her anger started to subside. A curious numbness dulled her hurt, and slowly her mind began to drift. She thought of the home she shared with Max in Los Angeles, of their garden there, the mango and pawpaw trees loaded with green and yellow fruit, the frail hibiscus flowers, the bougainvillea in thorny red clusters trailing along the sandy-coloured garden walls, the palm trees shooting up so high with their untidy, clustered fronds. She envisaged the house itself, full of light and colour and the beautiful objects Max had given her. There was the Mayan head, the Toltec figurine (an early present) and the Hokusai woodblock print to welcome her return.

He'd been so obviously delighted and relieved to have her home again.

Home.

She recalled coming back from London in her double grief after both her mother and then Violet had died. The garden had been heavy with the scent of citrus. Max had thrown a barbecue party, inviting a group of friends, to cheer her up.

She remembered the noise of vigorous splashing in the pool.

It was the first time she saw Narayan. He was moving in a strangely seal-like, twisting way, the floodlight flashing over his supple body, the lucent water swirling as he broke the surface.

'Who on earth is that?' she had asked Max, who seemed surprised. His answer, she realised now, was a touch dismissive.

'Oh, a guy I met at the gym. His name is Narayan. He's an Indian university academic… a physicist. He's only just come out here. I invited him because he knows no one and he's lonely. A bit of a mad joker.'

He laughed at the incident and led her away from the poolside, past a number of guests who looked on, bewildered yet amused.

'Let's be by ourselves, darling,' he said. 'Narayan can look after himself all right. He's got loads of confidence. Let's leave them to enjoy themselves and go.'

Max drove them to their beach house in Malibu. The moon above the highway was veined and icy, the ocean to the left brokenly reflecting it.

'I wanted to be alone with you,' he said, his hands firm on the wheel.

'Even if it means walking out on our guests?' Clare asked.

'They know about your grief,' he replied. 'Besides, I got a friend to host the party. We don't need to be there to keep it going. Talk to me. Tell me about Violet.'

Clare took a sharp intake of breath.

'Okay,' she said. 'Yes, I suppose I should. She was at home. She began struggling to breathe and I tried to give her the kiss of life. I'd called an ambulance and we got her to hospital, where they placed her in intensive care. She was put into an oxygen tent but it was too late. I was with her for several hours before she died.'

'I'm sorry,' Max said simply.

Clare knew he would be remembering his own mother's death, from emphysema, some years earlier. He had sobbed when he told her. He was able to release tears on rare occasions, and she respected him for this.

Max parked the car at the side of the beach house, and they walked down to the jetty, where their speedboat was moored.

This was their special place, their very own patch of beach. Clare loved the Los Angeles beaches, wide and windswept as they were. She liked to watch the black-billed gulls wheeling in the air above and around the palm trees. She remembered how they'd once walked under the old pier at Santa Monica, the rumbling carousel above them, the tide sweeping in around the wooden piles, scored by the sea and thickly barnacled.

It had been dark there. Max had kissed her with a quickly mounting passion that had excited and touched her deeply.

The old beach shack that they'd repaired together five years before – sawing, hammering, creosoting and painting for hours every day – stood in stark contrast to the supercharged, streamlined and very modern speedboat. Clare thought it was a little flashy, but she never said so.

They'd created this place so they could be alone.

They climbed into the boat and headed rapidly out into the ocean, the waves thudding below them. Max had taken the wheel, and Clare stood with her arm around him.

Fifteen minutes later, Max stopped the boat and switched off the engine. He picked up his binoculars and peered out at the sea, waiting for something, barely restraining his excitement.

And then it came.

At first, it seemed as if a solitary wave was rising from the sea. It sank and then rose again. The water was heaving, rolling and breaking, as if it was about to deliver some dark secret. Then out of the water rose a streaming apparition, the water cascading down its massive flanks. It sank again.

Moments later, the head of the great mammal, its mouth agape, broke the water's surface just in front of the boat. The surf boiled within its massive jaws. Its eye was like a flash of phosphorescence in the moonlight. Its powerful flipper hit the water, and its ribbed tail swept the air like some huge, glistening wing. The boat heeled over, flinging Clare against the stern.

Max threw himself across to grab her. Soaked and giddy, she clung to him. Another wave rose at them and hurled itself down before sweeping on. Clare caught one more sight of the whale as it plunged, its tail thrashing, sending a shivering last cascade of spray into the air.

'I guess that was quite scary,' said Max, as he secured the wheel.

'Scary, yes,' Clare agreed. 'But it was so beautiful.'

She felt the tension leave her body. As it did so, she began to shiver. Noticing this, Max put his hands on her arms and began to rub them to warm her. Then he touched her face, moved his hands to her breasts and began kissing her, his mouth urgent as he loosened her clothes. Reaching down, he began to caress her, to enter her with his fingers. He yearned to arouse her, something always so essential to his own pleasure. Clare kissed him back. The memory of Violet as a child sprang involuntarily to mind, making her think of having a child herself, something they'd put off for too long.

They made love in the stern. She heard his breath quicken as he whispered her name and then the huge gasp as he came, his body stiff and shuddering, her own cries mingling with his. She thought of the whale plunging onwards. She listened to the wind, the rippling of the sea. She looked up at the stars, at their unimaginable distances away. They usually made her feel so small and negligible but now strangely enhanced the idea of their being so close together, so intimate; the indifferent, cold infinitudes of space and time seemed purposeless and meaningless by contrast.

For a while afterwards, they lay on the deck, Max on top. She loved his weight on her, the reassurance she got from his body, his mouth on hers again, his quiet breathing. He rolled off her and she reached over to fondle his now-soft cock, the feel of it in her hand only intensifying her sense of his vulnerability and the beauty of the release they'd given each other. She held his head to her breasts, feeling a dissolving tenderness within, as if he were that child she might conceive through him. She thought of the whale swimming in the distance, having heaved up to the surface like a sudden dream before plunging down into its fathomless dark world, moving slowly, inexorably away.

So much in life was receding from her, she now thought. She lay alone in bed in this ancient town in Southern India. Max was sleeping in another room, and she recalled with acute nostalgia that night only eight months ago, remembering the intensity of her happiness with him.

She thought back to a similar time: that night in the castle when they had made love for the first time, A nightingale was singing in the valley below, giving off its extraordinary varied notes, very clear and fast, as if it hastened towards the climax of its song in hope the ecstatic moment might endure forever. The next morning she and Max had gazed out through the mullioned windows, watching the swallows swinging off with a flutter and flash of pointed wings in long downward loops and quivering ascents. The birds threaded the valley with their exultant flight, swooping down to the bright river before hurtling up above the wooded hills. As Max and Clare kissed deeply, she thought what marvellous chance had brought them here together to fall so dazzlingly in love.

She heard a noise in next room. It was a thud. Someone falling?

The cripple came to mind, falling down while trying to reach her on his crutches. She felt haunted by two very different and conflicting memories of him: his evil manipulation of a dependent and naive young man who he'd urged to commit an act of bloody murder, and the tenderness he'd shown towards his fragile little daughter. Clare also recalled his forgiving words to his anguished wife. The woman had a sensitive but worn face, as if she'd suffered much. Clare had been touched by her motherly and wifely love, and hoped the cripple was always as kind to her as he'd appeared.

There were sounds of more awkward movements from next door, and then Clare heard someone call her name; it was Tammy. She threw on her dressing gown and opened the door to see him rising to his feet, a shamed expression on his face. She came out and closed the door behind her.

'I'm sorry,' Tammy said. His voice was slurred. 'I'm very drunk, I'm afraid. I've been feeling terrible because of what I told you about Max. Don't think I did it out of malice. I know you can't love me back but I can't bear it that you don't accept my love.'

'Quiet, Tammy!' Clare urged, her voice low but sharp. 'Max is next door, asleep. Accept your love? Don't be mad.' She felt a throb of exasperation. 'It's a bit arrogant to suppose I would. Don't you think it's a touch insulting too?'

'I shouldn't have said anything. I wish I'd been told nothing.'

'Narayan told you, I suppose?'

Tammy nodded in acute discomfort, and this slightly softened her. Just when her marriage to Max was under threat, here was Tammy making these amorous declarations. Clare found him pathetic in this intoxicated state. She hated his loss of dignity, in spite of his attempts to recover it.

'You'd better go,' she said.

Tammy moved his arms in a gesture of frustration.

'I shouldn't have come on this trip. I only came because of what he told me,' he said. 'Maybe he exaggerated something out of proportion. And now look at the stupid mess I'm in. It's my fault, I know. Yes, it has been arrogant of me. I didn't mean it to be insulting, though.'

He stopped, but obviously wanted to say more.

'What?' asked Clare.

'Don't worry about what's happened. Veerapan's a real alarmist. They won't be pursuing us. I promise you'll be safe.'

He left then, and Clare went back to bed. She wondered if Max, sleeping alone, was dreaming of her – or of Narayan.

∴

Max woke alone and immediately missed Clare's presence in the bed next to him. He would often wake in the night and loved to feel her back up close against him. They often slept with his arms around her, the muscles of his stomach against her buttocks, his hands upon her breasts. He loved the way their bodies fitted together, his hardness and her softness, the beating of her heart and the motion of her breathing.

He thought of her vulnerability now that he was alone, and she was on her own in another room. He knew that he'd caused her enormous pain, and this knowledge cut deep into his conscience. He couldn't stop tracing in his memory the outline of events, the interrupted process of the development of his love for Narayan.

Memories flooded back. He'd contacted Narayan in Los Angeles a week after his return from London.

'I hate the idea of Clare staying behind,' Max told him as soon as they met. 'I want to introduce you as soon as she gets back. I'd like you to be friends.'

'I'd like that too,' Narayan replied. 'She sounds real cool.'

'Real cool? You're picking up our lingo quite impressively.'

Narayan smiled at this. Max was nervous of sounding too keen to meet him again, afraid of scaring him away.

'Would you like to go surfing one of these days?' he found himself asking. 'It'd be a real Los Angeles experience.' He was banking on Narayan's adventurous spirit. 'It's be a challenge,' he added.

Narayan hesitated. Max wondered if he'd pushed his luck too far, but then Narayan agreed, suggesting they meet at Venice Beach. He'd seen people surfing there when he'd met José.

When Narayan arrived, he was in a mildly combative, jokey mood; he claimed Max was leading him far astray with his American obsession over sport. But he took to surfing and learned quickly. They rode in several times together, but soon Narayan fell quite badly, gashing his shin against the board. He was stoic about it as he limped up the beach.

'I've only myself to blame for trying to keep up with your really terrible showing off. It's all this American competitiveness,' he went on, mock plaintively. 'I'm allowing it to corrupt my pristine Indian soul. You look disgustingly impressive, shooting around like that. I've become so envious. I want to look as good. Appearances, Max! Deceptive, vain, physical appearances! And to think my religion calls them mere illusion, while your civilisation's built upon them.'

'Oh come on,' Max retorted. 'What about all those ostentatious Indian palaces and monumental tombs? Are you sure your leg isn't hurting badly? Or is your pristine Indian soul above mere pain?'

'Total yoga may deliver one from pain,' Narayan said. 'I'm a long way from that, though. My flesh can hurt like bloody hell.'

'Then perhaps you might stoop to taking some painkillers. There's a drug store round the corner, full of those potions and pills we swallow endlessly. This shameful American obsession with the body, with the material world in general, by which you soulful Indians are, of course, quite uncorrupted.'

'Mocking me again, Max,' Narayan chided. 'I hate airs of spiritual superiority; they always sound suspiciously like material sour grapes. There's some terrible corruption in India, where the new middle classes are as avaricious as the middle classes anywhere in the world. Even I am not exactly a paragon of self-denial. My problem is I'm greedy, as I've said before. Greedy for a few base material advantages but more, I confess, for some love and admiration.'

Max was taken aback by this admission. Shortly afterwards, having bought a bandage in the drug store, he swabbed Narayan's wound and tied the bandage around it. Their physical proximity as he tended to him caused him a stab of both tenderness and desire, curiously commingled. He recognised his attraction to Narayan was growing rather than diminishing. His feelings were enhanced by Narayan's unexpected words of encouragement, however casually he'd uttered them.

Had he spoken them out of emotional loneliness? Was it because he genuinely liked Max's admiration of him, just as long as nothing sexual followed? Max really had no idea but, as he drove home that evening, he suffered a sharp attack of conscience over Clare. He summoned up the memory of her beautiful face in an effort to counteract, to somehow erase, the handsome face of Narayan, a vision that threatened to haunt him equally with its very different but equally immense appeal.

Max rang Rick, saying he wanted to discuss some problems, but Rick had more urgent matters of his own to attend to. After countless affairs, Rick had settled down with an older man, Mike, who proved, with his stable ways, a perfect foil for Rick's mercurial temperament. Rick told Max that they had agreed to have a HIV test and Rick had found himself to be HIV-positive.

He'd taken this badly at first, and it had required patient persuasion from Mike to restore his confidence.

Max was much depressed by Rick's news at first, but he knew something of the advances in medication and he decided to find out more. He recalled his affair with Rick with nostalgic tenderness and regretted that he'd ended it so badly. He was glad they'd never had penetrative sex, although he didn't feel at all self-congratulatory about it; he worried far too much about Rick's condition.

'I have a photo session to complete in San Francisco,' Max told him.

'What did you want to talk about?' Rick asked. 'I can still listen and offer advice, you know… if you need it.'

Max sighed deeply.

'Oh, nothing,' he lied. 'Nothing that can't wait until I get back. I'll be thinking of you.'

'You sure you're okay?'

It felt absurdly wrong to burden a man recently diagnosed with HIV with more to worry about, least of all the complexities of Max's own love life.

'I'm okay,' he said.

∴

The time in San Francisco afforded Max the opportunity to think things through as he was working. He decided to donate a large sum of the money inherited from his father to an AIDS charity. His father would undoubtedly have disapproved, but he didn't let that worry him.

When he got back to Los Angeles, he was still torn about his feelings for Clare and Narayan. He called Clare often, loving the sound of her voice, reassured by its closeness and intimacy. Even so, his charged relationship with Narayan continued. Every other evening, they swam in the pool together or went surfing.

When Clare phoned from London to say she was catching a plane, she sounded strained. It was understandable, given that she'd stayed behind to look after Violet. When Max met her at the airport she broke down in his arms and told him that Violet had died. He held her tightly, desperate to console her.

'Why didn't you tell me on the phone?' he eventually asked.

'I didn't want you to worry,' she said. 'You didn't need to attend the funeral.'

'Didn't I?'

She didn't respond to that.

'I felt guilty about Violet… I still do,' she said.

Max admired her honesty but felt sorrow for her pain, and her vulnerability again intensely moved him.

∴

At the party Max had arranged to welcome Clare home, he wanted to introduce Narayan to her straightaway, but he didn't arrive until very late. Max discovered later that he'd thought it amusing to slip into the pool, unobserved. When Max saw Narayan's floodlit face surfacing in a stream of bubbles, he recognised an involuntary surge of delight and hope inside himself, and it alarmed him.

It was partly that rush of feeling that prompted him to leave the party with Clare and to drive out to Malibu. Of course, he wanted to be alone with her and to help with her grief. Getting away from Narayan, and from the turmoil his presence provoked, was not his primary motive though. He knew driving fast to the coast always raised Clare's spirits. When the whale had surfaced, invoking awe and some degree of fear, the lovemaking that followed had been extraordinarily intense for both of them. It was the memory of this that allowed Max to feel unthreatened by any feelings for Narayan when they spoke on the phone the next day.

'Hey, Max,' Narayan greeted him. 'Why leave last night as soon as you set eyes on me? People might've thought I was an interloper.'

'I'm sorry. I hope you're not too sore at me.'

'I'm so sore, it's really hurting. There I was, dripping from the pool, and all those smart people staring at me, wondering who is this mysterious, dusky stranger. A terrorist perhaps, sabotaging the swimming pool? Like in one of those wild soap operas. I mean, what with you rushing off in your swanky, high-tech car in the very middle of your own party. Such a dramatic style of life you have. It's no wonder I find you so peculiar.'

'And what about your own peculiar behaviour?' Max asked. 'Secretly entering the pool to thrash around like a zombie! Clare thinks you're definitely cracked.'

'So when are you going to allow me to meet her properly, so she knows I'm not cracked. From the glimpse I caught of her at the poolside, she looks a gorgeous broad.'

'You don't say "broad", Narayan,' Max chided. 'All this low American slang you're picking up, you must learn to use it a bit more accurately. I wouldn't overdo it or people might think it was my vulgar influence.'

'Then you must teach me classy correct American. If you come out to India, I'll be helping you with classy Tamil, after all. You will be coming out to India sometime, yes?'

'Oh yes, I'm sure we shall. Sometime.'

'That doesn't sound too enthusiastic. I'm not starting to bore you with my endless chatter and idiotic antics, am I? Or are you just too busy now that Clare's here?'

'Of course not,' said Max. 'I really want you to meet her. Would you be free this weekend?'

∴

Clare took to Narayan immediately. He behaved with all the easy courtesy that seemed second nature to him. He talked with her about Max, saying what a good friend he had become, and how open-minded and full of curiosity about India.

'So,' she began, after he left, 'I like your new buddy. So you met at your gym? What started you off getting to know him? His being Indian, I assume.'

'I've always been intrigued by India. Look, let's go there some day.'

'I'd love to.'

'Narayan can help us when we're out there. He knows a lot about his country and he's a practising Hindu. And he's a really nice guy.'

'I can see that. And, unlike some of your sports freak friends, he's not just about macho vanity and self-absorption. It's good he has a soul. When are you inviting him again?'

Max asked Narayan over two days later, and soon he was coming round at least twice a week. Eventually, Max broached with Clare the idea of their working together on a book about India. She thought it an excellent idea, and soon they started a course in Indian civilisation, offered by a university department. After a while Clare asked for a sabbatical from her job, and she and Max provisionally planned to go out to India the following year; they would stay with Narayan in Chennai.

Max continued to be disturbed by reluctant erotic fantasies of Narayan's hard male body. He would often visualise that body swimming underwater in the pool or shooting in on a breaker, thighs flexed, plunging down the wall of a toppling wave. Max tried to confine these fantasies to a corner of his attention, admissible but unthreatening, concentrating instead on the reality of his sex life with Clare and the undiminished fulfilment she would always give him.

Chapter Six

Max and Clare drove back to Chennai, three hundred miles north of Madurai. Clare felt some relief as soon as they reached the huge city, where it was far less likely the assassins could track them down. Although Veerapan had cautioned Clare and Tammy about a possible risk and Tammy had discounted it, Clare was torn between their conflicting attitudes.

She knew she could not go on worrying about the problem, as it would ruin their time in India. They had to focus on what they'd come out to do: research the book that was so important to them both. She believed the shared endeavour might help their marriage. She could insist they went home to Los Angeles, away from the assassins as well as from Narayan. But that would be cowardly and evasive. It was better to stay, despite the possible danger. She moved away from thoughts of being attacked, instead focusing on the gratitude and concern the cripple had directed towards her. There was no faking that, she thought. It had been real.

She and Max were looking forward to going to a performance of classical dancing. A Professor Subramaniam, an elderly relative of Tammy and Narayan, had invited them. The Professor was a retired historian in his late eighties. Narayan had phoned to say he was working late at the university and couldn't come. Clare wondered if he was putting off seeing Max and, if he was, what the reason might be.

Tammy took them in a taxi to pick up the Professor, who seemed delighted to meet Clare and Max, en route to the theatre. The theatre had a balcony upstairs, with an ornately carved, gilded balustrade, and a wide aisle. The Professor, leaning on a stick, chatted with them amiably as they walked to their front-row seats. The place was crowded.

The faded velvet curtains eventually parted to reveal a dancer already in position. The musicians sat alongside their stringed, big-bellied instruments. A rapid rhythm was being beaten out on little drums. A song began, and the dancer started to move.

Professor Subramaniam leant across to whisper rather loudly in Clare's ear.

'This is Radha, and she's complaining to the Lord Krishna.'

The song rose in pitch. The neck and head of the dancer moved from side to side, and she stamped her feet with mounting vehemence. The notes of the sitar swelled, vibrating loosely, and then trembled into silence.

The dance ended, and the audience began to applaud in a respectful, even mildly reverent, way. The dancer stood still, her face flushed, panting. She stared into the spotlight, the mascara around her eyes giving her a somewhat ferocious look.

'An Indian love dance,' said Subramaniam, delicately rearranging a tiny fold in his dhoti. He smiled reassuringly.

'This is the Bharata Natyam, the classic dance of India. And now she returns. I shall explain it all, don't worry.'

The dancer recommenced, slowly and imperiously, with a touch of condescension, as if she wasn't quite sure her audience deserved it. The Professor leaned forward with one hand cupped to his large, whiskery ear. He spoke again in a resounding whisper.

'Her mood is different. She is very sad.'

The dancer glared at him for an instant, in his vulnerable position in the first row. But she was soon again transported into her mythic world, evincing a fierce passion that didn't entirely suit the plaintive, gentle words he ascribed to her.

'She is saying, "My mind is restless. I can't sleep when my brave lord is away." Ah, but he does not come to her, the Lord Krishna. She says, "Come, sweetheart", but he does not come… he will not come.'

'Please sir, it is your kindness not to talk,' said a woeful voice from behind, but Subramaniam, perhaps intent on not hearing it, seemed determined to go on.

'Now the amorous Radha says, "The sun goes down and still my Lord Krishna does not come. Come, beloved. My blue god." He is blue, always is shown as blue. It's a mark of his very passionate nature. But still, the blue god Krishna does not come.'

There was considerable shushing from the rows behind. The old man gazed around for a moment, with an air of bewildered innocence, as if surprised by all the fuss and somewhat pained by it. Meanwhile, the dance continued, the dancer in a state of lofty ecstasy now, the drumming frantic but then falling into a more delicate beat that eventually faded out.

The performance ended. The audience clapped with greater determination. The dancer responded in a trance-like manner, just about able to notice the acclaim before gliding off in a majestic daze.

The evening continued with several performances by other dancers, but the Professor remained quiet during these.

'Tammy and Narayan have asked me to tell you something of our religion and our history' the Professor said to Max and Clare as they walk out of the theatre. So. Well, it's nice to have Tammy back from UK. Good to have Narayan back from USA. All these young men going to their wonderful foreign parts, and I am eighty-eight and have never been. Oh no… I'm eighty-seven,' He chuckled warmly. 'I'm so ancient I even forget my age. Anyway, what is age? Does it really matter? When you think of the aeons that have gone and are yet to come.'

'That's a good way of looking at it,' Clare said. 'I'll remember that when I next forget my age myself.'

'Very funny for one so wonderfully young. So, what are you thinking of our Indian classic dance? The love of Radha for Krishna is so very touching, is it not?'

Clare made some appreciative comment, but she hadn't really enjoyed the subject of the dance – a woman fruitlessly pining for her lover – because it had intensified the numbness she was feeling at the thought of Max being in love with someone else. The hurt still pierced her from time to time, and she felt jealousy and anger.

'I see Krishna as a figure of myth indeed,' said Subramaniam, responding to a question from Max as they reached a waiting taxi. Tammy helped the old man into it. 'But one who feels to me a living presence. So near and so consoling. A god with many aspects, often surprisingly at variance with each other. A handsome youth, full of mirth and mischief, stealing the clothes of milkmaids when they bathe in the river. But then, in contrast, Krishna's love for Radha is often thought of as symbolising the pining of the soul for God. In the Bhagavad Gita, he counsels us on our duties to society, and on the elimination of our bad, imprisoning desires. He's playful and amorous but also very serious and wise.'

The old man waved his long, thin fingers in the air. They rose and fell as he carried on speaking. Max and Clare were grateful for his help with the background for their book, especially as he'd been an active member of the Congress Party during the struggle for independence from the British. He had even been a witness to Gandhi's assassination in 1948. Venkataraman's assassination in the present had horrified him.

Clare therefore supposed he could be of some support to her and Tammy. On their return to Chennai, Tammy had been contacted by Inspector Veerapan, he of the wig-like hair and doleful manner. Tammy was wanted for another identification parade as the police had come under increasing pressure from the government and the media to identify the assassins. Clare couldn't bear to think of the knife thrust and the pain Venkataraman must have felt, not just the physical pain but the terror of the realisation that his life was ebbing away, with all his aspirations and goals now never achievable. She felt great empathy, as she'd done with her dying father, who'd been similarly frustrated, and it now occurred to her that her horror at Venkataraman's death owed something to that devastating loss eight years ago.

The taxi drove along the seafront, prompting Subramaniam to speak.

'Over there you will see Saint George's Fort. You British, who called this town Madras, built it. In the eighteenth century, the British and French fought for domination in Tamil Nadu, turning it into a battleground. Thousands of Tamils were killed. There was a Tamil uprising, but it was crushed, and the temple enclosures were filled with Tamil prisoners. We rejected the name Madras because of its imperialist associations and began to use an old Tamil name, Chennai.'

'So this was where the British Raj began?' Clare asked.

'Yes, oh yes,' Subramaniam replied. 'But the British Raj was very wrong. Forgive me, but I'm afraid it was. It depressed the spirit of us Indians. It damaged our self-respect, our dignity. The British, with some rare exceptions, learnt little of our feelings and thoughts. They knew little of our ancient holy books, our Rig Veda, which is older than your Bible, or of the Mahabharata, our national great epic, which contains the Bhagavad Gita, the glory of Hindu speculative thought.'

'And then there's the Ramayana,' Max interposed.

'A wondrous story,' said Subramaniam, smiling. 'It tells of Rama and his beautiful wife, Sita, who was abducted by the demon king of Lanka. The monkey god Hanuman flew with his monkey army to get her back, the reason, no doubt, for our partiality for monkeys, mischievous as they can be. The Divali festival is in honour of Rama and Sita. Some of the Mughal emperors found the Ramayana fascinating, even though they were Muslims. But the British? They weren't interested in our religion.'

'Surely some of us were,' Clare said.

'The majority saw Hinduism as superstitious and idolatrous. It was so arrogant and ignorant of them,' said Subramaniam, raising his hands in a quiver of protestation. 'No wonder they lost their empire. I mustn't be angry about it, though. I was when I was a young freedom fighter, but even then I had some kind friends among the British. It's just I hated the insensitive imperialism…'

His voice trailed off as he stared out of the taxi window, but he suddenly became animated again as something caught his eye.

'We're passing the aquarium,' he said. 'At one time, there were seahorses in there but now I think they've gone. I saw them sixty years ago, when I first married. My wife was just fourteen. She thought them marvellous. Little tiny horses from the sea, so very touching.'

He sighed as if to imply that even though the world went on without them, they had been a wondrous detail in it. Clare felt he saw his young wife as wondrous too. Sadly, she had passed away.

They drove alongside a railway line. Tammy and Clare sat in the back, with Max and Subramaniam in the front. A train was hissing slowly past, hooting shrilly and shooting out blasts of steam. The carriages overflowed with passengers, and several small boys could be seen crouching on the roof, the braver ones among them recklessly scampering from carriage to carriage, defying a fat policemen with a whistle that he furiously blew to no great effect.

'We rid ourselves of British rule through ahimsa,' Subramaniam continued. 'That is, non-violent resistance. It is what Gandhi taught us. Although it worked against the British, it wouldn't have succeeded against Hitler. But would it have worked in South Africa and Ireland? Resistance was sometimes very violent there and this provoked even more oppression.'

'Do you think non-violence would've brought freedom to the people in those countries any earlier?' Max asked.

'Well, we Indians won our freedom through ahimsa, although the British were quite oppressive. My uncle was shot in the Amritsar massacre, just after World War One. Four hundred men and women were killed. My father survived, but some years later he was arrested for being on Gandhi's salt march. That was in 1930, when I was thirteen. The salt tax was a symbol of our oppression. Two hundred miles we walked to collect salt from the sea. I remember the long and dusty road, with villagers standing by the roadside, gently cheering. And then the sea at last! Such a sense of liberation! But sixty thousand people were imprisoned as a consequence. My father was locked for six months in a single cell.'

'Were you imprisoned too?'

'No, I was too young.' Subramaniam waved his fingers once again. 'All long past now, but we must not forget. Forgive, but do not forget. We must learn our lessons from it. There must be the right to protest, just as long as it's non-violent. There's been such violence since, though. Yes, indeed. And now poor Venkataraman, knifed to death by a mere boy.' His voice rose. 'How could he have done it? Giving Venkataraman a flower, pretending to be devoted. Oh, so very false and terrible.'

Subramaniam stopped talking and gazed pensively up at the sky, as if he sought consolation in the windblown clouds. He began to chant softly to himself, his fingers ascending from his lap to tremble in the air at the more sonorous moments; they hovered and made tiny dips before alighting on his knees again.

The car slowed down because of a large and unwieldy procession. They passed a couple of vehicles carrying enormous cardboard statues of Ganesh, with dangling trunks and slowly flapping, elephantine ears. A line of sadhus, wearing holy threads around their torsos, held their hands together. They were quietly intoning, picking their delicate way forwards. Some boys dodged nimbly between the onlookers, selling glasses of syrupy-looking tea, thick with milk and sugar. One of them wobbled along on an antiquated bicycle, chirruping his bell and balancing trays of oozing sweetmeats precariously on one hand.

The taxi had to slow down more to avoid hitting an overloaded cart that was being pulled by two half-naked, sweating men. A garlanded cow, with silver-tipped horns, chewed its cud musingly and meandered across the road with all the stately freedom the reverence of India allowed it. As it passed a vegetable stall, it seized some cabbage leaves in its frothy mouth with a lordly tossing of its head, to the startled dismay of the stallholder.

The taxi moved slowly forward again and then stopped at some traffic lights. A large, throbbing motorbike pulled up alongside. Clare noticed the rider was looking over at Tammy, whose face was turned outwards, his arm on the ridge of the open window.

Suddenly she thought she recognised, behind the Perspex of the crash helmet, the troubled eyes of the boy assassin!

She saw the knife in the rider's hand and shouted out. Tammy reacted fast. He pulled his arm in from the window and wound it up at once. The knife struck the glass and rebounded. The driver pulled up on the clutch and the car lurched forward, through the red lights. A car was crossing the junction, and the driver had to swerve to avoid a collision. There was a scream and a shudder of wheels, followed by rasping shouts of protest and horns blaring out in anger and confusion. The car skidded towards a bullock cart; the animal jerked up its head, the whites of its eyes bulging. It emitted a terrified high bellow. The motorbike hurtled away with a reverberating thrum, leaving a trail of bluish fumes in its wake. The rider crouched forward, his body looking so thin and fragile on that vast machine, with its blazing headlamp.

The car had hit the bullock cart. It was only a glancing blow but the animal had been knocked down. It lay on the tarmac, bleating. The cow Clare seen earlier ambled grandly by, waving its great head as if in solemn deliberation and loftily preparing to overlook the incident. A policeman soon appeared, but no real damage had been done to the bullock or the cart.

Tammy was typically cool, surprising Clare with the assumption that the young man had merely been trying to cut the watch from his wrist.

'This happened to me once,' he said. 'The strap was sliced off with impudent expertise. The young thief dashed off with a cheeky grin, which made the theft even more infuriating.'

While Max took photos, Clare led Tammy aside and spoke to him.

'That might've been the assassin making an attempt upon your life.'

Tammy smiled incredulously.

'I don't think so,' he answered.

'The knife was far too large for what you suggest. And did you see the naivety of those eyes? Or the delicate, thin body? He was just like the assassin!'

'That's a very mild coincidence. Thinness isn't exactly uncommon in India. Nor is criminality among the young. It's a symptom of growing urban unemployment, desperation, lawlessness and social breakdown.'

Subramaniam was showing some solicitude for Tammy, although rather more, Clare thought, for the poor buffalo, whose owner Tammy now stepped forward to console with some much-appreciated banknotes.

As they got back into the car, Max looked inquiringly at Clare, curious about the closeness of her talk with Tammy. But she didn't wish to share her fears with Max. He would be over-anxious on her account, as he always was, and she felt too hurt and angry with him over Narayan to want his concern now. However, as they drove on, she thought again about the crippled beggar and the motorcyclist, and about their being hit men determined to murder Tammy in his turn. But how morbid was her fear for him! And how melodramatic! Perhaps she was falling in love with him, she pondered with vague irony, and her anguish only measured how far she'd fallen. That was absurd, though. She merely found his attention reassuring; she liked his strange courage and his nonchalant, dry wit.

She gazed at the car window, at the scratch on the glass where the knife had struck. She imagined the blow again, and the motorbike leaping forward with its raging engine. Then she thought about the cow with its flower-strung head, as if it travelled to some grave and peaceful ceremony, well away from all the noise and speed and violence.

Chapter Seven

Max hadn't seen Narayan since he got back from Madurai, and he'd missed him at the dancing. He was thinking back to the vicissitudes of their relationship when on his home ground in Los Angeles. Narayan had once left Los Angeles to visit some married friends of his in Mexico. Max had then thrown himself into his studies, trying to ease the dismay Narayan's absence caused him. He sent him texts but got back nothing in reply. When Narayan returned, Max did at last manage to reach him by phone.

'I'm driving over to see you,' Max said.

'I'm not sure that's a good idea right now,' Narayan replied, sounding guarded and reluctant.

'I really need to see you,' Max said, hearing frustration in his voice, and worrying about how he was coming across.

'If you're sure,' Narayan replied.

'I'm sure.'

Max drove too fast to the university campus. He loathed his feelings of uncertainty over Narayan, even more than he hated his guilt about Clare. He convinced himself that Narayan felt bad and wanted to put an end to things between them. To a certain extent, Max welcomed the idea. He hated being so much in someone else's power. He longed to be free of what he thought in his worst moments was a demeaning obsession that threatened his marriage.

Narayan was apologetic, though, when Max arrived.

'You took me by surprise on the phone,' he said. 'I'm sorry if I sounded a bit dim. I'm also sorry I didn't answer your messages when I was down in Mexico. I left my wretched mobile phone behind. I've only just read them. Sometimes I'm ridiculously scatty.'

'Oh, that's okay,' Max said. 'You sounded as if you didn't want me to come today, though. I thought I was maybe pushing you too much.'

'You certainly do push, but that impresses me. You're always reaching out at life, bursting with American achievement complex. If you're not rushing about controlling things, you don't feel quite alive, I imagine.'

'Oh,' breathed Max, with a smile. 'So I'm full of aggressive, misdirected energy? Like our president?'

'I'm just joshing,' said Narayan. 'No, not at all like your president. You love being on the move and self-improving, though, while I lazily stagnate. I was pretty active down in Mexico, mind. I climbed Popocatepetl, as I told you on my postcards.'

'Postcards?' said Max. 'I never got any postcards. You climbed Popocatepetl? Wow!'

'I sent two postcards,' said Narayan. 'It seems you and I are doomed to a state of non-communication! Oh well, maybe they'll turn up eventually. Anyhow, while I was there I got you this.'

And then he produced the gift. It appeared to be an ancient Mayan head figurine but Max at once knew it was a fake, a well-made fake but definitely a fake. It would have cost a fortune if it had been genuine, but Max decided not to reveal it wasn't. He smiled warmly as he took it. He was touched by Narayan's generosity, ashamed of his unspoken grievance and impressed by his climbing skills (having no head for heights himself, he'd always been impressed by mountaineering exploits).

'The antique shop said it was pre-Columbian,' Narayan added.

'Really?' Max feigned being impressed. 'It's incredible, thank you. I love it.'

'I wanted to check it out at the Getty museum first, so I could learn more about it. That's why I didn't want you to come today. But as you're here, I might as well give it to you now.'

It mattered nothing to Max that the head should be a fake. It was the giving that meant so much. Impulsively, he took Narayan's hand, surprising him. They just stood there in silence for some seconds. Max eventually found his voice. He seemed to drag it husky and disused from somewhere deep inside.

'I can't stop thinking of you,' he said. 'I can't help it.'

'I think of you, too.'

'Do you? Do you really?'

'Yes, Max. I really do.'

'I think of you in my arms,' Max blurted out. 'I want to make love to you. I suppose you'd hate it.'

'I don't know,' Narayan answered candidly, not at all offended, or so it seemed, by Max being so direct. 'The truth is, I've never made love before. Not to anyone. I've done a bit of frustrated snogging but that's all.'

'I can't believe it.'

'Our women are so dauntingly virginal.'

'Well, isn't it time you started?' asked Max, smiling and recovering his confidence. 'At twenty-six, you're getting on a bit.'

'I know,' Narayan laughed.

They were still holding hands.

'It's such a waste,' Narayan went on. 'I'm quite disgracefully immaculate.'

Both men laughed then, and Max released Narayan's hand.

'So you can't stop thinking of me. How boring for you,' Narayan teased. 'What on earth can you possibly see in me?'

'God knows!' Max replied with a grin. 'You're as ugly as a…' – he fumbled for the joke – '… as a toad and just as charmless. So anyway, tell me… do you like me back at all?'

Narayan raised his eyebrows.

'Or have I become a horrible embarrassment?' Max continued. 'Have you become all American and cool? Am I being schmaltzy?'

'Oh yes, definitely schmaltzy… disgustingly schmaltzy. I'm far too cool and cynical to have human feelings of any sort. I've become just like those silent majority American males you're always criticising: tough-minded and impenetrable, terrified of being thought sensitive and soulful. You've no idea how hard and mean I am. Beneath my toad-like surface, that's to say.'

Despite his joking, Narayan seemed embarrassed now. He appeared to lose his humour suddenly and to become vulnerable without it.

'I like your wanting me, Max,' he said. 'But I feel very bad about Clare. If it weren't for her…' His voice trailed off.

'Yes,' said Max dolefully. 'I know.'

'These feelings between men… I know they're not wrong. But back home they're thought of as unnatural. It's such a relentlessly heterosexual culture, fixated on marriage and having children to support one in tottering old age. So it's not just to do with us being two men.'

'Then what?'

'It's mainly Clare who worries me. If you want me, then you can't want her. Or can you? You'd be cheating on her. But I'd feel I was cheating on her too… and being a fraud.'

'Look, I still love Clare deeply. I always will. This'll make no difference to her and me. Anyhow, it's all your fault.'

'What? How so?'

'You shouldn't have given me this fantastic present. How did you expect me to react?'

'In that case, I'd better take it back,' Narayan answered, his smile returning. 'You know, it's not just that I feel bad. I also feel a fool. I've no idea what we actually do in bed… what two men do, I mean. You're dealing with a virgin, as I've told you. Unmentionable in your society, I'm sure, where sex is apparently so obligatory, although everyone starts out as a virgin. Even you!'

'Do you think I did?'

'But you're so attractive, in your highly suspect way. I daresay it wasn't for very long.'

Max had longed for encouragement but hadn't expected anything this explicit. He moved closer and put his lips to Narayan's mouth. Narayan didn't react at first but then very gradually began to return the kiss, which slowly deepened. They put their arms around each other. Max took off his shirt; Narayan, taking the cue from Max, did the same, stripping it from his back with an oddly touching awkwardness, grinning shyly. They undressed and lay on the floor together. The lovemaking that Max initiated, although constrained and lacking confidence, was to some extent reciprocated.

As they held each other afterwards, Narayan turned to look at Max.

'What are you thinking?' Max asked him.

'It's instinct, I suppose,' Narayan said. 'Or maybe I've made love in a past life, though God knows what the body was I did it in. It might've been that of some hairy gorilla whom you wouldn't have fancied much.'

He laughed at his own joke, which Max found curiously appealing. His laughing and talking about their sex delighted him. In the days that followed, Max went to see him several times in his hostel room on campus. The physical side of their lovemaking improved, Max feeling more actively desired. His own confidence grew. Eventually he told Narayan he loved him, which seemed to add to Narayan's ardour. His breath came tremblingly. His legs moved as if not under his volition. His eyes glazed over. Max felt the thudding of Narayan's heart as if it almost came from his own body. Narayan's spine arched backwards. His legs stiffened. His breathing was a series of rough gasps. With a shuddering of his entire body, Narayan came at last, crying out as from some convulsive pain.

As their mutual passion grew, so did the humour they brought to it. It seemed this was some necessary element to make the passion more acceptable. It made the guilt they both felt about Clare somehow easier to deal with. Narayan joked about his possible previous incarnations, which had set him down this terrible path of sensual desire.

'Maybe I was a deviant figure from the Kama Sutra, someone whose activities were expurgated even from that masterpiece of erotica. What will happen to my soul in my next reincarnation, I wonder? By the law of karma, I'll be reduced next time round to something unimaginably frustrating.'

'Like what?'

'A lustful spider, perhaps. A spider who's eaten her husband and suffers badly from second thoughts.'

'Are you having second thoughts?'

'No.'

'The Kama Sutra,' Max said, shifting his body slightly. 'I've heard so much about it but I haven't read it yet.'

'Oh really? I might've assumed you had.'

Max smiled at the implication.

'It says no guilt is attached to sex as such,' Narayan told him. 'Women are men's sexual equals. It's a paradox that Indian women have become so prudish on the whole since then – some of the middle class ones, at least. They can be so stodgy and respectable, like my harpy aunts.'

'Village women worship a phallic emblem in the temple sanctum, I've observed,' said Max. 'And yet kissing in public is frowned on. Another paradox.'

'Yes, it's strange that our culture venerates the sexual instinct, and yet there's this belief in the sanctity of chastity. As with Gandhi in his later years, his aim being moksha and not kama.'

'Moksha means spiritual enlightenment, right?'

'You've been doing your research,' said Narayan, pleased. 'Yes, and kama means the delights of love and sex. Dharma means virtue. All of these are part of being a good Hindu, such as I'm trying to be – but without spectacular success, I must admit.'

Their humorous fantasies grew as their intimacy grew. They spent time together in Narayan's room, in Max's car or on the wide windy beaches where they surfed – and the sense of privacy added to the charm Max found in them. Max wanted to keep their whole affair separate, inviolate, outside the equally charmed circle of his life and his love for Clare. Consequently, when circumstances came to threaten it eventually, he had notion how to react.

The first threat came about by accident. Max had given the fake Mayan head pride of place in his collection. When one of his friends dropped by he immediately spotted the new addition and picked it up, subjecting it to his sharp scrutiny. Jimmy, a corpulent, shaven-headed man with wandering eyes, thought he knew more than Max about Mexican art, and a knowing smile spread across his glossy face. Narayan smiled in return, pleased that his present had been singled out for such attention. Max stiffened slightly. He knew what was coming, and he dreaded it.

'Of course,' Jimmy said, 'you know this is a fake, Max, don't you?'

The air grew strained. Max changed the subject swiftly, not answering the question but instead bringing the subject around to the proposed visit to India. Jimmy, realising he'd made some sort of gaffe, tried to make amends.

'I visited India ten years ago,' he said. 'I loved the Buddhist murals at Ajanta, and the erotic carvings at Khajuraho were incredible. I remember well the noble, painted elephants, not to mention the quite impossibly handsome people.'

The strained atmosphere was not alleviated. Jimmy concocted some reason to be elsewhere and hurriedly said his goodbyes to the two of them. As soon as he'd gone, Narayan turned to Max, his eyes flashing with hurt pride.

'You knew it was a fake, Max, didn't you?' he exploded.

'Yes, but I like it,' Max conceded. 'Fake it may be, but I genuinely like it.'

'You didn't respect me enough to tell me.'

'How does my not telling you it's fake show disrespect?'

'It means you don't think I can take the truth,' Narayan said. 'You kept it from me to protect my wretched feelings.'

'And what's so wrong about protecting your touchy feelings?'

'It's patronising. It's treating me like a child.'

'Oh, for fuck sake,' said Max, exasperated. 'At the present moment you're acting very like one.'

'Damn you, Max! How dare you say that! I loathe all this pretence and secrecy, our horrible false positions. Why couldn't you be bloody straight with me at once?'

Narayan quickly left and drove away. In his desire for independence, he had bought a second-hand car that was ancient, noisy and unpredictable. Max was left alone, staring at Narayan's present, which he fancied was staring back as if it

105

mocked him. The row, he thought, was surely of his own making.

'I guess I overreacted,' said Narayan, when Max turned up on his doorstep the next day. 'It's bad enough deceiving Clare. I couldn't bear you deceiving me as well, even over something pretty trivial. I dislike myself for giving in to trivial grievances. If only I could wipe them completely from my mind.'

'But it was stupid of me,' admitted Max. 'I did always want us to be honest with each other.'

'Honest with each other, but not with Clare,' Narayan pointed out. 'That's not very noble of us, is it, Max? You're not going to get to heaven for that, and I'll probably come back as something really daunting, possibly a fat, lascivious warthog.'

'What makes a warthog lascivious?' Max asked, relieved they found refuge so quickly in their joking fantasies. 'What's the sex life of a warthog like, do you suppose?'

'Rather scratchy, I imagine. The faces of warthogesses, with all those warts, and whiskers, and nasty little tusks! Frankly, they don't seem all that seductive. Anyway, thanks to you, I'll probably be a gay warthog.'

'There might be gay warthogs for all we know,' said Max.

'Seriously, Max, the dreadful things you're doing to my soul. There's nothing in the Hindu scriptures against being gay, I think, but the Hindu ideal is to renounce the world and lust, despite the Kama Sutra, and you don't exactly encourage me in either. I mean, look at you.'

'Look at me?'

'Look at you, Max, with your terrible and conspicuous consumption. It's madness that I've fallen for you a bit. Your lifestyle is so materialistic: jacuzzis and swimming pools, supercharged aggressive sports cars and noisy, fuel-guzzling speedboats. This decadent obsession with flashiness and speed, wilfully ignoring the dire effects on the environment.'

'I get your point,' Max said, taken aback a little. 'So you've fallen for me a bit. Well, that's good news.'

'No, it's pretty bad news really. I was taken in at first by your being so sexy and self-assured. I was seduced by your wicked, superficial charm. There was I, an innocent young Indian, whose virginity you robbed so cunningly. Oh well, when you come out to India, I shall lure you into an ashram, where everyone takes vows of poverty and chastity, like with your Saint Francis. It'll do wonders for your consumerist persona.'

There were only three months left before they were due to leave for India. A fortnight Jimmy's visit, he discovered from Clare that Narayan had given Max the fake. He rang Max.

'I'm really sorry for making such a gaffe the other day. I didn't know Narayan had given you that fake and thought it genuine. But how delightful to be given a fake in such a manner! I wish I'd been given one or two by someone with such good looks and charm.'

Max found him funny, and blurted out what he maybe should not have said.

'I'm kind of in love with Narayan. Clare doesn't know yet. So for God's sake be discreet about it.'

Max didn't know how difficult Jimmy found discretion, and indeed Jimmy was soon unable to resist telling one of his most reticent of friends, who'd expressed curiosity about Narayan. Within a week, a group of the most discreet people knew about it, and one of them approached Narayan in the gym.

'I'm giving a gay party next Saturday, to which you've very welcome. Jimmy will be coming. Do bring Max along if you so wish.'

Max and Narayan had agreed to go surfing again next day. They met on the beach, where the wind was blowing hard. Narayan angrily told him about the invitation.

'You shouldn't have told Jimmy about us. That's something absolutely private. Look, I don't mind being thought of as having a few homosexual feelings. But I loathe being seen as the underhand destroyer of your marriage. I'd lose all dignity in other people's eyes. I'll lose all dignity and all self-respect.'

'That's ridiculous. You're being paranoid.'

'I resent that. Why can't you be honest with Clare about us?'

'It could destroy our marriage. What the hell do you expect?'

'She ought to know. If you don't tell her, I think I shall myself.'

Max was horrified by the threat.

'That's emotional blackmail,' he said. 'If you feel like doing a lousy thing like that then let's not meet any more.'

'I agree,' said Narayan. 'It's not fair for you to go on cheating on her like this. It's all so hole in corner… so degrading and contemptible.'

Max momentarily lost his temper, even raising his hand as if to hit Narayan. Although Max immediately controlled himself, Narayan was incensed by this reaction. They left the beach, neither of them feeling in the mood for surfing. Max felt ashamed but was too proud to say so in the face of Narayan's hostile stare.

'I won't be seeing Narayan for some time,' Max told Clare later. 'He feels he's spent too little time on his research, and he needs to concentrate more fully on all that.'

'Have you quarrelled with him, darling?' she incredulously asked.

'To be honest, yes,' said Max. 'I have slightly. He gets over-sensitive.'

'Much better than getting under-sensitive,' she quipped. 'What was it about?'

'That business over the fake Mayan head. He's a bit thin-skinned and can have real downers from time to time.'

'Don't we all? I hope you'll make it up. You don't lose friends easily. You're so loyal and tenacious, like with Rick.' Clare paused. 'Incidentally, how is Rick? Any more news?'

Such had been his involvement with Narayan that Max had not been seeing Rick as much as he'd intended, but now he contacted him again.

'I've taken up visiting AIDS victims in hospital,' Rick told him. 'I met a former lover of mine there. Ben. It was quite a shock.'

Max remembered Ben from the past.

'Can I come with you on one of your visits?'

Ben at first seemed more cheerful than Max had remembered him, telling various blue jokes and risqué stories, a habit he'd obviously picked up from Rick, although he lacked Rick's multicoloured imagination. When Rick left the room to visit someone else, Ben spoke.

'I appreciate Rick and I were only together for six months, and that was three years ago, but none of my other lovers have kept up with me. Rick comes every other day, but I don't want to become too dependent.'

Max felt ambivalent about this. The intensity and depth of Rick's emotional life impressed him. Although he knew he could develop AIDS himself, he refused to avoid awareness of its realities. On the one hand, Rick's involvement with Mike and his care for Ben encouraged Max, who was working through feelings he'd imagined he'd suppressed, and made him yearn to see Narayan again, despite his conscious resolution not to. On the other, and although he felt no shame at all about loving his own sex, Rick's commitment to his former lover, difficult and brief as it had to be, inspired Max to devote himself exclusively to his marriage with Clare, which was far easier and more enduring.

Chapter Eight

As soon as the taxi reached Narayan and Vijaya's seaside house on the outskirts of Chennai, Subramaniam announced that he would like to have a siesta.

'I get tired a lot these days,' he'd said before retiring.

The others went into the living room. The room was long and dark, with shutters covering the windows to keep out the heat. The house was very old – Narayan described it as 'trembling on the verge of dilapidation'. On the walls hung ancient wooden carvings, impressively worn and fissured. A sideboard had a rough crack in the middle, as if to boast about its dilapidation too.

'A evening raga,' Vijaya announced, holding a sitar. She plucked at a string, allowing the note to swell in quivering vibration. Her finger slid on the string, its delicate resonance diminishing. She played for a just a little while, with Max listening intently.

'I really loved that,' said Max. 'Please play more.'

'Max is really keen on Ravi Shankar,' added Clare. 'Back in Los Angeles he bought a couple of CDs of his concerts. He was always playing them and I enjoyed them. But my ear is not as finely attuned as his.'

'Indian classical music is perhaps a bit of an acquired taste for you,' Vijaya suggested.

'A taste I much want to acquire,' Clare replied. 'Yes, do go on.'

'I shall play more later,' Vijaya replied. 'Narayan will be here in a jiffy,' she added, her smile lighting up her soft features. Unlike Narayan, she spoke with a sometimes old-fashioned English slang, but her idiosyncratic humour was not dissimilar to his. She'd made the charming gesture of Namaste when she'd finished playing, something Narayan had resumed after his year in the America.

'Narayan loves to hear me play,' Vijaya went on. 'He loves Indian music, as he loves most things Indian. All that time with you in super-modern Los Angeles, and yet he's kept his roots here in his country. Of course I'm mad with envy of his time there. I feel my own life's been so narrow and constricted.'

Clare was only half-listening to the discussion. She had only partly recovered from the shock of the threatened knifing incident an hour ago. She was not convinced by Tammy's supposition that the youth had been merely out to slice the watch from his wrist. Why inspect his face so closely just beforehand? But if it had been a murder attempt, the rider must have followed them from the dance performance, making her wonder if they were constantly being followed? Had the cripple been following them ever since his appearance in that small hotel? Given that she and Tammy had been marked as prime witnesses, why would the youths risk carrying out another killing unless they were under some new and urgent pressure?

The police were certainly under increasing pressure. Commentaries on the television and in the press were demanding that greater efforts be made to capture the assassins. Venkataraman was being lauded as a lost leader, whose assassination put the Indian democratic process at risk. His party was offering a huge reward to anyone who could provide information that led to a conviction. He'd been known as a politician determined to combat corruption at every level of Indian society: among licensing officials, traffic policemen; he even included school headmasters, who were normally held to be paragons of rectitude. A newspaper article had hinted at a shady industrialist and his association with a politician known to be highly venal, and one whom Venkataraman had started to investigate. But the article had not implied any connection between them and the assassination, for a lack of hard evidence as well as fear of being sued for libel.

Clare recalled something Tammy had said: 'The assassins could've been prompted by some bitter sense of communal oppression, such as those that motivated earlier political assassinations, as well as by the crushing poverty in which they probably live. This makes them vulnerable to being seduced into being potential hit men. But of course there's no firm proof of any of this.'

Sometimes Clare longed to have the whole terrible affair forgotten. But she remembered Veerapan's resolve to find the assassins, fuelled by his belief that corruption and terrorism were the scourge of modern times, his sharp determination consorting oddly with his scrupulous manners and soft melancholy. She hoped that the killers would not be panicked into any further killing by all this publicity and pressure.

At Veerapan's request, Tammy was now at the police station, a grim concrete structure overlooking the sea front; he'd pointed

113

it out to her the previous day. He had been asked to take part in an identification parade. Before he went, he'd asked them not to tell Vijaya of the knifing incident. He didn't want her to worry, and Clare was impressed by his concern for her.

Vijaya began showing them her temple images. Before they'd gone to Madurai, Max had asked her to find some piece for him, and she gestured towards the four-armed image of Shiva on the sideboard.

'It's Shiva in his cosmic dance,' she declared. 'One hand is in a gesture of fearlessness, while another points at his foot, symbolising freedom and release. It's a very inspiring image. Narayan found it for you. It's a nineteenth-century reproduction. The original dates from Chola times, a golden age of Tamil art.'

'It's magnificent,' said Max. 'I'm over the moon about it.'

'Good, good! That's exactly what I said to Narayan! And there was Narayan, such a bag of misery.'

'A bag of misery?' questioned Max.

'Yes,' Vijaya went on. 'You left on the trip to Madurai, and he wasn't able to go with you because of his interminable lecturing. He was really in the dumps. He was looking everywhere for something for your collection. He kept saying that we must give you something special from Tamil Nadu. Shiva is much venerated here.'

'How do you mean, give me?' asked Max. 'Naturally, I'm paying for it.'

'Oh no,' Vijaya said, shaking her head. 'This is a present from us both.'

'But I commissioned you, as it were, to find something for my collection. It was a professional arrangement. I wouldn't dream of accepting it as a present.'

'But you must, or we might dream of taking it back again,' Vijaya said, the tone of her voice jokey but determined. 'We don't understand what you mean about a professional arrangement. We only know that we're your friends. Narayan's always saying you're his best friend, his buddy. There's no question of paying. That would be too awful.'

'But it must have cost a real bomb.'

'Really? But I've no idea what real bombs cost!' Vijaya laughed, smoothing her sari. 'So tell me, anyway, will this go well with your collection? The trouble Narayan went to in order to find something good enough for your top-notch collection… he worried himself crazy over it. But now, let's look at this, which Narayan gave me for myself.'

She pointed to a figure of a woman suckling an infant.

'This is the infant Krishna being suckled by Yashoda. It's an unusual subject. I find it rather moving.'

The child was reaching for Yashoda's breasts with tranquil expectancy, and Clare found the image moving too. She was moved also by Narayan having given it to his sister, who was doubtless yearning to have a child with Tammy. Clare was saddened to think how little he wished to marry her. She felt an involuntary stab of guilt lest she were in part the cause of this, despite her reluctance to return his feelings.

'When's Narayan coming back?' Max asked, breaking into her thoughts.

'Oh,' breathed Vijaya, thinking a moment. 'Ah, he said that he may be held up at a faculty meeting, where they'll be discussing too many things, no doubt. What chatterboxes people are, especially all these clever-clever scientists.'

'But did he definitely say it was a present?'

'Oh no, what he really said was "Max is to give me a million dollars for it, and I want it in ready money, please!"' She laughed delightedly. 'Look, what a chatterbox I am myself, and such a dreadful hostess. I must get you your whisky, or else you'll pack your bags and run off in a huff. Narayan got some in for you. He says you couldn't survive without your swigs of whisky.'

'I'm not sure we're quite as bad as that,' said Max.

'I'm only joking. I'm a dreadful tease. Narayan's made me become a tease in self-defence. He's always pulling my leg and laughing at me. Now, I must be off to get the drinks.'

Vijaya left the room, and Max turned to Clare as if appealing to her. Telling her of his feelings for Narayan seemed to have released him from the reticence she'd hated, from the inhibiting unease between them. His sympathy for her being in possible danger had also made him far more open with her, and she was glad at least for this small mercy. He decided to tell her more.

'Narayan and I had a really lousy row before we left. It was about my putting him into such a bad position, in relation to you... about his guilt.'

'Didn't he put himself into this position?' Clare retorted. 'Doesn't he indulge his precious guilt?'

'No, it genuinely makes him feel bad. He's extremely fond of you, you know. He hated my deceiving you about him.'

'Extremely fond of me!' scoffed Clare. 'Don't kid yourself.'

'He admires you, Clare… especially your courage. Why don't you believe me?'

'If he admires me that much, why has he gone with you behind my back?'

'He's only gone with me with great reluctance. I talked him into it.'

'He should've resisted going with a married man, but I see you're determined to defend him. So what did you row about, exactly?'

'Oh Christ, the screwed-up things we've sometimes said to one another. He loathes the slightest idea of being patronised by me… of my being the superior one in our relationship. He has a thing about my money, I suppose. He's not comfortable about my American money. He's got a bit of a love-hate thing about America, for sure, admiring its scientific progress but resenting its top nation arrogance. I tell him to hell with my money. We're absolutely equal in every way. He tends to be so instantly defensive, but in the end he longs to make things up.'

'So now this wondrous peace offering.'

'It's a magnificent present. I'm really grateful. I'm immensely grateful to you too. I don't know what I'd do if you weren't so understanding and supportive. As little as I deserve it, I couldn't exist without our marriage.'

∴

Max and Clare both needed to be alone at times, even when they were happy with each other. In his solitude, Max often thought of their times of special closeness. He'd always loved the physical closeness before they made love – the caresses, the murmured words, the hushed half-spoken language of their intimacy. His dread of its destruction was what held him back in his love for Narayan. Yes as his desire for Narayan grew he felt it was part of his true nature, and repressing a desire so basic and involuntary would be dishonest, even though he hated cheating on Clare, whom he desired just as intensely.

Max recalled the strange course of events during Narayan's last fortnight in Los Angeles. Paradoxically, it was Clare who reunited them by suggesting Max call Narayan. He resisted the idea at first, but that only made her more determined that he sort things out with him.

'He's so witty and amusing,' she said. 'I find his being Indian intriguingly exotic, and he's so well informed about his country.'

Eventually Max swallowed his defensive pride and rang Narayan.

'I felt too strongly but now am more detached. I hope we can be friends again.'

'I'd like that very much,' Narayan answered.

'I lost my temper with you. I hate to lose to lose my temper. It makes me feel a fool. I'm really sorry for it.'

'We were angry at each other. We were both at fault, I think.'

They agreed to meet; this time Clare was present, as she'd planned. She invited Narayan round for a vegetarian meal she'd specially prepared. She teased him, and her joking greatly eased the situation.

'You're a compulsive boffin, Narayan,' she said. 'You abandoned us on behalf of your wretched molecules. They sound so boringly predictable. Or is that my disgraceful ignorance of science, which secretly makes me feel a bit inferior?'

After that, Narayan and Max met twice alone. The first time was at Venice Beach, Narayan's favourite place in Los Angeles, where the two men watched the high-speed roller-skaters, the muscle-bound narcissists of Muscle Beach and the incredibly tall basketball players who leapt high in the air, hurling the ball jubilantly about. They ate in a cheap restaurant with bohemian pretensions, where José had taken Narayan. The burgers there were named after American literary figures: Max ate a Scott Fitzgerald while Narayan had a vegetarian one called Sylvia Plath. Narayan had read Plath's poems, at José's prompting.

The second time was on Narayan's last day. Max suggested they drive out to the beach house in Malibu, where they could surf together. By the time they got there, it was raining heavily, the wind was scouring across the sea and the waves were rising high. Max was surprised by the savagery of the ocean, and went to check on his speedboat, which was moored down by the jetty.

As he walked towards the jetty, he noticed a dinghy some way out to sea, its sails wildly flapping. He recognised it as belonging to a young married couple from a nearby beach house.

'They're obviously in trouble,' he shouted at Narayan. 'We could take the speedboat out and rescue them.'

Max ran along the jetty, with Narayan following him. The sea hurled its weight onto the thick wooden structure, making it creak beneath its heavy pounding. His speedboat was bucking on the waves and getting battered by the water. A wave descended and exploded onto the deck. Max was swept over the side of the jetty before he could climb on board. He grabbed at the stern as he fell. It rose with a jerk and came back down again. And then a sudden darkness overcame him.

He was in a place of swirling movement. He gasped for air, but there was no air! He felt a mouth on his mouth, and then a heavy sucking at his straining lungs. He could hear his name being called, as if from far away. His lungs laboured in pain. He was being held by someone, then the mouth made contact with his mouth again, filling him with streaming air. He fell into unconsciousness once more.

∴

When Max came to, it seemed as if a long time had passed. The wind had died down. He couldn't hear any crashing of waves. He was lying in a bed in the beach house. He remembered the couple in the dinghy: the woman with her blond ringlets and sensual mouth, the man with his thick biceps, unshaven face and dark blue eyes. He thought of their mutual absorption that had so struck him with its intensity.

Narayan was there, beside him.

'What happened to me?' Max asked.

'You were hit on the side of the head. Just a glancing blow, but it knocked you out. I pulled you out of the sea.'

'And then gave me the kiss of life, I think.'

Max felt gratitude course through him. He wanted to touch the mouth that had given him air and given him back his life – but suddenly he imagined the dinghy keeling over, swamped and sinking.

'Do you think that couple have survived?' he asked.

'I don't know. I rang the lifeguards in the area. They came round but have seen nothing.'

'You took a bit of a risk you took, fishing me out,' Max said.

'Not really. I'm glad to have been of help,' Narayan answered. He paused before adding, 'I'm glad to have been able to show you something of what I feel for you.'

Max looked at him.

'And what do you feel for me?' he asked, with feigned, jokey casualness. 'Apart from my being tolerable when not making embarrassing emotional demands.'

'Look, there's more to me than being feebly embarrassed.' Narayan seemed slightly indignant at Max's irony. 'Why didn't you ring before? Why wait until just before I left?'

'Couldn't you have rung me?' pointed out Max, recovering his strength and wits after almost drowning. 'Wasn't it you who was scared of getting too involved? You, with your idiot conformism. You, who couldn't bear the thought of loving another man. Oh so unnatural and disgusting. And so inadmissible.'

'You know it wasn't mere conformism,' Narayan protested. 'Of course I think it's natural. We're part of nature, aren't we? The disgust is mere social conditioning. No, it was guilt over Clare. But I overreacted, stupidly. I'm really sorry now. What a bloody awful waste it's been.'

Narayan smiled then, touching Max and gently kissing him. Max responded passionately. It was as if the danger of near death had filled him with the desire to hold on to life in its most exciting form. He and Narayan made love with mounting ardour. It was as if the lost time could be retrieved, as if they could make up for all that had been wasted, all the passion rejected, all the desires unfulfilled. Max felt his excitement gather. He heard the beating of the waves outside as though they were the beating of the blood in his own veins. Outside their private world, the night with the storm blown over seemed strangely peaceful, as though reflecting the peace that came over them once they had reached their mutual climax. Max let his mind drift to the couple in the dinghy; he imagined them lying equally at peace in each other's arms, their mouths pressed together. Through the window he saw the stars in a glittering diffusion, the moon casting its frail glimmer on the sea.

Narayan's head rested on Max's shoulder, and Max looked down the length of their two naked bodies, admiring the contrast between their differing colours.

'I'm so boringly colourless compared with you,' Max joked.

'Oh well, I know you were born that way. You can't help it.'

'You're leaving tomorrow,' Max said suddenly. 'I don't know what I'll do without you now.'

Narayan paused a while before replying.

'I hate the idea of deceiving Clare but I hate the prospect of losing you far more. I hope you'll tell her about us, though I fear she's going to say you shouldn't see me again. I know that is the likely outcome. I appreciate your dilemma now, as I failed to do before.'

∴

It was two in the morning when Max suggested they go for a swim. As they swam out to sea, Max recalled the night he and Clare had sighted the whales: the water swelling and splitting open, the soaring bulk of the enormous creature, its piercing eye and thrashing tail, and how they'd been in awe of its dark magnificence. His though of his lovemaking with Clare, saw its passion and its beauty, even as he swam to Narayan's side to float with him in a loose embrace. Clare's face came vividly to mind – her rapturous eyes and feminine soft mouth – as he faced Narayan alone in the sea, with his muscular arms and masculine features.

As they walked along the beach after their swim, they both spotted something in the distance. At first it seemed like a glistening white shell among the seaweed, washed up on the sand. But no.

'God,' was all that Max could say. Narayan said nothing but exhaled slowly, taking in the sight.

It was a face, with an arm stretched out above it. The body lay where the waves hissed on the sand. They rippled over the face, with its dead mouth and open eyes, stirring the blond, tangled hair. It was as if the woman had been delivered up by the now quiet waves in the position she was in when life had left her. It was as though she was reaching out for someone.

Narayan closed the woman's eyelids, then lifted the body over his shoulder. Her head fell back, the soaked hair dangling, the shirt half torn away. Her breasts were unmarked, though, as if the sea that had seized and drowned her had carefully preserved her skin. When they reached the beach house, Narayan gingerly arranged the limbs, the head, the strands of hair.

'She's beautiful,' Max said. 'What a tragedy. I suppose her partner's drowned as well.'

'He must have,' Narayan replied. 'And to think they were parted as they drowned.'

Narayan then knelt and prayed. Max, in his own form of silent prayer, offered up thoughts for the young man. Max knew he could have suffered the same fate were it not for Narayan. He imagined the woman desperately reaching for the man, and wondered where his body might be floating. Then his prayer turned to matters closer to him: his feelings for Narayan, his concern for Rick, his sorrow for Ben and, most importantly of all, his deep and enduring love for Clare.

∴

A month after Narayan's departure, Rick called.

'My affair with Mike has ended. I told him I was in love with Ben again. I said I still needed Mike and hoped he'd tolerate this love that unexpectedly recurred, brief and sexless as it has to be. I was astonished when Mike said he couldn't. I was shocked by his jealous anger. The next day he packed his things and left.'

Max found himself thinking ever more seriously about the new direction his life was taking. After Narayan returned to India, he exchanged texts with him several times a week. In those texts, Narayan revealed that he couldn't stop thinking about Max and longed for him to come out to Chennai. Max thought of him incessantly, although he also thought of Rick and Ben and the happiness they'd resolved to seize from what little time they had left together.

Max thought of how Clare had liked Narayan so much that she'd helped to reconcile them when they'd fallen out. She was grateful to Narayan for saving Max's life. She knew the immense importance Max attached to their marriage and might concede the respect Narayan had for it. But he wondered if she would keep reacting with anger, pain and grief. Max felt anxious about this but knew he had to face up to reality, to live his life in accord with his divided nature. His love for Clare seemed only to intensify the more he loved Narayan. He dreaded losing his wife, but he could also lose Narayan. When he thought about not having Narayan in his life, he felt it was better to have loved and lost than never to have known this difficult but wondrous passion, to never have taken the risk at all.

Chapter Nine

'I've had a good sleep,' Subramaniam said, addressing Max and Clare. 'And now I'm looking forward to a nice, long chat. Narayan says you want to know more about our history, to help you with your book. Western people do need to know more about our old civilisation and ancient wisdoms, I believe.'

Max sat down beside him.

'We do know that India achieved much more than the British thought,' he said.

'Indeed, yes,' said Subramaniam. 'In the fifth century, it was an Indian mathematician who pioneered the use of zero. One of our astronomers divined that the earth went around the sun, a thousand years before Galileo. Under the Gupta kings, we had an advanced iron technology, but no capital punishment, no slaughtering of animals. The British never recognised any of this, being so wilfully Eurocentric. They wished to justify the Raj, you see.'

He paused, smiling at Clare a little awkwardly.

'You are British, aren't you? And your good husband is American. A most interesting mix.'

Narayan came into the room then and shook Max's hand with his usual warmth. Then he kissed Clare fondly on the cheek, a kiss she couldn't easily refuse.

'What a terrible experience you had in Madurai... you and Tammy,' Narayan said. 'I hear you were very brave. I can't tell you the enormous sympathy I feel.'

Clare found that difficult to accept when she hated the falsehood that she saw in him. Narayan, though, was delighted to hear that the present of the Shiva image, the Nataraja, had pleased both Clare and Max. After Max thanked Narayan, perhaps a bit too profusely, Vijaya touched the figure.

'It's so beautiful as well as so significant,' she said, adding jokingly, 'I have to confess, I'm really envious. I wish now that I'd kept it for myself.'

'Envious?' Narayan repeated. 'But you have the figure of Yashoda and the infant Krishna. You're so greedy and demanding.' He turned and smiled at Clare. 'You don't know how much I'm hen-pecked, Clare, or rather chick-pecked. Chick-pecked by my little sister, who's very bossy! She's taking after the virago aunts. If you don't look out, Vijaya, Tammy may take fright and have second thoughts.'

'Really, Narayan,' Vijaya retorted, too abruptly. 'The ridiculous things you say.'

'Narayan, my dear fellow,' interposed Subramaniam, 'all this you say about being chick-pecked and Tammy taking fright… some of your chatter is such nonsense. I wonder what America has done to you. Oh, no disrespect to you, Max. It's just these young men go to their foreign places and come back so changed… it's most confusing for me. And now he says Vijaya is a bossy boots. And yet he jokes. He is a funny chap, our Narayan. Always joking, always laughing. Even as a little boy, he was always teasing poor Vijaya. And now he is so suddenly grown up.'

Vijaya had left the room, and so she hadn't heard Subramaniam's words. Clare was wondering when Tammy would

127

arrive. It was just as well he hadn't heard that joke of Narayan's about his having second thoughts, which had caused Vijaya's mood to change so quickly. She returned with a tray of drinks, soft with one exception: a bottle of whisky.

'Of course, Vijaya imagined I'd come back from the USA a totally American creature,' said Narayan. 'She thought I'd become a sort of Hollywood cowboy, swaggering into bars and endlessly knocking people out, or else a decadent pop idol with skin-tight, spangled trousers, saying "Yeah, man, yeah!" each time I gave myself another fix. Or maybe she saw me as a militant fitness freak, with gym-cultivated muscles, luridly covered with tattoos.'

'He's always mocking me,' said Vijaya, assuming an air of confidence as she poured out alarming amounts of whisky for Clare and Max. 'But Narayan came back with a definite American accent, and he started using all sorts of funny expressions. He talked of nothing but you, Max. Max says this… Max says that. Who is this Max person? Who is this mystery American always haunting you? All this fitness freakiness; he never did it so much before coming under your influence.'

'I'm a bit of a fitness freak myself,' said Subramaniam with one of his little chuckles. 'I've always done hatha yoga. Yoga means union in Sanskrit – it's about being at one with the universal spirit. Two thousand years old, our yoga is, while modern science is so very new, coldly trying to explain the world away and taking no account of its great mystery.'

'Yes, the world is mysterious and ultimately inexplicable,' said Narayan, 'as many modern scientists might agree.'

'Indeed, indeed. We live in a state of maya, of illusion. The physical world you study is full of freakish strangeness.'

Vijaya now turned enquiringly to Subramaniam.

'Yes, Vijaya,' he said. 'I'd like some nice refreshment. Mango juice, oh yes.' He eyed the whisky, making a little joke. 'And I'd like it neat, as well.'

Tammy arrived then. He's brought Maria, a colleague from the university. Clare had met her briefly before the expedition. Maria was fat and jovial, with a wide mouth that was plastered with crimson lipstick, and black curly hair that tumbled down to her shoulders. She'd brought her baby boy along, and occasionally suckled him when among her friends. This didn't always put a stop to the infant's vociferous complaints, although they were generally replaced by appreciative little burps and gurgles of delight.

Tammy had picked up Maria and her baby on his way back from the identification parade, about which he now complained.

'None of the young men in the line-up bore the faintest resemblance to the assassins. Some were too old, with balding heads and heavy paunches. Others were obviously chosen only because of their scowling looks. Well, I'm not as impressed as you are, Clare, by the Inspector. Sorry about that, since I know you wish to believe in his effectiveness.'

Tammy looked unsettled, which could have been because, that morning, he had received a long email from his Muslim friend Shahpur, saying he'd had a bitter row with his Hindu girlfriend's father, who'd forbidden his daughter Kalyani to see him any more. The father threatened to turn her out of the house if she persisted. This had caused his wife to break down in tears. She was in timid rebellion against his patriarchal despotism, regretting Kalyani's love for a Muslim but wanting to keep her beloved daughter in the family. Near to despair, Shahpur was trying to persuade Kalyani to go off with him without her father's blessing, and she was painfully undecided.

Maria kissed Vijaya before taking the hand of the old man as she coaxed her reluctant child towards him.

'Professor Subramaniam, you once told me you love little children.'

'Did I say that, dear lady?'

'Yes, you said that was the bit you liked most in all the Christian gospels, about not getting into the kingdom of heaven unless one became like a child. But Jesus had no children, so how could he really know what they are like?'

'He was a great moral teacher, one we Hindus enormously admire,' said the Professor. 'We especially love his sermon on the mount. Christians see him as the third part of God, like our Hindu trinity of Brahma, Vishnu and Shiva – all different aspects of the same divinity. What Jesus said about the little children, I think he meant that as a metaphor.'

'How do you mean?' asked Maria.

'I mean our minds are too full of adult confusions: rivalry, vengefulness and greed. Surely, Jesus meant one needs to have the simple mind of a little child to enter heaven, although our idea of heaven is very different from your Christian one, with its separate souls. For us, it's a state without individual desire and suffering, all our souls being merged into one great spiritual union.'

'Children can be even greedier than adults and often just as vengeful,' Maria murmured, before turning to Clare to ask her about her trip.

Clare was about to answer but her attention was captured by the old man, who was smiling at the inquisitive, roly-poly infant, whose hands were making little grasping motions. The child reached for Subramaniam's spectacles; frustrated in his attempts to seize them, he began to whimper ominously.

'The infant's too hot, which always makes it cross,' Maria commented, forgetting that she'd just asked Clare a question. 'It really can be quite ferocious sometimes, in which respect it takes after Antonio, not me.'

'You shouldn't call him it,' said Vijaya. 'He's him.'

'Oh, for me it's usually it. I love to think of this as my little thing, all warm and cuddly, which won't grow up into some lustful and deceitful male, leaving its fat, old mother in the lurch.'

'Antonio?' asked Clare.

'Its horror of a father,' Maria sighed. 'I see I'll have to tell you the gruesome story. I left the brute in Rome. I really couldn't take him any more.' She lowered her voice, and leant over to whisper in Clare's ear. 'He's got more sexual stamina than is probably desirable, but he's not so well endowed with other talents, such as the ability to resist other women. In fact, he's an animal of monstrous promiscuity. So he remained in Rome and I came here.'

Maria was interrupted by a bellow from the child, who had a plastic toy in his hand, raised menacingly above his head.

Apparently, it was just about to be hurled at someone. The old man smiled with determined benignity, but Maria remained blithely unperturbed.

'You mustn't allow it to annoy you, Professor,' she said. 'Non-violent resistance may've been fine when dealing with the faintly civilised British, but it shouldn't apply to savage little children.'

The infant began to howl in an agony of frustration. Maria, with a martyr's sigh, scooped him up, still grimly clutching his toy missile. After an interval of not very tuneful crooning, she went on to tell Clare something of her recent life, while thumping the infant lovingly upon his back to deter the aggressive belch he threatened to emit. She spoke with a cheerful lack of reticence and possibly a certain exaggeration for the sake of the narrative appeal.

'I'm Italian-American in origin,' she declared. 'I read Italian and French literature in the United States. When I graduated, I went to sacred Italy. I lived with the profane Antonio, who abandoned me six months after I bore his child, a man-child, from his very loins. Such tears, such sentiment, such treachery. He was lured away by a predatory female, loaded with disgusting lucre. She was captivated by his physical charms but had no idea how generously he offered them around. I ceased repining after a while and applied for work at the university here, which is where I've been for the last six months.'

The infant had wriggled his way out of his mother's arms. He threw the missile down on the floor in a fury of displeasure and squirmed against Maria with redoubled energy.

'It's still too hot,' Maria said. 'Let's get its clothes off. It always behaves better when it's innocently nude. Give me a hand, Vijaya darling.'

Vijaya moved to help her, holding the boy as still as she was able to.

'Ah, there's its little cock,' Maria said as she removed the infant's little yellow pants. 'Trés charmant but inclined to be so unpredictable.'

Maria talked about being abandoned by her man in spite of the demon he'd turned out to be.

'I should've known from his eyes, so glistening and predatory. But I refuse to be maltreated by a man ever again. I'll forget about that brutish egotist and find some selfless Indian who's quiet and contemplative, and who rises above all temptations of the flesh – apart from mine, of course! I'll find someone who'll dedicate his life to my total happiness. You're looking sceptical, Clare.'

Clare said nothing.

'You don't think such a being could exist in raw reality?' pressed Maria. 'Not even in miraculous, sweet India?'

She heaved a mockingly self-piteous sigh. She held her infant close, and then patted his pink bottom with her ring-encrusted hand before opening her dress and offering him one of her large, blushing breasts.

'I believed in suckling till very late. I'm convinced most of the neuroses of the modern West sprung from being torn from the breast too early.' Clare wondered if they could also spring from having it thrust upon one for too long, but she kept that opinion to herself.

Across the room, Tammy and Narayan were drifting into an argument.

'I think it's down here in Tamil Nadu that Hindustan is at its purest,' said Narayan.

Tammy sighed impatiently.

'Tanjore, the capital of the Chola Empire, was the Athens of India, with its bronzes, its frescoes and its literature. Our kings undertook huge irrigation schemes. They sent armies to Sri Lanka and as far north as the Ganges.'

'Our country is called India, not Hindustan,' said Tammy, greatly annoyed. 'We also have Muslims, Sikhs, Jains, Christians and Parsees. With 1.2 billion people, we've a greater diversity of language, race and religion than any other country in the world. We stay together, despite separatist extremism in Kashmir and the Punjab, and the regional prejudice of the sort you're sentimentally expressing.' He seemed moved by an intensifying frustration. 'The Cholan Empire's bloody well over. All this ancient history, it's so divisive. Your whole attitude's so fucking backward looking.'

Surprised by his own outburst, Tammy looked around in some embarrassment. Vijaya lowered her face while Subramaniam gazed at him reproachfully.

'You shouldn't use such horrible words,' said the old man, 'especially in front of gentle ladies.'

'He only uses them because he feels so strongly,' Clare said.

'Nonetheless, he shouldn't use them in front of ladies,' Subramaniam insisted. 'I, too, have felt strongly about Indian unity. I, too, don't call India Hindustan. Thinking that way makes for faction and for strife, such as tragically happened over the long years. Those Partition riots that Gandhi tried to stop by fasting… I'll never forget when he was assassinated.'

'Narayan tells me you witnessed it,' said Max.

'Yes. One moment he was walking among us in his garden, his nieces on either side of him. And then this man appeared out of nowhere: a mad extremist who hated Gandhi's attempts at reconciliation with the Muslims. He bowed and made the gesture of Namaste before he shot him. People tried to go to Gandhi's aid, but it was too late: the wound was a fatal one. The news spread like wildfire. People of every faith were weeping in the streets. The assassin was hanged, something Gandhi himself would never have approved of.'

Subramaniam paused a moment, then looked at Clare as he spoke again.

'This young assassin the other day. He seems to have come out of nowhere too. Nobody knows what his motives were.'

'Unlike when Indira was assassinated,' said Tammy. 'She was also shot down in a garden because she ordered the storming of the Sikhs' Golden Temple. Indira had become a bit of an autocrat, suspending democracy in the Emergency of seventy-four.'

'An autocrat?' said Subramaniam, shaking his head. 'Nonsense, my dear fellow. She was mainly a good woman… her father's daughter. But she'd tragically lost her elder son, and the emergency was a temporary mistake. Our democracy recovered. It has the largest electorate in the world, which is most marvellous. Yes, the storming of the Golden Temple was very wrong but to be shot by her Sikh bodyguard? That was most terrible.'

'It caused widespread revenge against the Sikhs,' said Tammy. 'Thousands were massacred. All this mass, knee-jerk retaliation! It's appalling.'

Subramaniam nodded in agreement.

'All these assassinations in our recent history. Indira's second child, Rajiv, cruelly blown up… and by a suicide woman! Just imagine. Murder and suicide together… that was something we never had before. It's a terrifying feature of our times. And now Venkataraman, knifed to death by a mere boy. Why did he do it? He must've been hired. He must be punished when he's caught, but I hope he won't be hanged like Gandhi's assassin. Ahima means respect for all living things. It's wrong to kill, and two wrongs never make one right.'

'He was obviously pressured into it,' Tammy replied. 'He can't be held entirely responsible. As one of the oppressed and dispossessed, he had nothing in the world to lose. Great poverty drives the really desperate to crime and terrorism.'

'You seem to think all crime is the result of poverty,' Narayan objected strongly. 'That's utter nonsense. Most poor people don't resort to crime and terrorism. If they did, society could not exist at all. Everything would be violence and murderous confusion.'

'Societies with extremes of wealth and poverty have far more crime than those with more equality,' Tammy answered. 'The new affluence is largely confined to the top twenty per cent of the population, drawn mainly from the upper castes. There are still four hundred million without electricity. What's spent on public health is among the lowest in any country anywhere: only 1.2 per cent of GDP. Compare that to the world average of 6.5 per cent. Opportunities for the lower castes are better now than they were, but they need to be enormously improved.'

'I know it's your profession, but how you hold all these figures in your head amazes me!' Subramaniam exclaimed. 'But violence is no answer to social unfairness and oppression. The answer for my generation was non-violent resistance to British rule. Perhaps it could be for your generation too, in resistance to all these inequalities. We Congress people used to lie down in the streets to stop the soldiers marching. And we lay on the railways tracks to stop the trains. The British put me in prison for sedition. I spent six months in solitary confinement.'

'Did they allow you books?' Clare asked.

'Yes. I read the Bhagavad Gita many times. I read Tolstoy's The Kingdom of God is Within You. Its basic Christianity greatly influenced our Gandhiji; it told us to control our natural egotism, our pride and rivalry. He believed Hindus and Muslims should never fight each other. Muslims should know more about Hinduism, and Hindus should know more about Islam. I think it's a beautiful religion, though it's not mine. The Koran acknowledges Abraham, Moses and Jesus. It says that our God and your God is one and the same. I've known Muslims say that if Mohammed had known about Hinduism, he'd have included our sages too. Islam should be regarded with respect and not misgiving.'

'It's surely the world's number one problem,' Max said. 'It's a problem that there's this ignorance and fear of Islam, and that it should be so mixed up with politics and power.'

'Indeed, indeed,' the old man continued. 'We never expected to have three leaders murdered for political-religious reasons… and now a fourth in Venkataraman. He was probably killed for his brave opposition to political corruption… all this terrible corruption.' His voice rose. 'It is so destructive of good government, so demeaning of our high ideals.'

Subramaniam paused to control his indignation, which seemed to have rather taken him by surprise. 'It wasn't always like this,' he went on, his voice calmer. 'The times we knew… the good people who have gone. How fast the years have sped by, how sadly vanished.'

He looked a touch exhausted by his fervour and slumped back against a cushion with a little sigh. Tammy began to speak.

'When I came back from Cambridge, I felt so rootless and cut off. I went everywhere, wanting to feel I really was an Indian. Shahpur and I slept on rope beds in the open. He carried a small prayer mat for worshipping the single God he loves so loyally. Yet he also loyally loves this Hindu woman, who worships many gods. He says one God or many, they come to the same thing in the end: our endless search for spiritual light.'

'I don't agree,' said Narayan. 'The two religions are fundamentally so different.'

'You think so? Anyhow, we slept one time in a converted buffalo shed in a poor little Hindu village in Rajasthan. Some of the younger villagers accepted him as a Muslim, but their elders didn't. India is still seventy per cent villages, you know. Most of them have open drains and intermittent, unreliable electricity.

The women are so beautiful, though, and move so gracefully. And the children are so high-spirited. We walked through fields of yellow mustard to the local primary school, where they were taught to be proud of being Indian, to be proud of being citizens of an undivided country.'

Maria's child had now finished suckling, and had mercifully fallen asleep in her arms, judging by the end of his feisty burps and dulcet snores. She handed him over to Vijaya, who began to rock him in her arms.

'You're going to make a wonderful mother, Vijaya dear,' Maria said. 'You're going to have fabulous children, you and Tammy. But when oh when is Narayan going to show interest in another woman? It's the sweetest brother and sister relationship I've ever seen, but he's so wrapped up in you that no other woman can get a look in.'

Clare was surprised Maria could be this outspoken. Vijaya clearly was too, for she looked quite disconcerted. Clare wondered if this could be part of the reason for Narayan's responsiveness to Max. Had there been no other woman in his life apart the sister he adored so much? As she sipped her neat whisky, she found herself wondering how she might dispose of some it other than by drinking it, without offending Vijaya's over-generous ideas of hospitality. Max had already drunk half the contents of his glass, but then he had a harder head for alcohol than Clare had.

'Hindu prayer must be very different from Christian prayer,' Max said to Subramaniam, 'in view of their different ideas about the godhead.'

'Some pray to an elephant god,' Subramaniam replied, 'and some pray to a monkey god. They all worship an aspect of the divine that has a wonderful infinity of forms. God is in an elephant and in a monkey. It makes us feel tenderness towards animals when we know there are animals in God as well.'

Clare gazed around the room at Vijaya's carvings: a frieze of Sarasvati being bathed by two fat little elephants, their coiling trunks raised up above her head, Hanuman, with his monkey paws stretched out, symbolising loyalty. Luminous in the glow of the oil lamps that Vijaya treasured, the figures threw shadows around the room.

The old man continued.

'You are asking me how I pray, Max. I imagine the world and God as being one and the same. I am part of the same. There is no separation between the world and me, so there is no desire, no striving, and no frustration. There is no further passion; there is only peace. I feel myself in God and I feel God in me. Death and destruction don't exist at all.'

He sat back. There was a long pause before Tammy replied with some impatience.

'Forgive me,' he said. 'But it's attitudes like yours that drain away our energy and effort. Desire and need cause us to struggle and improve our lot. Passion and frustration are what make us strive and live. The spiritual passivity you've just described encourages mere enervating dreams.'

Subramaniam nodded sharply.

'In a purely secular society, one that worships only science, all is greed and material go-getting. Death will kill all this when it comes. Oh my dear boy, you may know a lot about your economics and statistics, I am sure, but what is life without some form of spiritual dimension?'

Subramaniam accidentally knocked over his glass of mango juice. Tammy picked it up, then stooped to touch the feet of the old man, in that traditional gesture of respect for age. Clare was glad to see his respect, its simple dignity, and yet she felt for Tammy in his frustration. She'd been moved by Subramaniam's prayer, but the search for peace touched only a part of her: the longing for no desire and to see no endeavour as depressing. Her glass of whisky was almost empty, and she realised she'd drunk too much. A wave of languor came over her, and she wondered about Tammy: his bruised divided spirit increasingly appealed to her, and his passionate convictions stirred her sympathies.

She lay back against the cushions, on the verge of sleep. A succession of memories came to her: the river beneath the castle walls, an ancient bridge with fireflies all around. She and Max had picnicked on the bank of that river one night, with Max playing the guitar and singing. The sparks from the fire had shot and crackled, the flames reflecting on the swirling water. Their shadows leapt among the rocks and flickered on the stonework of the bridge. She remembered the nightingale again, with its hypnotic song that mingled with the sound of the rippling, falling water. She remembered thinking, as Max kissed her, that this was the happiest moment of her life so far.

She fell asleep and dreamt.

The temple was huge, covered with gesticulating gods and heroes. The cripple was standing motionless. Clare recognised him. She looked into his pitiless eyes.

'I told you to keep away,' he said, pointing at Venkataraman high above, with his bloody shirt and a terrified, lost expression in his eyes.

The dream kept changing. Clare's father was lying on his deathbed, reaching out for her hand, seeking reassurance. Then a frightened little girl had fallen down, gasping for air in a panic-stricken crowd. Clare was desperate to hold her close, to keep her safe. The cripple took the child and gently kissed her.

The child was Violet. Then she was gone, and the whale was diving in the sea while Clare and Max were making love in the boat. She longed to be impregnated by him. The next moment Tammy was there beside her in the car, and through the window a long thin knife was striking, and blood began pulsing from his chest.

Clare woke with a start, feeling a recurrence of her fear that the assassins were pursuing them. It surfaced in her mind like an evil she was desperately trying to forget. She also felt a sharp return of her anger at Narayan but hoped she'd not allow it to be overwhelmed with hatred.

Chapter Ten

When Clare woke next morning, she was in bed but had no recollection of how she got there.

Max was fully dressed. He bent to kiss her.

'You had a drop too much last night, darling,' he said. 'I guess all this is proving a real strain for you.'

'Well, mine's not exactly an easy situation, is it?' she said. 'With you and Narayan. But it's weird; you seem to need my support with him somehow.'

'I suppose I do,' he answered. She felt he was appealing to her, although she vowed to resist it.

'You're being wonderful about it. I guess you must really hate me sometimes. But you've no reason to hate him.'

'Why not? Is he being as wonderful as I am?'

'Don't laugh at me,' he said. 'Look, it was never his doing. From the start, as I keep saying, he's loathed deceiving you.'

Clare had no time to answer because Maria burst into the room with her child and a plate of mangoes. Max moved to kiss her – Maria was a rather insistent kisser – but he looked frustrated by the interruption.

'I hear there's an expedition planned to Sandeha,' Maria said.

'What's at Sandeha?' Clare asked.

'This temple by the sea,' Max explained. 'Tammy's coming, and he's brining Subramaniam. Vijaya won't be able to come, though. What about you, Maria?'

'I'd love to come if you can all put up with the horrible infant.'

Max laughingly took his leave. Maria began to prepare a mango for Clare to eat. The child, quite nude – seemingly his favourite condition – was picking up various things of Clare's, and casting to the floor those that displeased him most. Maria cut the mango open and offered one juicy wedge to Clare, taking the other herself.

'Darling,' she said, between mouthfuls, 'I do hope you're not seriously taking to drink.' She laughed to emphasise she was joking. 'Do look at the Putto. Isn't it deliciously absurd? Come here, you little horror. Come and stuff your angel mouth. At once!'

The infant lumbered towards his mother, gurgling in anticipation. Maria, perhaps not in the mood for his ravenous suckling, offered the infant a dripping piece of mango in lieu of her soft breast. She inserted the fruit decisively into his mouth. He spat out bits of thready pulp with an air of scornful disappointment.

Maria peeled another mango, and Clare decided to ask her about the night before.

'What did happen last night… after I fell into my drunken stupor?'

'Not a drunken stupor,' said Maria smilingly. 'More of a modest slumber. Anyhow, there was another argument between Tammy and Narayan, and Vijaya got a bit upset. She adores them both and hates it when they quarrel. You know, Tammy will never marry her in my view. I dread to think how Narayan will react when Tammy summons up whatever he needs to say so openly. Narayan's in a funny state these days.'

'Oh really? How?'

'Colleagues say he's become very unsettled. He worships Max, obviously. Perhaps it's the lack of a loving father in his own life. Of course, there are only a few years between them, but perhaps he needs the friendly guidance of an older man. I think he relishes the culture shock as well. I mean, for someone so traditional in his own country to enjoy the brash modernism of Los Angeles – Western civilisation taken to its ultimate extreme. It's odd, to say the least.'

'I suppose it is,' agreed Clare, feeling quite uncomfortable.

'Tammy wants to Westernise his India, yet he's always running down the exploitative, greedy West. Narayan likes his India traditional but finds himself seduced by its total opposite. Well, I do go in for the attraction of opposites myself, hence my fatal falling for The Animal.'

For the next two minutes, Maria regaled Clare with an elaborate account of Antonio's appalling deceitfulness, as well as his avid sexual prowess, both apparently inexhaustible. Before she could tell her any more, she was interrupted by someone knocking at the door. It was Vijaya.

'Vijayalakshmi,' said Maria, smiling. 'We oughtn't to shorten it. It's the loveliest name I've ever heard.'

'Oh but it takes so long to say,' Vijaya replied. 'Vijayalakshmi Patabiraman. By the time people have got to the end, they've almost forgotten the beginning. No, I won't have a mango, Maria. I'm not dressed for one.'

145

'Dressed for one?' Maria echoed. 'So what's the best dress for eating mangos in?'

'One's birthday suit,' replied Vijaya.

'Really?' Maria's fingers dripped with juice, as did the blotchy face of the infant, who seemed disappointed by the mango stone Maria had given him. It was all slithery and hardly very suckable, and he had already thrown it on the floor, with yet another expression of displeasure.

'I often eat mangoes in the bath,' said Vijaya. 'They're so juicy, it's best to be clothed in a readily washable birthday suit. So very fashionable!'

'My trouble is, I'm a terrible glutton,' said Maria. 'And my birthday suit is hardly the latest fashion.' She roared with laughter, then suddenly stopped. 'Oh my God, that dread child! Do stop it, quick, Vijayalakshmi! I'd better take it into the garden where its destructive instincts might do less damage.'

The child, tired of being so wilfully ignored, had seized one of Vijaya's figurines and was about to hurl it to the floor in indignant protest. Maria didn't wait for Vijaya to react and quickly rose to her feet, seizing the child herself. After prising the object from his tenacious grip, she rushed him downstairs, the little boy howling at the intolerable frustrations he was being made to suffer.

Vijaya stayed on to talk to Clare, who had come to really like her style of humour. She felt solicitous towards her, even protective, which she thought was probably the effect of guilt about Tammy.

'Why aren't you coming to Sandeha?' Clare asked her.

'I can't. My ferocious aunts would disapprove. You see, Clare, I'm not as free and emancipated as I like to make out. I wouldn't be able to bathe in a bathing costume, exposing my legs, or lie on the beach sunning them black as ink. So what would I be doing while you're all gadding about the place?'

'There's the sea temple for you to look at,' Clare protested. 'Anyhow, Narayan will be with you as a chaperon.'

'In the view of my aunts, Narayan as a chaperon wouldn't be much use. He's too chic and cool, and too Americanised. They'd imagine him tanking me up on cocktails and persuading me to wear tiny little bikinis. They'd think me full of chutzpah, slinking about covered from head to foot in suntan oil.'

'But surely you can come?' Clare persisted. 'Tammy is your fiancé, after all.'

'That, in the opinion of my aunts, would make the whole thing infinitely worse. They'd think we were endlessly jumping into bed together. My spotless reputation would be ripped to shreds. Besides, I don't think Tammy even wants me to come. Yesterday I vaguely hinted I might, and he wasn't at all encouraging.'

'Surely he'd be happy about your being with us?' Clare asked, with a sinking feeling.

'No,' Vijaya replied, shaking her head sadly. 'Tammy's funny that way. He agrees with me about the emancipation of Indian women, and yet I'm still supposed to be sublimely virginal and pure, even with him. Oh yes, despite his lip service to sacred feminism, there's a chauvinist male pig inside him still. Men want women to be virgins when they marry because of male egotism and pride.'

'And yet they're secretly – or sometimes not so secretly – proud of their own pre-marital and extra-marital conquests,' said Clare. 'Unlike us, they don't think badly of each other when they hear of them. Appalling double standards! We're not all that emancipated in the West. There's still a long way to go.'

'So what's a thinking modern Indian woman to do?' asked Vijaya. 'Tammy expects you all to be going to see the sea temple and me to be kowtowing to the harpies who are even more male supremacist than he is, paradoxical as that may seem, in view of how they try to boss their male relations.'

'Maybe you didn't insist enough with Tammy?'

'Insist enough? If he doesn't want me there, I'm not going to beg. Anyway, one thing I don't crave is getting sunburnt. The way you Europeans lie sizzling in the sun, it's a wonder you don't get burnt to a frazzle.'

'Some do,' said Clare.

'Why do you do it? It sounds so uncomfortable. Western ways seem so peculiar at times, it's no wonder Tammy and Narayan have come back slightly bonkers.'

Vijaya smiled, and Clare felt a growing affection for her, but she also felt encouraged. Tammy not being keen to have Vijaya with him was sad and predictable, given what Clare knew, but she decided Vijaya wasn't nearly as vulnerable as she'd feared. Tammy might well never marry her, but, with her humour and lively common sense, Vijaya was resilient enough to survive the upset.

∴

Some time later, Clare went out to wander around the garden. A boy was vigorously watering the plants and grinning at her with a certain impishness. She came to the banana patch, and was looking at their dangling fruit when she heard Tammy call her name. She turned to see him walking across the lawn towards her. She could tell something was agitating him.

'I got a text message from Shahpur this morning,' he said. 'Kalyani is agonising about whether to run off with him. She's pleaded with her father again, who's repeated that he'll disown her if she doesn't give him up. I hate patriarchal despotism and the appalling subordination of our women.'

He then went on to talk of the coming expedition to Sandeha.

'There's a modest hotel there, so I gather. The sea temple is apparently the main thing to see, but there are also some rock carvings, ancient enough to please you.'

'Tell me, how much has Max said about Narayan?' he asked hesitantly.

Clare was taken aback by his directness.

'Quite a lot. Why?'

'I wonder why you never guessed about them.'

'Well, I suppose I developed a blind spot. I didn't want to know.'

'Not that I'd have guessed myself that Narayan could be gay, however gay he is, which in my view may not be very much. I think he's been sort of flattered into it.'

'If it isn't in you in the first place,' Clare said, somewhat irritated, 'no amount of flattery will put it there.'

'So being gay himself, why did Max marry you? Wasn't that pretty irresponsible?'

'He was in love with me… and he still is. There are lots of gay men who fall in love with women, but Max is bisexual. It's far more common than people want to think.'

'Well, I don't know much about it. It's put a bit of strain on my relationship with Narayan. We've had a couple of arguments recently that went further than expected, partly to do with Vijaya, but then he told me today… he asked me this morning…' His voice faltered.

'What, Tammy? Go on.'

'He asked when would I be marrying her.'

'What did you tell him?'

'I put him off with a vague reply. He went on to do the whole big, protective brother act, though. He said he wanted me to make a definite arrangement. I asked him why the sudden hurry.'

'What did he say to that?'

'He said he had to make a crucial decision about his own life, one that depended upon when I'd marry her.'

'What decision?' Clare asked, her voice sharp. When she got no reply, she repeated the question.

'What decision?'

'He said it might involve him going abroad again.'

'With whom?' she asked at once. She felt breathless. 'With Max?'

'Yes,' said Tammy. 'He said he's in love with him. He thinks he wants to live with him.'

'How can you be so brutal?' Clare said, appalled and furious. 'You've made this up.'

'No!'

'You're trying to destroy my love for Max, so I'll turn to you instead.'

Tammy opened his mouth to protest his innocence, but Clare, feeling a rush of blood to her face, raised her hand as if to strike him. But then she turned and ran into the banana patch. Tammy pursued her.

'Leave me alone!' she shouted at him. She tripped over something and fell. Feeling Tammy's hand at her elbow, she turned her burning face to him.

'How could you bloody tell me a thing like that?'

An enormous sense of humiliation seized her.

'I love you,' Tammy said quietly. 'I love you very much.'

Clare tried to calm herself and her outrage ebbed slightly. Tammy put his arm around her and she didn't push him away. For a few minutes he just held her. Then he kissed her hand.

'I love you,' he repeated.

She looked at him, surprised. The simple words seemed to come at her from a strange distance, and yet they moved her with their earnestness. She thought about how she hadn't wanted this and hadn't sought it. She was immensely hurt by Max: what could Tammy's feelings possibly mean to her? What was she beginning to feel about him? A mild increase of sympathy? A sense of consolation? Vaguely she wondered if her feelings might grow further and if she conceivably could want them to. She closed her eyes for a moment. When she opened them, the sunlight flashed on the banana leaves, and the grove was a dappled maze of light and shadow.

'I do love you,' Tammy said once more.

Clare felt something inside herself give. It seemed to her that some of her anguish and confusion could yield to the plain but difficult words Tammy spoke. He touched her face with his nervous, and rather beautiful, hands. He put his lips to hers, and she accepted the gentle kiss. She wrapped her arms around his neck. They kissed very softly for just a few moments. It felt strange to be kissing a man other than Max. She felt awkward and uncertain and pulled away from him.

As she looked over Tammy's shoulder she saw a face peering through the banana leaves.

It was Vijaya, Clare realised with horror.

∴

'Someone was looking at us just now,' she whispered'. 'I think it was Vijaya.'

He too was horrified.

'Oh God, it can't have been. You must've imagined it.'

'It might have been a trick of the light. My eyes were dazzled,' she said, hoping to reassure him.

It might have been an illusion, she thought, the dreamed-up effect of her sense of guilt.

'It could've been the garden boy,' she suggested. 'His face is young and smooth as well. His curiosity was probably aroused by seeing us enter the banana patch.'

But then she thought it could have been that other face, also smooth and young and innocent looking. She tried to dismiss the supposition. At times that face haunted her. She recalled the look of urgent determination the first time she'd seen the boy, the look of panic on his face as Tammy had gripped him around the waist. But it was absurd to think the boy assassin had come to this garden. It was far more likely to have been Vijaya. Her mind went from one probability to another in her distress.

'I'll leave by the side gate that leads out onto the lane,' said Tammy. 'You go out onto the lawn as if you've been merely resting in the shade.'

She agreed. As she emerged she saw the garden boy watering a flowerbed, and he again grinned impishly at her. Did that mean anything particular or was it just the cheeky spirit of so many Indian boys? But surely he was darker than Vijaya, and his hair was short. Had not the face she'd glimpsed so briefly been framed with long and glossy hair?

The garden boy was still watering the plants. He directed the jet of water joyfully at the shrubs and trees, and even a chirpy mynah bird, which flew away with a flash of splattered wings. He managed to soak a cantankerous fat dog, which sent the boy into a gurgle of laughter; the sodden dog made a hasty retreat, whimpering in complaint.

Then Clare noticed another face above the hibiscus hedge at the end of the garden. She saw the eyes – their piercing gaze – and her heart pounded. She remembered those eyes. They were the same cold, resolute eyes of the boy on the motorbike, which she'd glimpsed behind the visor of the crash helmet. They were the eyes of the boy who'd tried to stab Tammy but had only succeeded in striking the window of the taxi. Tammy had explained him away as a watch thief when it was far more probable he was the boy assassin and he'd meant to kill him.

And here he was. Or was he? Confused, Clare saw the eyes blink, the mouth move. It was as if the face became more ordinary. Had she been carried away by fear? Surely it couldn't be the same boy. She was falling prey to paranoia. People often stared at her in India, after all. Her fair European looks prompted many long, unflinching gazes that should not be mistaken for more than innocent, fascinated curiosity. Nothing more.

She decided to act in order to dispel her fear and walked across the lawn towards him. The face seemed to lure her on. The eyes were mesmerising. She again recalled the eyes of the boy assassin, which had turned from fear and bemusement into ruthlessness. She felt herself sway, a heavy dizziness coming over her. The palm trees reeled. She felt herself about to faint but put up a fierce resistance to it, hating such weakness in herself.

Her dizziness went. She looked across at the hedge again. The face had gone. The boy must have slipped away.

Turning her head in confusion, Clare gazed at the banana patch, at the glistening green boles of the banana plants with their delicate tube-like leaves. Then she turned her attention to the hibiscus flowers, with their veined, translucent petals. The garden was so luxuriant and beautiful, she thought, and yet that face came back to her with its terrible ambiguity. She wondered what force of human evil could transform a naive youth into a brutal killer. What desperation? What uncontrolled spirit of destruction? But then the memory faded. The face in her mind dissolved away.

Taking a deep breath, Clare turned and began walking towards the house, feeling the whole experience might have been a hectic illusion, but this made her worry about herself. Was she imagining being stared menacingly at? Was she hallucinating? As she climbed the steps to the veranda, she recalled with sudden sharpness what Tammy had so recently told her about Max and Narayan. She didn't entirely believe him, but the anger the idea revived in her diminished her feelings of self-doubt. She would tell Tammy about the face she'd seen – or thought she'd seen – but she wouldn't tell Max. Telling him would only weaken her in the stand she now intended to take. She would confront him with what Tammy had said about him and Narayan to discover whether or not it was the truth.

Chapter Eleven

As Clare went back into the house Max came forward to kiss her.

'Where've you been?' he asked, concern in his voice. She evaded his kiss, turning her face away. 'I wondered where you'd got to. I was worried.'

'Were you, Max?' she replied, a note of irony in her voice. 'Well, how very flattering.'

'Hey, why that tone?' he asked, evidently hurt. 'Look, I really am appreciative of how you're handling things. How many women would have shown half your sympathy and understanding, or a fraction of your sensitivity and courage?'

If only she had greater courage, she thought, and less sensitivity. She needed to be insensitive to the fears that still haunted her.

'You know,' she said, 'I wonder how far being the sensitive, sympathetic wife is getting me.'

'You sound really sore with me. I love you more than ever! Don't you see that?'

'The way you love me frankly sounds quite selfish,' Clare retorted. 'You get the excitement, the highs and the romance, while I provide the emotional security. That's it, isn't it? The truth is, you want to keep our marriage of convenience going until Narayan chooses to make up his bloody mind about whether to live with you or not.'

Max put out a hand urgently, on an impulse of denial.

'That's not so,' he said. 'Our marriage is absolutely vital to me. I've told you about his conscience over you.'

'His conscience over me is fake,' Clare said, her eyes flashing. 'I wonder why even you don't see through it.'

'Damn it, Clare!' said Max, frustrated. 'It isn't. He's said he'd never be responsible for breaking up our marriage. Twice he's tried to finish things between us.'

'Christ, that old gesture of false renunciation. Is this his brilliant conscience or his wonderful hypocrisy?'

'False? Hypocrisy?' He seemed astounded at the words. Increasingly frustrated, he now exploded in sudden rage.

'Damn you, Clare! Fuck you! There isn't a trace of hypocrisy in him.'

'Oh isn't there?' Clare shouted back. 'How naïve you are, Max. How pathetically ingenuous! My God, you make me sick!'

She turned and walked away, her outrage at its height. She was glad she'd hurt him to the point of fury. She couldn't bear his making these excuses for Narayan and was revolted by his so-called conscience.

'Don't follow me,' she said, not looking back.

She went into the bathroom, where she proceeded to bathe Indian-style. She filled the small brass bowl and began pouring the water over the nape of her neck, the stream enclosing her body like a sheath. For a minute she continued, then reached for the towel and dried herself, surprised by the confidence she felt now that she'd spoken out.

When she returned to their bedroom, Max had left. She went over to the mirror and looked at her reflection. There was a strained look in her eyes, but otherwise she quite liked what she saw. She'd never felt she was vain in any real sense; she was more concerned about her power to attract the man she loved. Surveying her breasts, she'd often imagined Max's hands caressing them, a habit of hers when they were apart and she was in need of comfort and reassurance. She was proud of her breasts. She loved how he admired and fondled them. This time, though, the hands in her imagination were Tammy's. She closed her eyes and dwelt on the image.

She opened her eyes again and for a second saw surprise on the face reflected back at her. She turned away from the mirror, disturbed by the morphing of her daydream.

As she set about getting dressed to go back downstairs, she worried about whether it had been Vijaya who'd seen her and Tammy kissing. She hoped it had been the garden boy instead, getting a quick voyeuristic thrill.

In the hallway, Clare came face to face with Narayan. She'd known for some time that she had to confront him. After Tammy's revelation, she knew she had to do so now.

'You're trying to destroy my marriage!' she blurted out at once.

'That's not true,' he said quietly, obviously shocked by her furious assertion.

'You're in love with Max.'

'Yes, I am,' he answered without hesitation, as if doing so enormously relieved him.

Clare hated his admission but liked his honesty after all the falsehood and deception.

'Tammy tells me you want to live with Max,' she angrily went on. 'Where the hell does that leave me?'

'I shouldn't have told Tammy that,' said Narayan.

So it was true, Clare realised. Tammy hadn't been lying to her.

'It was just a pipe dream,' Narayan insisted. 'It'll never happen. Max loves you far more than he loves me.'

'Why've you encouraged him, behind my back?' Clare asked, her voice sharp. 'Why don't you have a girlfriend? You're twenty-six, for God's sake. Why don't you get yourself a wife?'

'I will, in time.' Narayan swallowed hard. 'Look, I'm extremely fond of you. You must know that,' he said with obvious earnestness. 'Yes, I love him, but I feel huge guilt about it. Do you know what it's like to fall in love against your will?' She thought about how she may have fallen in love with Tammy against her will, and the idea somewhat curbed her fury with Narayan.

Tammy came into the hallway just then. It seemed obvious he'd overheard the confrontation and was uneasy that he'd been the cause of it by breaking Narayan's confidence, and Clare felt embarrassed that Tammy had seen her in the middle of such an argument. The three went into the living room, and Narayan tactfully changed the subject.

'Vijaya's doing you a mutton curry,' he said quietly, addressing Clare.

'But you can't have meat dishes just on our account,' she said.

'You are our guests,' said Narayan in a conciliatory tone. 'You gave me vegetarian dishes in Los Angeles, after all. Anyway, Tammy eats meat. He's such a reprobate. Vijaya's doing vegetarian food for us two, though. She's in the kitchen now, cooking away like a mad thing, and better left alone.'

The table was set with knives, forks and all things Western. In the middle, like a decorative centrepiece, was the inevitable bottle of whisky. This time, Clare looked somewhat askance at it. So did Max when he saw the bottle. Maria was already there. She grinned at Clare, obviously in fond anticipation of the meal.

Narayan wagged his head very gently, beckoning them to sit. It was strange how he'd reverted to his Indian gestures, and even lost his slight American accent. He smiled at Clare as he led her to the table. His smile exasperated her, although she knew it was his way of apologising. He couldn't express his regret any further with the others present in the room, so he was attempting to do so with his relentlessly sweet manners.

Clare sat at the table and gazed at all these foreign objects. Could the bottle of whisky, potentially so lethal in Narayan's eyes, and the imminent mutton curry, so fleshy and unholy, be tokens of his attempt at reparation? And what reparation could she make to Vijaya if it had been she who'd seen them kissing? Her recollection of accepting Tammy's kiss, whatever her initial reluctance, made her feel less solidly assured about acting towards Narayan with such indignant fury.

Eventually Vijaya entered the room, bearing a large dish. She set it on the table and returned to the kitchen to fetch further dishes: rice, dhal, onion bhajis, leathery strips of dried fish – all the elaborate accompaniments of an Indian meal. Clare watched Vijaya's face but couldn't read anything untoward in her expression.

Courteous and competent, Vijaya served the curry.

'I've practised cooking this dish in Kolkata,' she said. 'Some of my old relatives are given to eating meat occasionally. Odd as the practice is, at least the sheep aren't cruelly raised. I've no doubt one could get used to the peculiar, greasy smell of it. You know, a traditional wife doesn't even eat with her husband. She crouches on the floor and serves him first.'

'That's dreadful,' said Maria. 'How can women tolerate it?'

'Yes, the wife eats only after he has stuffed himself,' Vijaya went on. 'It's demeaning not just for the women but for the men as well, who must feel so pampered and piggish.'

'It's demeaning for everyone,' Tammy insisted. 'It still goes on in backward areas. I've been at a meal where the wife crouched on the floor until her self-satisfied, fat husband had gorged himself stupid. She ate only what he had left.'

'The traditional ideal of Indian womanhood is appalling,' said Vijaya. 'The level of marital oppression is disgraceful.'

'Things are getting better for women, thank God,' Tammy said.

'To some extent,' Vijaya answered. 'But there's all this sexual harassment going on, and people don't take it seriously enough. Harassment often leads to rape, and there's more rape than ever in our cities. I've heard men say raped women ask for it. Victims internalise the shame because of such male attitudes. A girl was recently sexually attacked, and not one man came to help her.'

'We saw her on television,' Narayan added. 'Her face was badly bruised. She said she felt degraded and so no one would want to marry her now, when the shame and degradation should be felt only by the rapist.'

'Yes, a man with any decency should be proud to marry her,' said Vijaya. 'In the big cities, women are afraid to go out at night. They're expected to stay at home, ministering to the vanity of their menfolk – cooking, sweeping and slaving away. The men want to be big shots, and boss women around. Boys see how women are treated in the home and then follow the bad example set them. Women and men should be seen as completely equal right from the start.'

She paused then, relenting slightly, and added with a trace of humour, 'Well, when I get married, whoever my husband will be, if anyone at all is crouching on the floor and eating last, that very stupid person won't be me.'

Everyone laughed, if uneasily. Clare saw Tammy was impressed, and yet a slight perplexity had touched him. That little phrase – whoever my husband will be – had been casually, almost jokingly, uttered, but it seemed apparent to Clare that there was a challenge in it. Vijaya was stronger and more modern than Tammy had assumed.

The meal flowed on, Maria complaining that the food was alarmingly delicious.

'I've put on so much weight since coming out to India,' she moaned. 'Italy was bad enough for my figure, with all its succulent pasta and irresistible ice cream, all slyly thrust upon me just when my defences had been momentarily lowered. How inconsiderate you are, Vijaya, dear. If only you'd taken the trouble to cook something really horrible, I might've resisted the temptation better.'

Tammy smiled at Maria's joke and then spoke to Vijaya.

'Women in modern India are now far more emancipated. There are women judges, academics, journalists and politicians.'

'They're the exceptions,' Vijaya argued back. 'I'm talking of the generality of women, unqualified and unheard.'

Having made her point, she fell silent. Clare suspected what was on her mind and dreaded finding out for certain.

At last Vijaya began to clear the table. Tammy made a point of helping her, awkwardly, as if not at all accustomed to it. Clare helped Vijaya as well, carrying some of the plates into the kitchen. The two women made a couple of journeys each until the remains of the mutton curry had been cleared away and the inoffensive fruit set out.

Eventually, Clare and Vijaya were alone in the kitchen. Vijaya stood by the sink in silence, her face averted.

'Will you play the sitar for us later?' Clare asked, mainly to break the silence. 'Please, Vijaya. I love to hear you play.'

Vijaya turned to face her. She spoke with vehemence, her mouth trembling.

'What's the matter between you and your husband?'

Clare impulsively leant forward to take her hand, but Vijaya snatched it away.

'You with your dreadful Western ways,' she said. 'Why do you come out here, you people, and cause us such unhappiness?'

'That's unfair. I'm sorry, but I never started anything.'

'You've been our friends. We liked you so much. You've lived with us in our house, our parents' house. You've had enjoyed our hospitality; you've even had our present. And now? Now you destroy everything for me.'

'I never started it,' Clare repeated. 'I'm sorry, Vijaya, but I won't accept this. I like Tammy very much, but I tell you I've resisted him repeatedly.'

Clare hated herself for saying that because Vijaya's look wasn't one of disbelief; the shaking of her shoulders revealed grief instead of anger.

Clare's defensiveness gave way to pity.

Vijaya lifted her head, her face contorted with pain, tears streaming down her cheeks. Clare reached out, putting her hand on Vijaya's shoulder.

'Look,' Clare said, 'there's nothing between us. I'm still very much in love with Max, and anything you saw today was nothing but a foolish little accident.'

Maria entered the kitchen and stood staring, astonished. Clare was still touching the weeping Vijaya, but now she noticed, over Vijaya's shoulder, that someone was standing by the garden gate, beside a motorbike, looking up at the house. She saw his face, but it was not the face that had previously haunted her. It seemed more like that of the plump man with the unkempt moustache. As Vijaya recovered her composure, Clare recalled the flick-knife the man had drawn on Max, then his attempt to stab at Tammy, an attempt that had been thwarted by that tall woman, her blood-red betel juice staining his white shirt.

The accomplice, if that was what he was, turned his gaze towards the garden. He made a beckoning gesture, mounting his motorbike as a boy walked slowly towards him. It was surely the boy who'd gazed at Clare over the hibiscus hedge. The man revved the bike's engine, coaxing the boy to climb on the pillion seat. He seemed reluctant at first. The man continued humouring him, affectionately taking him by the arm, and the boy acquiesced. The pair rode off, the boy now laughing, clinging to his companion. So it was the two of them, Clare now knew for sure. She had to warn Tammy as soon as possible.

'Let's go outside,' Narayan said to everyone except Vijaya, who had gone upstairs. Clare and Maria were back in the dining room. 'Come on, you ladies, where are your romantic feelings?' he teased. 'Wasting the beautiful night, sitting indoors. All this drink, smoke and savage wolfing down of animal flesh… it's all so decadent.'

He waved his hands in the air, as if humorously wafting away all the unholy odours defiling the purity of his beloved ideal of Hindustan.

'Guzzling this wasteful form of protein and inhaling the smoke of these inedible plants. It's all so unecological! Now if we go outside, where there are breezes from the sea and the scent of jasmine, we might even imagine ourselves in Los Angeles.'

'God forbid!' cried Maria, defiantly lighting a cigarette. 'You and your barbarous dream city. Surely it's the ultimate in savagery and decadence. How come an innocent Indian like you got so hooked on wasteful and wicked, polluted old LA?'

'Clare and Max were very good to me there,' Narayan answered. 'I had a wonderful time. I love its beaches, the sunshine, the surfing and the marvellous art galleries. Anyway, the wickedness you think is there is mainly unreal: all these dream-filled soap operas, science fiction films and Westerns, full of pseudo macho heroes. In a weird sort of way, it's all very childlike.'

'Well, children can be pretty fiendish sometimes, as we unfortunately know,' Maria asserted.

The infant had been put to bed, much to his disgust when there were so many fascinating people to climb over and explore. His howls of complaint had become pathetic whimpers aimed at getting his own way, although Maria turned a resolutely deaf ear to them.

'Your tinsel paradise has one of the highest crime rates in the world,' Maria went on. 'Really, Narayan, America was just an exotic adventure for you, not more than a romantic fantasy. Oh you Indians, you're slaves to strict convention in your actual lives but revolting romantics in your dreams. Look at your Bollywood films, which are so unreal and fanciful.'

'Look,' interjected Tammy, in mild protest, 'people need unreality at night to make up for the grimness they have to face by day.'

They went into the garden. Clare was thinking about those two young men. She felt distanced from Max, or she might perhaps have told him. Her hurt had put up a wall between them. She'd already taken Tammy aside, wanting to speak with him alone. She had to tell him about the boy in the garden, the man on the motorbike. It was no one's business but theirs, a danger temporarily driving them together. They shared this as they shared the horror of the murder and the mystery of the cripple, and she felt the need to keep it to themselves.

As she walked across the lawn, the palm trees towered in the darkness. The moon hung in the sky, a disc of icy brilliance. She reached the end of the garden, and gazed down the lane beyond. It seemed empty save for the moon shadows of the eucalyptus branches. The two youths wouldn't be lurking here, but where would they have gone? The boy's appearance by the garden hedge had presumably been his own idea and his accomplice had now taken him away. Had the boy intended merely to frighten her? She recalled his laughter as the bike sped away, and it had seemed innocent enough. He'd appeared even more dominated by the older youth, good humoured though it was. So what were their intentions? Were they preparing to rid themselves of her and Tammy, but waiting for a less risky time?

Tammy would be sceptical about what she was about to tell him, but she knew she must stay cool and appear reasonable. Behind her, she could hear chattering and laughter, but as she kept walking and these noises died away. She knew Tammy had followed her, and then realised that she hadn't told him about Vijaya yet. She wondered how he'd take the news, and her own decision.

A dog was howling somewhere, a mournful outcry on the wind. Clare heard Tammy call her name but didn't turn, staring instead at a snake delicately moving across the path. She wasn't scared of it; she was more in awe of its beautiful, patterned skin, and with the unhurried dignity it displayed as it proceeded on its solitary way.

The wind was whispering in the eucalyptus branches as Tammy came up close. Clare did turn then, determined to tell him of her resolve as well as of the danger she thought might threaten them. But he was the first to speak.

'What happened in the kitchen?' he asked.

'Vijaya broke down. She wept. I felt terrible.'

'Clare, darling, please…'

Tammy tried to take her in his arms, but she flinched. She knew he was too shy to thrust himself upon her, though. She wouldn't need to fight off his physical advances. If only they were all she must resist.

'I'm sorry, Tammy. From now on we mustn't see each other alone. We must put an end to this.'

'Put an end to what?'

'This must be the last time,' Clare said, steeling herself.

Tammy said nothing. He just stood, listening. Waiting.

'I think you're wrong about the boy on the motorbike after the dance performance,' Clare told him. 'I think he was the assassin, and he's since been lurking round us. I saw him in the garden after you had left. I saw them both ride off on a motorbike together. Thank God we leave Chennai tomorrow to go to Sandeha. But, please, can't you get Vijaya to come too?'

'I love you,' he replied, total conviction in his voice. 'I'm not going to marry Vijaya. I've finally decided that and I'm telling her tomorrow.'

'Don't, for God's sake,' urged Clare.

Her voice had gone hard as a form of defence. She told herself that she hadn't known Tammy long, and she wasn't in love with him. She'd been wrong in allowing that brief and foolish kiss.

'Tell her that,' she said, 'and I'll be the one to have destroyed her.'

'You're being dramatic. Vijaya's much tougher than you think. Not marrying me will not destroy her.'

'You should've seen her this evening,' Clare said, the memory of Vijaya's desperate sadness coming back to her. 'I wouldn't want to witness that, or her to experience it, again. She's an attractive woman, Tammy, with intelligent, strong beliefs. We heard her articulate them this evening. She's amusing and she's loved you for years.' Clare paused, just for a moment. 'Is that the trouble? Has it gone on for too long? Has it become stale? Do you feel trapped? Did your family force you into it?'

'I admire and respect her very much,' Tammy said quietly. 'I've just never loved her.'

'I wish to God you did. I don't want you loving me. I fear I'll hurt you. We need to return to the others. We need to go now.'

Abruptly, Clare started to walk away. She glanced back, and saw him standing in a forlorn and stricken attitude. Her looking back induced him to come up to her, although she'd not intended this.

'I can't stop loving you,' he said. 'I can't get you out of my wretched mind.'

He tried to pull her gently towards him, his face moving close. Clare knew he wanted to kiss her, to express his tenderness, but she would not allow it. She could not allow it. She raised a hand, warning him to keep his distance. He had begun to weep, and she hated to see the pain she now caused him.

She walked resolutely on till she reached the garden. The others had gone back inside. Clare thought she heard the noise of the sea in the distance, but perhaps it was the wind. She heard the howl of that dog again. A bat swung out of the darkness, twisting, looping in the air. Another came hurtling from the sky and seemed to pause an instant in the air before, with a tremor of its delicate wings, it skated with a flash into the night.

I've loved Max too much and for too long, she thought. I'll always be in love with him. Tammy was behind her, but she refused to turn this time. He whispered something to her imploringly, but she didn't catch what he said and found herself uncertain what to do.

Max had come back outside and was calling her name. She could see the shadow he cast upon the lawn. She thought he sounded really anxious. As she moved towards him, leaving Tammy alone again, she felt as if she were returning from some foreign, dangerous country to one whose claims on her were still far too compelling.

∴

The following morning, as the party prepared to depart for Sandeha, Clare glanced out of an upstairs window and saw the man with the moustache sitting astride a stationary motorbike. He was about to put on his crash helmet. She picked up her binoculars to observe him more closely as he forcefully kick-started the engine. It roared and the headlamp glowed, a menacing bright eye in the morning light.

The boy appeared and ran towards the motorbike, giving the impression that he feared being abandoned. He began pleading with the older youth and seemed close to tears. The man affectionately patted him on the shoulder and, laughing teasingly, beckoned him to climb up behind him. They rode off together on that great machine, the stutter of his engine vibrating stridently. The boy, himself laughing now, had his arms tightly around his companion's waist, tenaciously clinging on.

Max had gone downstairs with their light luggage. Narayan was loading up his car. She met Tammy in the hallway.

'You haven't changed your mind about getting Vijaya to come with us?' she asked him anxiously.

'No,' he solemnly answered. 'I'm just about to tell her what I said I would.'

'I can't bear to think how she'll react… what she'll be feeling.'

'I'll do it kindly, I promise you.'

'I wish to God you wouldn't do it at all.'

He went upstairs, and she heard him walk along the landing to Vijaya's room. She felt sick with dread at what he was about to say to her. She walked outside and, to her astonishment, found the cripple waiting, smiling apologetically. He approached, looking deeply concerned, and handed her a note. Before she had a chance to speak, he made the gesture of Namaste and swung away hurriedly, as if he wanted to get away before she read it.

The note was in English, and brief.

My wife and I have not forgotten you saved our dauhter.

Do not wory.

We wil not harm you.

Clare took a deep breath and looked up at the sky, trying to decide what to do next. Should she tell Tammy? She decided in an instant that she wouldn't. The note didn't mention him at all, so she thought it likely he was excluded from the reassurance and still at risk. Even if she did tell him, he would scoff at the prospect of there being any danger to his life at all. Besides, they were leaving for Chennai, in ten minutes. She decided to call Inspector Veerapan from her mobile.

As she waited for the Inspector to pick up the phone, Clare resolved to tell Max too. He would feel a lot easier to know that she at least would not be harmed. The phone clicked through to an answerphone. Clare felt impatient as she waited for the recorded greeting to end.

'Inspector,' she began, 'it's Clare. I've seen the assassins again. They're definitely following Tammy and me. I've seen the cripple too. He came up to me and gave me a note in English. It says they won't harm me but it doesn't mention Tammy. So I don't think he's safe at all. I'm only safe because I saved the man's daughter from being crushed and trampled in the crowd. He's obviously grateful. We're going to Sandeha now. Bye.'

It suddenly occurred to Clare that the cripple had taken quite a risk in giving her the note. His handwriting could surely help to identify him. But then she realised he could've got a professional scribe in the bazaar to write it. He didn't seem to have much English after all. Although the spelling had been poor, the note hadn't been all that badly worded.

She thought of Veerapan's solicitous determination and gentle manners, which lent her reassurance, although she couldn't help incongruously still supposing his hair was too impeccable to be naturally his own.

Chapter Twelve

Max found the journey to Sandeha uneventful, or perhaps he had too much on his mind to fully to take it in. On their arrival they booked into a hotel that was sufficiently modest for his liking. Sandeha, this place of the sea temple and the rock carvings, was a hundred miles south of Chennai. Subramaniam had told him that Sandeha meant doubt in Sanskrit. The old man had decided to come along, but Vijaya had not. He hadn't seen the temple for fifty years and wanted to see it one more time before he died. An hour later Max went down to the sea alone, with his camera, leaving Tammy, Maria, Narayan and Clare back at the hotel.

The temple, about twelve metres in height, was much smaller than the one at Madurai. The waves were throwing themselves against the rocks around it, sending up a delicate thin spray, flecks of which just reached the stonework of the temple, with its eroded vestiges of carvings.

As he stood watching the waves, Max found his thoughts turning to Clare, as they always did. He'd seen her moods fluctuate in last few days: sometimes she was remote and hard, other times vulnerable and nervous. He didn't really understand what was happening. Why that strange scene with Vijaya when they'd left? Was there something wrong between her and Tammy? Max hadn't wanted to ask and didn't want to appear suspicious. Anyway, he had other things pressing heavily on his mind. Just before leaving Chennai that morning, he'd had a long text message from Rick.

Ben was dead. He'd died in Rick's apartment. Rick had brought him there when they knew the end was near. They'd had a small party the week before, during which they'd drunk a lot of Californian champagne, which had helped Ben to laugh at Rick's ribald jokes. It was not Ben's inevitable death that hit Max so hard but what Rick wrote later in the message:

> *I hope I'll have Ben's courage if things go bad for me as well. I've lost weight, you see, and I've got this little scabby growth on my shoulder. The treatments are much improved these days, I know. I shouldn't be complaining, but I've lost Mike for good now. He's got someone else. He can't bear being alone in life. I don't blame him.*
>
> *I'm having some tests next week. I'll let you know when I get the results back. Don't worry in the meantime.*
>
> *Good luck with your research! Rick. x*

∴

'The phenomena of this world are all one vast, mysterious illusion,' Subramaniam had once said to Max. 'Time and space are all illusory. They are without form or significance until experienced inside a human mind, or an animal mind for that matter, or even, according to the Jains, the mind of an insect.' Max wondered, though, if they'd include, in their all-embracing veneration, a virus that attacked the defences of a body and brought a human life to cruel destruction.

'Hinduism has an actual god of destruction,' Subramaniam had gone on. 'Shiva the Destroyer. But Shiva's also the Preserver, doubtless the reason for his being a god of sexuality. He's venerated in the lingams, those phallic symbols you see in the temple sanctums.'

Destruction. Sexuality. Preservation. Death.

These ideas moved around in Max's mind, in painful contradiction and confusion. The waves beat on. The rain fell and the winds blew. On either side of the temple, which had been scoured away for centuries, the beach stretched away into the distance, with the odd piece of driftwood brought in by a high tide, stranded now among the shells and piles of seaweed.

Max set off in search of the bas-reliefs, some two hundred metres away. On the huge rock surface was carved a group of elephants, with noble, heavy heads and curling trunks, figures of gods and goddesses and depictions of ceremonial cattle. The light fell on the surface and shimmered in the heat so that the carved rocks took on a curious, insubstantial quality. It was as if their enormous presence was as elusive and transient as the clouds dissolving in the sky above him. Max sensed the passing of time, which sometimes seemed to have gone by with extraordinary speed, as in a sudden disturbing burst of wind, and sometimes with a silent gathering enchantment, as in the solemn coming of a summer dawn.

Enchantment? He thought of the enchanted times of his own life… with Clare… with Narayan… with Rick. The future was unknowable. He tried to imagine living with Narayan in Chennai, or back in Los Angeles, with his marriage broken up and Clare gone from him. Clare gone and irretrievable! The idea froze him, but he had to confront the fact that he had a choice to make – in fairness to Clare, to Narayan and indeed to himself. Life without Narayan seemed like a kind of death in life, but life without Clare felt like non-existence.

Would Rick live on for years? Or would he, like Ben, become very sick and need someone to look after him? The thought of his dying was devastating. Max thought of his old feeling for Rick and the memories it conjured up. He remembered being kissed by him in a foam of bubbles in a jacuzzi one night. At Clare and Max's wedding reception, Rick had crooned, in mock romantic fashion, one of those old thirties songs that satirised the painful claims of half-requited love. How vibrant the memories of him seemed, with his jokes and songs, his tearaway rebelliousness and masculine wild charm. The sacrifice he'd made for Ben, giving up Mike so he could devote himself to Ben, touched Max with an appalled sorrow at the possibility of his own destruction.

Max had asked Subramaniam about pointless death, with both Rick and Ben on his mind. The old man had gazed at him through his small, round spectacles.

'You think of life as merciless and fearful,' said the Professor, with that sense of tranquillity that Max yearned for in himself but mainly failed to find, 'attended, in the end, by pain and fear and death. But these will not endure. Death is like a dream that's quickly over. These things vanish like shadows in the rising sun, when our lonely souls are ours no more.'

The remembered voice now died away, like the temple life had died away. Max tried to imagine the temple full of worshippers, with their urgent prayers and the blare of trumpets. It was now empty and alone, the mournful cries of gulls echoing around it, subject to the crashing of the never-ending waves.

A bell clanged. Max looked around and saw a little, whitewashed temple not far away. A sadhu, with a gaunt face and emaciated body, approached. He whispered for alms. Max gave him some money, thinking of the traditional Hindu attitude to material possessions: the sanctity of poverty, such as Jesus and Saint Francis had also preached. He imagined with dread the thinness that might overtake Rick's body.

The bell tolled again. Max took hold of himself. Worrying like this would be the last thing Rick would want him to be doing.

And then he saw Narayan approaching. He strode with casual vigour, the sea glittering behind him. He waved at Max in his impulsive way, seeming so very physical, so substantial. Max gazed again at the rock carvings, in all their beauty and solidity, and wondered about his quest for happiness. But what about the happiness of spiritual tranquillity?

'All is maya, illusion,' he recalled the old man saying. 'Look at this material world. What can it signify?'

Max reflected that the bas-reliefs – those images of gods and elephants and holy cattle – were part of maya too, yet they had lasted a good twelve hundred years.

∴

Max lay on the beach, asleep. He woke to the sensation of Narayan trickling sand onto his chest.

'Not content with blackening my karma for my next incarnation,' Narayan said, a broad grin on his face, 'you have to blacken my poor skin in this one. You have to drag me out to sunbathe with you, so that you, a white American, can be impressively dark brown.'

He laughed and dropped down next to Max, who smiled back at him.

'Isn't it perfect here?' Narayan asked. 'Didn't I say it would be a paradise?'

'It's wonderful,' Max said. 'It really is.'

'Yes, but Tammy wouldn't think so. He'd say that the village had undernourished children and that someone had died of typhoid yesterday. I once asked him if he thought it was ever right to be happy in this country with so much misery around.'

'What did he say to that?'

Narayan shrugged.

'He goes on about the miserable poverty in India, hating the huge disparities of wealth, but these disparities exist throughout the world.'

'In America especially,' Max said. 'What did he say about being happy in the midst of misery, though? It's quite a question.'

'He didn't answer. Well, it can't help the misery to add to it. What do you think?'

'I think we have a right to happiness but that other people's misery can often make that difficult to attain.'

'People's misery in general?'

'Yes, but also the misery one's own attempts to reach happiness can cause.'

Narayan fell into an absorbed silence. Max looked across at the temple. A single rock stood halfway across the beach. It had been carved with the outline of figure, which was much eroded by the wind and waves – the vestige of a god, maybe, scoured beyond the point of recognition.

'You know what I hope for most?' asked Narayan. 'It's for you to stay here with me. Clare could stay too, if she's willing – or is that being absurdly unrealistic? Do you think you could ever give up LA?'

'It depends on you. Could you ever give up Tamil Nadu?'

'When I was in LA, I thought I could... when I first came back and I was really down. Now? Well... now I think I'd never leave if you would stay here with me.'

He brought himself up short, as if he hadn't meant to say this.

What an admission, Max thought. It had come out so spontaneously, but it had the clumsy ring of truth. Narayan was never much good at polite pretence.

'I'd love to stay here with you,' Max replied. 'But Clare would not, of course... not under those circumstances.'

'And if she left, you'd be thinking all the time how you'd made her miserable?'

Max nodded.

'Things are bad enough for her with the assassins still at large,' said Narayan, 'even though Tammy insists there's little cause to worry. I feel enormous sympathy for her, but she resists my telling her so. I can't get through to her any more. The reason's obvious, and it makes me feel horrible.'

Narayan gazed at the sea, looking guilty and unhappy, as he always did when talking about Clare.

'At least Clare's making friends,' he went on. 'Maria's taken a real shine to her, and vice versa. She seems fond of Vijaya too. She tried to kiss her this morning, although Vijaya avoided it for some reason. Odd.'

'I thought she really wanted to come with us. Why didn't you persuade her to.'

'I think she felt Tammy didn't want her to, not that she'd tell me if that was the case. We may seem close, but she's very proud and reserved at times. Either she's chattering and joking away or she cuts herself completely off. Well, anyway, Clare's made quite a pal of Tammy. Maybe that's half the reason for Vijaya being so strange this morning. Perhaps she's jealous.'

'Jealous?' Max echoed.

'She's got absolutely no reason to be, of course. In all these years, he's never looked at another woman. He's obviously attached to Vijaya, even if it's hardly a blinding passion. But then he's never been blindly passionate about anything, except the problems of modern India, about which he makes me feel so ignorant and guilty. No, she'd never foolishly imagine anything like that between them. She might feel slightly jealous of Tammy having more in common with Clare than he has with her, though.'

'That's possible,' Max answered briefly, feeling as if he was being probed.

'I had a word with him a day or two ago… about when he'd be marrying Vijaya.'

'What did he say?'

'He was typically evasive. Not that I'm worried about whether or not he'll ever marry her. It's unbelievable he'd let her down at this stage. I only wonder about when.'

'Well, you can ask him again some time,' said Max. 'Do you want to go for a swim?' he then asked. He was keen to shake thoughts of Tammy and Clare from his mind because he was, at that moment, imagining something he really didn't want to take shape in his head.

'Why not?' Narayan answered, quickly dismissing his preoccupations. 'Come on then!'

As they walked down to the sea, Max spoke about something he'd been deliberating on for quite some time.

'You know, I want to donate to famine relief in India. I have too much money, too many undeserved, ill-gotten gains.'

'I hope you haven't been taking my joshing too seriously,' Narayan replied, casually kicking at a mound of seaweed. 'About your vulgarly expensive lifestyle, I mean. We don't exactly live in poverty ourselves, Vijaya and I. We have a fair-sized house and garden; and a car, however antiquated. They amount to relative riches here in India. Whether our gains are ill gotten or not, I'm afraid I'm greedy. I know the story of Jesus and the rich man, but I'm less of a true Hindu than you're an ethical, agnostic Christian, as you describe yourself. I can't see myself about to give up the things I have.'

They reached the sea and waded in. As they swam out, Max hoped he wouldn't live to regret voicing his intention, although the thought of giving to such a cause gave him a distinct feeling of relief. A wave swelled towards them and they both dived beneath it. The sun pierced though the water to irradiate their bodies, which now touched and intertwined, their mouths joined in a slow subaqueous kiss. As they rose to the surface it seemed to Max that this moment of his happiness, transient as it might be, was a spot of time he would remember in the years to come. It would actively revive his spirits when he succumbed to the despair that sometimes dragged him down.

He'd always felt ambivalent about his inherited money, although he'd made full use of it – as anyone would, he thought. That little Christian story remained at the back of mind, sometimes like a nagging challenge, at other times an awkward inspiration. Was he capable of giving away most of his wealth? He'd miss the benefits it brought him and it certainly would prove quite a wrench.

But his spirits soared once more as he embraced Narayan again and they began to swim back to the shore.

Later Max began wondering about Clare and Tammy again as he recalled the scene with Vijaya when they'd been about to leave. Max had been in the garden with Clare, and Tammy was upstairs with Vijaya. He'd heard the sounds of a hushed argument and then a little stifled wail. He'd turned to Clare but she was hurrying away as if she couldn't bear to hear it.

At this point, Narayan had appeared with Subramaniam, who'd told them of a dream he'd had that morning: 'There was this procession descending to the sea to gather salt. A man was praying for peace and love. The dawn sun was ascending.' Then he'd waited in the shade of a frangipani tree, happily chanting in snatches beneath his breath.

When Vijaya appeared at last, she was her characteristically amusing self, joking about the harpy aunt with whom she was to stay when Narayan had gone.

'The Battleaxe phoned this morning, demanding to know why she's not been allowed to meet these decadent Western guests. She asked if Clare chain-smoked and had a long black cigarette holder. She wanted to know if she made up her face in public, and if they talked about sex without interruption, and if they had both gaily married and divorced several times already!'

Max thought that the bizarre practices of Western people – as seen through the jaundiced eyes of these viragos – had become for Vijaya quite a successful form of joke exaggeration. As they got into the car to leave, though, her joking petered out. Clare had tried to kiss her, but she'd turned her face awkwardly away, leaving Max to wonder what this portended.

Chapter Thirteen

Clare was lying on the beach, a short distance from the temple. Maria was with her, generously anointing the infant, and then herself, with sun cream. Earlier in the day, Clare had insisted upon knowing the child's name – 'assuming he has a name,' she'd said – and was told it was Sam. Despite having rather reluctantly revealed this, Maria still referred to Sam as 'it' and called him by whatever other amusing names happened to appeal to her capricious nature at the time.

'Let me rub some sun cream on your back as well,' she said to Clare. 'You know, you do have a gorgeous body.'

'Thank you,' said Clare, blushing a little.

'No wonder Tammy finds you irresistible…' Maria's voice trailed off as she squinted to see into the distance. 'My God, look at him! I hope he doesn't swim out too far. There's a nasty undertow on this coast, so I've heard.'

Clare followed Maria's narrow-eyed stare and saw Tammy striding into the sea, being pushed back by waves as they broke against him. Eventually, he flung himself forward and began to swim.

Clare could not stop thinking about the cripple's note, and what its omission of any reference to Tammy might imply. On the radio that morning there'd been an announcement that the police were getting closer to tracking down the assassins, whatever that meant in actual reality. Clare thought that if they really were on the verge of making arrests, it would make the assassins all the more desperate to strike at Tammy so as to silence him as a damaging witness. On the drive to Sandeha, she'd seen a number of motorbikes, each one causing her anxiety in case it could've been the two young men. But as she realised the riders were nothing like those she feared, she would relax, dismissing her anxieties, even embarrassed about allowing them to haunt her.

'You're crazy about him, aren't you?' Maria said, interrupting Clare's thoughts. 'As mad for him as I am for Antonio.'

'Who? Tammy?' Clare asked defiantly. 'No! I most certainly am not.'

Having seen Vijaya in tears, Maria had been filled with an avid curiosity ever since. Clare resisted many of her questions, either answering them obliquely or not at all. But she did tell Maria about Max and Narayan, which Maria unconvincingly claimed to have guessed at already. Hesitant at first, Clare also found herself revealing the brief encounter between herself and Tammy. She soon wished she hadn't, because Maria then became determined to urge her on.

'Why not?' she said. 'Max has Narayan after all.'

'But I feel very badly about Vijaya.'

'You've no reason to,' said Maria. 'You're not at all to blame for what's happened.'

Nonetheless, Clare couldn't get the sound of Vijaya weeping upstairs out of her mind. She recalled her own brief argument with Tammy afterwards.

'I said I'd never marry her,' he'd told Clare with very evident distress. 'I respected her greatly but we were not compatible.'

'You shouldn't have told her that,' Clare had replied, appalled. 'It was cruel.'

They could not discuss it further then because they'd had to join the others, who'd been waiting by the two cars, Tammy's and Narayan's. Vijaya had come downstairs then, feeling compelled to say goodbye. She'd joked about the wretched aunts who seemed to tyrannise her, however much she laughed at them, bravely covering up her enormous hurt regarding Tammy.

It now seemed that Tammy had changed his mind about swimming in the sea and was making his way back to shore. Clare watched him anxiously, wondering what he might do next. Sam was climbing all over her, joyfully exploring this newly acquired territory, trying to probe her mouth with his sticky fingers.

'Stop him doing that,' said Maria.

'Oh no,' Clare said, shaking her head. 'He's so affectionate. He doesn't seem to know what an inhibition is, does he?'

'More's the pity,' said Maria as she put a pair of binoculars to her eyes and began to focus on something over towards the temple, or perhaps on the temple itself.

'A few self-respecting inhibitions wouldn't do it any harm at all,' she went on. 'My God, Clare darling! Look! Max and Narayan are climbing the temple.'

She handed the binoculars to Clare. She set Sam down at her side, and raised the binoculars to her eyes. She had to adjust them slightly before she could make out Max stretching up his arms to find a handhold. Above him, Narayan was moving his hands and feet gingerly across the stonework.

Tammy was back on the beach and heading towards the temple himself.

'Max isn't good at heights,' Clare said. 'Presumably Narayan is. I hope he is.'

'He's strange, that one,' said Maria. 'A bundle of contradictions. What a fantastic body, though! It's all that pumping iron, I suppose. If I writhed and grunted in a gym, heaving weights around, do you think I'd ever be reduced to a shape more like that? Oh baby, sweetie baby, tell me that it's possible! Go on.'

Maria lifted Sam into the air, where he cooed benignly at her, before gently putting him down again. She beamed at Clare.

'Antonio's such a brute,' she confided. 'What a dance macabre the monster led me! And then I lost him, even after I bore him a son! Now, though, it seems it may not be for good. He sent me a text to tell me the Innamorata is goading him past endurance.'

'The Innamorata?'

'That skeletal creature he ditched me for, lured by the reek of her abominable loot. Apparently, she's flying into screaming tantrums whenever he glances at another woman by accident, which probably happens only every half a minute or so, I'd say.'

Clare laughed. Sam was trying to remove the bung from a thermos flask that he'd pulled from the basket Maria had brought with them.

'My gin!' she cried out in simulated panic. 'My chilled gin and tonic!'

She uncurled the child's stubborn fingers from the bung, then unscrewed it and poured a dash of the contents into a cup.

Clare watched, astonished, as she gave it to Sam to drink.

'It makes it so much better tempered,' Maria gaily told her, although Sam sipped at it with a screwed-up face, obviously not approving of the taste at all. 'Little angel monkey,' she added, kissing the child lightly on his lips. 'Monstrous little putto. Can you imagine it, Clare, painted on a Renaissance ceiling, all plump and rosy? Imagine its cherubic fat wings, and sweet little leer, hovering over some large sexy lady who is trying to forget her horrible butch lover and longing for some delicate, sweet substitute.'

Clare picked up the binoculars again and looked towards the temple. Tammy was now standing at its base, apparently readying himself to begin the climb. Max was halfway up, and Narayan was still above him. Clare thought it was typical of Max to want to climb this derelict temple, the element of danger adding to the romance of it, no doubt. Would they not be damaging its surface, though, however lightly? Was it not a form of desecration?

Tammy started climbing.

'I think it's boozing time,' Maria announced. 'Come on, let's have some gin and tonic to celebrate the downfall of the dread Innamorata, cast into the outer darkness by the maddened animal.

'Here's to The Animal!'

'I toast to him,' Maria cried, handing a cup to Clare and taking a swig or two from her own. She gazed at The Putto – her current favourite name for him – but he wasn't hovering over her with a sweetie leer at all. Instead, he was stumbling around in a most unfriendly sulk, letting off cross little squeaks that Maria airily ignored.

Clare turned and noticed Subramaniam was approaching them, leaning on his stick, his shadow hobbling before him as if it lured him on across the windblown sand. She took a sip from her cup, and shifted her focus to the sea.

'The tide's coming in very fast,' she said to Maria.

Narayan was nearing the crest of the temple. Max was directly below him, and Tammy was about halfway up now.

'The temple's much smaller than I'd imagined it over all these years,' said Subramaniam as he reached the two women. 'I pictured it covered with a hundred gods and heroes. Maybe the sea has worn them away.' He sighed. 'It's more than fifty years since I last came here, you know, maybe even sixty. At my great age, time often seems so unreal; the distant past could have been in some other quite different life. Who knows what other lives I've led, or what other forms my wandering soul's inhabited.'

He smiled gently at the two women, as if suspecting they were sceptical of such beliefs.

'But reincarnation does pose problems,' he conceded. 'The idea of karma has its difficulties.'

'Bad luck in this life being down to sins committed in a previous one?' queried Clare.

'Indeed, yes. I had a son who was born deformed. He died when he was only eight years old. I hated to think that was because of sins he'd committed in a past life. That's so unjust. But no religion is perfect. All of them present us with their problems, in our search for transcendent meaning in this puzzling, often very painful, life of ours. So, so.' Subramaniam paused reflectively before continuing. 'I'm very happy to see the temple again,' he said. 'A reminder of my innocent youth. Why, though, are these young men climbing all over it? Is that entirely respectful of them?'

'I was thinking the same,' said Clare.

'It is a religious building, even if it has been abandoned to the wind and waves. Maybe they think of themselves as the modern equivalents to those mythic heroes: Tammy with his economics, Narayan with his physics, a subject that tries to reduce the entire world to the whirling around of tiny atoms, lacking in both mystery and meaning. Oh but we've had such discussions, he and I.'

'Surely Narayan sees the laws of physics as purely human hypotheses,' Clare suggested.

'Yes, they don't exclude the possibility of divine purpose, of ultimate spiritual significance,' agreed the Professor. 'Nor do they exclude the possibility of human goodness, such as we need so much in these bad times of terror and fanaticism. That young man, how could he have been so cruel? Narayan has never lost his beloved Hindu faith, as Tammy seems to have, the poor dear fellow. And which of them is the happier, I ask you? Which is the more understanding and secure? Does Tammy think we can save this ancient country with all these soulless forms of modern knowledge?'

While Subramaniam was speaking, Clare looked from time to time through Maria's binoculars. She saw Max lever himself up and stand on the summit with Narayan – and then she saw them put their arms around each other. She felt a sudden stab of exasperation, although she knew she was being jealous. Eager for distraction, she turned to catch Maria telling Subramaniam about Antonio, much to her surprise.

'He is an animal?' asked Subramaniam, determined to take Maria in his gentle stride. 'Well, many of our gods take the forms of animals. We find it a very touching notion.' He looked at the sea for a while. 'Look at the tide coming in so fast; the sea so rough.' He turned back to Maria. 'So what kind of animal is your husband?'

'A cross between a rabid tiger and a lecherous great ape.'

'Well, you joke about him, but even a tiger has its gentleness, and even the ape possesses a kind of beauty that is not immediately apparent to our human eyes. If he's your husband, though – animal or otherwise – why did he not come with you to these shores?'

'Because he deserted me for another woman,' said Maria flatly. 'Actually, I've a new theory to account for his philandering. I suspect he's a repressed gay. Not only repressed but very chauvinistic, and macho, hence his pathetic attempts to prove himself by being such a compulsive lady-killer.'

'The human spirit has always been repressed,' observed Subramaniam. 'It is the very condition of the finite, earth-bound soul. As for being gay, that is very marvellous! Every bit of gaiety brings us ever closer to the soul divine – and that is of a boundless happiness.'

'What I meant by gay is homosexual,' Maria apparently felt required to say.

'Oh,' said the old man. 'Homosexual? I didn't know that was especially gay. We have little of it in India.'

'You might think that,' Clare said on impulse, immediately regretting it.

'A great shame, in my opinion,' said Maria. 'It might solve some of your population problems. Far more fulfilling than vasectomy.'

'Vasectomy's no more the answer than being gay is. All this frantic desire, this pursuit of sheer physical sensation, when chastity is what is needed: more restraint and quiet contemplation.'

'Chastity!' exclaimed Maria. 'That's asking far too much. No, you ought to have loudspeaker vans touring the villages, advertising the joys of all non-reproductive sex.' She carried on, although Clare rather hoped that she would stop.

'Homosexuality should be positively encouraged,' she said, 'at least up to its natural limits. Seven per cent or so, I think it is. A most effective and natural means of birth control at a time when your population is over the billion mark.'

'You mustn't think I'm intolerant,' the old man replied, blinking mildly, 'but all forms of love are an aspect, however partial, of the divine love that is in us all. Abstinence, though, doesn't mean misery. Chastity can be very gay. The triumph of the soul over the body is a very happy thing indeed. The power of chaste love is infinitely greater than that of mere carnality, which can be so frustrating and tormenting.'

Clare was still intermittently looking at the temple, around the base of which the tide was now swirling. She saw Tammy clinging to the stonework. The sun dazzled her eyes for a few moments. The scene seemed to tremble and was lost to her, but then she found it again. Tammy looked to be about six metres up. He suddenly moved his head sideways, as if intending to look up at Max and Narayan.

There was a violent burst upon the stonework, just where Tammy's head had been. He lost his handhold. There was another explosion of stone dust. Tammy's body swayed across and was left hanging from only one hand.

Another explosion. He lost his grip entirely, his arms flew backwards, and he began to fall. Horrified, she heard his sudden cry.

Without a moment's hesitation, Clare ran. It took a minute for her to reach the water that now surrounded the temple (she later learnt it had been an abnormally high tide). As she ran, her thoughts were whirling. Were those bullets that had struck the temple? There'd been no noise, but a rifle could have been fitted with a silencer. Some fishermen and children were also racing towards the temple, stumbling in the loose, wind-driven sand.

Tammy had fallen into the water. He appeared to be unconscious, his head bobbing limply up and down as the water rose and fell. Had a bullet hit him? Max was climbing back down, fast; Narayan too. The fishermen had reached the temple, and Clare wondered if the marksman was among them. The waves surged on, and Max dived into them, ignoring any risk of danger to himself. Narayan followed. Both of them vanished, as if sucked down by a cascading wave. Seconds later, Clare saw them farther out, their arms beating hard in the driving surf. She watched as they desperately sought to save Tammy.

She scanned the fishermen. They were moving frantically about, pointing and shouting. There was a tall man noticeable among them, his back to her.

Twenty metres out, Max and Narayan converged. A wave seized hold of Tammy's body, and his head disappeared below the water. Above the spray, the gulls shrieked and wheeled about in fierce excitement. Clare heard a voice calling from behind her; it was Subramaniam, who was holding his hands together in prayer.

The sea was running even higher. Clare saw Max emerge from one of the waves and then saw Tammy's body slide down another before being thrown to the top of a splitting breaker. It was there that Max managed to get a hold on him. With one arm around his chest, he began to tow him back to shore. Narayan joined them moments later and helped to keep Tammy's head above the water.

Clare felt an enormous surge of gratitude to both men. It coursed through her body like electricity. She wanted to keep her eyes on them as they approached the shore but something, some instinct, compelled her to turn her head.

She saw the face of the tall man, lined, bearded and frowning intensely. Then she saw the crutches. She believed it was the cripple. Were the two youths with him? She looked around, searching frantically, but the group was breaking up. She couldn't make them out among the excited, moving fishermen. She looked back, but the cripple had disappeared. The number of onlookers was growing. People were hurrying from all directions, gathering in little awed clusters, as they watched Max and Narayan bring Tammy back.

A terrifying thought seized hold of Clare. What if someone on shore was waiting for Tammy? What if they would try to kill him in some other way?

Max and Narayan reached the shore. Max took Tammy in his arms and carried him a little way up the beach before placing him gently down by a clump of seaweed. He put his mouth to Tammy's and began to breathe into it. Clare and Narayan crouched down next to them. Subramaniam stood a short distance away, chanting his prayers, while the temple, silhouetted against the sky, threw its long, twilight shadow across the beach.

Maria had stayed behind with Sam, but now she advanced towards them, holding his squirming, protesting body tightly in her arms.

Clare concentrated on what Max was doing. She knew he'd been trained in First Aid resuscitation. She watched as he breathed hard into Tammy's mouth, and then leant his hands on his sternum, pressing several times in measured sequence. There was no response. Fervently she wished for that inert body to revive, for even a flicker of breath to stir his chest. Tammy had a cut on his forehead and it was oozing blood. His hand, now stiff and pale, rested on the straggling seaweed.

'Let me help,' Clare said, involuntarily recalling Violet's fight for air.

Max pulled back, allowing Clare the space to put her mouth to Tammy's and breathe into his lungs. Max positioned himself so that he could continue the compressions on Tammy's sternum. Between breaths, Clare put a hand to his forehead. It was a cut, not a bullet hole. It was bleeding profusely, though. She tried, ineffectually, to stem the flow with her hand, feeling his blood pulse beneath her fingers. She kept up the breathing, aware of Subramanian chanting his prayers, and the idea helped her. It served as an antidote to her bemused feelings about the cripple. She hadn't seen him again. She wondered why he'd tried to kill Tammy in that extraordinary way. She supposed he'd been watching Tammy for some time and had seized his chance when he saw him climb the temple. He'd be separated from her, alone and totally exposed.

There was still no response, still no movement of Tammy's chest. Lifting her head, Clare saw the fishermen and children in a circle around them, now watching silently. There were two or three youths among them, although she couldn't make out their faces in the fading light. She couldn't let herself think of the assassins, or the cripple. She couldn't afford to be afraid of them, not there and then. She had to focus all her energy, everything she had to give, on reviving Tammy. His lips felt cold and hard, but she kept going. She felt her own heart thud as she thrust all her breath into Tammy's saturated lungs till her head began to ache.

Tammy's eyelids flickered.

'Tammy!' Clare exclaimed, feeling the tears welling in her eyes.

His eyes began to open, his head jerked back, and water spurted from his mouth. He coughed convulsively. His back arched, and his hands beat at the sand. Clare watched with awe and pity as he fought for air, for life; it was as if he was struggling to return to her. Eventually, the coughing slowed, and his breathing grew more regular and strong. His eyes seemed to focus in dim bemusement and he mumbled a few incoherent words. Max moved forward, and Clare moved away to allow him to turn Tammy onto his side.

Clare remembered something Narayan had said to her about falling in love against one's own will.

She looked around and noticed that the two youths had now gone. They were probably innocent onlookers. If they were conceivably the assassins, they might still attempt to murder Tammy, although they were unlikely to try when so many people surrounded him. She realised they might make a move later on, when he was quite alone, and that must be prevented at all costs. The cripple still hadn't reappeared and she began to wonder if, in her fear and confusion, she'd imagined him.

It was only then they noticed Tammy's leg wound. His thigh was streaming blood. Narayan tore a strip from the towel he'd brought, and Max found a piece of driftwood with which they made a clumsy tourniquet. He tightened it around Tammy's upper thigh and the bleeding stopped. He tore another strip from the towel, which he used to secure the folded remainder tightly against the leg wound. He then loosened the tourniquet a little. The cut on his forehead had stopped bleeding.

'We can't move him,' Max said. 'Not for quite some time.'

It was another half-hour before Tammy sat up. Vaguely he asked what had happened. They told him but, not surprisingly, he didn't take it all in at first. As they walked slowly back to the hotel, a curious levity seemed to overcome them. This was partly helped by Maria's jokes, especially about The Putto. Strangely, he did not seem to have been upset by all the drama. Indeed, he seemed to approve, as if assuming it had all been put on for his entertainment. He waved his chubby hands in cherubic blessing and, after some gurgles of satisfaction and an appreciative belch or two, fell fast asleep in his mother's enfolding arms.

Subramaniam limped back, leaning heavily on Narayan's shoulder. Tammy, now being carried with in Max's strong arms, still appeared stunned, although he too laughed a little. It was only when they reached the hotel that Clare felt the full force of her shock, and she laughed and wept in relief. She knew now that she was in love with Tammy, but Narayan's gaze of curiosity made her see the need to control her feelings.

Chapter Fourteen

A doctor arrived within an hour. He attended to Tammy's leg wound and the cut on his head and gave him a shot of penicillin. Tammy's concussion was such that he couldn't remember anything from the time he'd begun to climb the temple, and the doctor advised him to stay in bed for a day or two. It seemed to Max a strange coincidence that both he and Tammy had been concussed and nearly drowned, Max from his failed attempt to save the couple in Malibu, and Tammy from a failed attempt upon his life at Sandeha, the latter assuming Clare's suppositions were correct.

Max didn't know what to make of Clare's idea that Tammy had been shot at as he climbed the temple. Max and Narayan, being further up the temple wall, hadn't seen or heard anything. Maria, meanwhile, had been too involved with her demanding little boy to notice. Clare said she'd seen the cripple standing among the fishermen, and possibly the two youths as well, while she and Max had been resuscitating Tammy. Characteristically, though, she was not without her doubts in view of the panic she had felt. Max had always admired Clare's ability to admit she might be wrong.

Max had phoned Inspector Veerapan in Chennai, and he'd issued orders to the local police to provide the group with protection. A police guard arrived that same night. He was a smart young man, with a pencil-thin moustache that he touched with concern from time to time, as if worried it might not be sufficiently admired. He fulfilled his duties with disconcerting zeal, vigorously saluting Max and the others on every possible occasion. He enjoyed ceaseless radio communication with his headquarters, the excited sounds of which leaked past his headset in a series of shrill jabberings.

The following morning, the police guard announced, with awe and enthusiasm, that a senior inspector was coming out to see them. It turned out to be Veerapan, of course. He arrived by helicopter. Clare and Max met him in the lobby of the hotel. Max well remembered him from Madurai; how could he forget his meticulously combed hair and woeful manner? This time, Veerapan was pleased to be able to set their minds at rest. He had surprising news.

'The evidence you gave at Madurai proved most useful,' he told Max and Clare. 'We deduced the assassins were part of a new, small group of hit men. Informed by a rival of theirs, we raided their headquarters yesterday. Four of them were killed, including the two we believe were Venkataraman's assassins.'

'How do you know that?' asked Clare.

'We made an identikit picture of the boy,' Veerapan went on. 'It was based on your description, madam, and' – he turned to Max – 'on your photo of him, good sir, albeit having been in quarter-profile.'

There was an awkward pause then, as if Veerapan was weighing up what he would say next.

'The boy had a bullet hole in his face,' he said, glancing at Clare.

'Don't mind me,' she replied. 'I can handle the gory details.'

The Inspector gave an embarrassed cough.

'It made identification difficult, you understand. We cannot be absolutely certain.'

He brushed at his immaculate grey hair with his fingers, as though nervous of a single strand being out of place.

'About this shooting you've told us of,' he now said. 'I understand it happened at the sea temple. Shall we go there now and you can tell us what you saw.'

'Terrorism's getting worse in India,' Veerapan went on, as the three of them walked down to the temple, 'as it is in the whole world. The Twin Towers, for example. There were only twenty suicide men involved – as few as that.'

'What that crime has done to the whole planet… it seemed to change everything, in a single day,' Max said.

'Yes, it was most terrible,' said the Inspector. 'These militant extremists! People prepared to commit horrifying murders in the cause of a fanatical ideology.'

'When most religions are supposed to be forgiving and pacific,' Max declared.

'Oh yes, the horrible things done from religious rivalry. Hindus, Muslims, Christians, Jews and Sikhs… even Buddhists. None of them should believe in retaliation, but people seem driven to get their own back, both personally and communally.'

'But we don't have to think it's instinctive and inevitable,' suggested Clare. 'Tell me, do you have any idea who hired the assassins?'

'Not yet, but we're working on it. It's more difficult now the assassins are surely dead. The mastermind is still alive, though. You think it was he who shot at this friend of yours? May I ask where he is now?'

'He's not yet fully recovered,' said Max. 'He's back at the hotel in bed.'

When they eventually reached the temple, Veerapan asked Clare to show where she was standing at the time she thought she saw the bullets strike. She was unable to do this easily, as the tide had obliterated any marks upon the sand, and the change in the position of some driftwood was confusing. They examined the surface of the temple for bullet marks, but the stone had traces of erosion all over, having been scoured and pitted in many places over the years. Veerapan seemed not to believe that Tammy had been shot at but he didn't like to say so at first.

'The government's trying to upgrade the country's anti-terrorist activities,' he said. 'There is a need to stop these mad conspiracies in time.'

'More should be done to penetrate terrorist groups,' asserted Max. Which should be far more effective than these Western crude military interventions. So, what do you think about the crippled mastermind? Do you think he was the marksman?'

The Inspector fastidiously polished his already glistening spectacles, as if to emphasise the need for clarity in his reply. He sighed and gave a weary smile.

'I don't believe your friend was really shot at,' he said, turning to Clare. 'You were confused by the sun, I think. It shone into your eyes, perhaps, and dazzled you. We shall keep this young man to guard you for a time, but, in view of the cripple's note, I believe there's little for you to fear.'

'For me, perhaps,' Clare conceded. Then she frowned. 'But what about Tammy?'

Veerapan finished polishing his spectacles, as if he felt they'd never be clean enough. He gave them his melancholy smile. As he drove off to the helicopter, he waved at them with a gesture of encouragement that contained just a hint of caution.

That evening the five of them gathered in Tammy's room, a blandly furnished, anonymous hotel room but one that had a wonderful view of the sea.

Subramaniam gazed at Tammy, who was sitting in a chair now, dressed in a long loose shirt and baggy trousers, a bandage around his head.

'Tammy, my good fellow, what have you learnt from your Muslim friend,' the old man asked.

'Mutual understanding in particular. Non-Muslims tend to think of jihadis as fundamentalist Islamic warriors. But Shahpur taught me that, at a personal level, jihad means the struggle against resistance to the divine law within us. In the Koran, wars of aggression are condemned. Allah is compassionate and merciful. Islam and Hinduism could, in theory, be combined.'

'The Emperor Akbar founded a religion of his own with that intent,' Subramaniam replied. 'He invited Christian priests as well as Hindu gurus to attend his court. But, Tammy, don't entirely forget you were born a Hindu and a Brahmin.'

'Why should I be the Brahmin I was born as? These caste divisions… how I hate the system! The outcasts, the Dalits as we now term them… at one time they weren't allowed to sit down in the presence of Brahmins or even to enter temples. That was monstrous.'

'That was in the bad old days. 'Gandhi called them the harijans,' Subramaniam insisted. 'The beloved of God.'

'Yes, but they're not the beloved of the other castes. In the remoter villages they're still made to have their own inferior wells. All right, we've laws against it, and we keep on hypocritically insisting that caste discrimination doesn't exist, yet there's still great prejudice against their marrying people from higher castes.'

'I too hate the idea of people being outcasts,' Narayan interjected, 'but it's not an essential part of Hinduism. Look, I don't think we ought to keep strictly apart as religious groups, but surely we're allowed to keep a sense of our identity.'

Tammy and Narayan continued arguing. It seemed amiable enough, but Max did wonder if anything further lay behind it. It was the second day after Tammy's accident, and Narayan's possible increased wariness troubled Max. Clare's distress at the time of Tammy's accident had perhaps made Narayan wonder about the nature of the feelings underlying it.

Max now understood more about those feelings. He'd seen the look on her face as they'd resuscitated Tammy, and it had seemed to be a reflection of his own grief at the prospect of losing Narayan. With great difficulty, he at last spoke to Clare.

'Tell me, are you in love with Tammy?'

'Yes, I am, Max,' she said with some caution, 'and he loves me back.'

'I'd thought this was coming, but it's still a shock,' Max said. He found his hands were shaking.

'It's something you've absolutely no right to resent,' she answered, but her voice was softer than before. 'You have no right whatever, not in view of you and Narayan.'

'I know it's caused you enormous anguish. I couldn't have felt more guilty.'

She smiled.

'And I couldn't feel more grateful to you both for what you did in saving Tammy's life.'

Max leant forward and kissed her on the cheek, a gentle kiss that began to heal the breach between them.

It was getting late now. Subramaniam was chanting faintly under his breath. He stirred, opening his watery eyes. His voice grew firmer for a while before his eyelids trembled and began to droop, and the delicate chant fluttered and died out. Tammy was still condemning the caste system:

'Those youths shot down the other day were probably Dalits. All right, Gandhi called them the beloved of God, but they felt more humiliated than beloved no doubt, and humiliation festers and corrupts. They were as much the victims of poverty and prejudice as of their own embittered bloody thoughts, and so more easily suborned to do this crime.'

Narayan seemed on the point of objecting but Tammy wasn't quite finished.

'I say this in attempted explanation not excuse.'

There was a long pause. The sea broke on the shore with a rushing surge. The old man's head was bowed in sleep. His breath came sighing from him as though in sleep he sighed his life away. Then he suddenly woke and began to speak.

'That young man who assassinated Gandhi… one of a group of Hindu fanatics. He killed him because he stood up for the Pakistanis, resisting hatred of our Muslim brothers. But Gandhi would've wanted us to pray for the assassin's soul. He'd never have approved of our hating him in return… for his being hanged.'

He lay back as if about to hover on the edge of sleep again, to experience some uplifting dream of reconciliation.

'Come on. Off to bed,' Maria said as she put her hand on Tammy's head to ruffle his hair. 'No more discussion, Tammy dear. You must be quite worn out.'

Tammy helped Subramaniam to his feet. Before he went to bed, Max thought of their visit to the ashram fifty miles away, and he thought about his time with Narayan.

'I'll stay behind in Sandeha to be with you,' Tammy said to Subramaniam.

'I'll stay as well, said Clare. 'If that's all right.'

Max was happy with this arrangement, since he wished to have some time alone with Narayan to talk about their future. Narayan spoke so inconsistently of this.

'Life without you is inconceivable. But where would we spend our life together?' he'd once said.

Max had been worrying about Clare's safety. However, he felt less anxious after what Inspector Veerapan had said, and what Clare had told Max about the reassuring note the cripple had given her. And, of course, they now had a police guard.

Max knew Clare wanted to be alone with Tammy, which both concerned him and made him feel better about his going to the ashram with Narayan. He and Clare were sleeping in single beds in the same room, and he stretched out a hand across the gap to touch her and felt her accept his touch. He knew she'd come to resent him, to hate him even, just as she'd come to resent and hate Narayan, but her attitude to them both had undergone a miraculous reversal since the two of them had swum out to save Tammy's life.

Max couldn't pretend that Clare's love for Tammy didn't make him feel deprived and insecure, but he was trying to accept that she loved Tammy. What he felt for her was a deep-rooted tenderness that had once allowed his sexual passion its full head.

The memory of her reaction to Tammy on the beach was becoming easier to contemplate. He recalled being on top of the temple with Narayan, with a dizzying drop either side. His fear of heights meant he'd had to force himself to climb it, which he'd done only for Narayan's sake. He'd felt a liberating sense of exhilaration as he'd stood next to Narayan and watched the sun streaking the sea with a blaze of light.

The memory changed. He was with his father. His mother had died a month before, and he was trying to get to know his father better, as if he could somehow fill that appalling gap. His father had been devoted to her, doubtless resenting Max's extreme attachment. However, he'd stumbled into a bitter argument with his father about the invasion of Iraq.

'Bush lied about Saddam's weapons of mass destruction. The enormous cost of the war should be paid for by increased taxation of the very wealthy. But Bush is cutting taxation to enrich his cronies. Paying for the war by borrowing money will have dire fiscal consequences later on.'

This had provoked an explosion of anger from his father.

'I worked my balls off for the money I've paid for you and your education. I haven't noticed you refusing to accept it. You're wasting your time trying to be a writer and photographer. You ought to settle down to a proper job. You've achieved nothing and are getting nowhere. And you have the fucking nerve to talk of high taxation of the rich. My God, you're such a lousy hypocrite!'

This touched Max's vulnerable point. He did feel hypocritical taking advantage of his father's money and did indeed feel he'd achieved very little. He blamed himself for blundering into that futile row, especially since his father's health was failing. He'd craved his father's encouragement and affection. Clare had been in London at the time, and Max had longed for her return. Their love had seemed all he had to keep him going.

He reached out for her again. He still loved her: a changed love but a strong one, which he still didn't think he could ever do without. He began to speak about Rick.

'I'm really worried that he'll develop AIDS… as his former lover did.'

'But there've been all these new advances,' she reassured him. 'Things are so much better with this combination therapy.'

This slightly encouraged him when he thought about Rick, but the idea of the disease becoming so widespread in the Third World, affecting women too, filled him with a sense of frustration and dismay. He recalled asking Subramaniam about the pointlessness of so much suffering and death and the answer he had ventured with its quiet equivocal assurances.

'Why worry about what happens in this confusing world, which often seems so cruel and merciless? Do the seabirds worry? Do the strange seahorses care? Humankind feels pain and fear and passion, but all these things will disappear very soon… like a noise in the quiet night that wakes one from a sleep… or a distant cry that disturbs a peaceful dream.'

As Max began to fall asleep, he heard the surf roll in the distance, and from the room next door came the sound of the old man singing. His voice rose and fell, sometimes high and sweet, sometimes low and solemn. Was his song a hymn of exultation at the mystery of things… or a gentle call for his deliverance? But then the singing died slowly out, and there remained the noise of the endless waves.

Chapter Fifteen

Max and Narayan had departed for the ashram, leaving Clare behind with Tammy. They were now in bed together, and she pulled his sleeping head against her breasts. She thought about the sea temple and how he'd fallen from it, and remembered Max and Narayan courageously diving in, swimming through the beating waves to seize his body and tow it to the shore. Her renewed admiration for Max and Narayan had wiped away the rancour and jealousy she'd felt. She even felt a strange, vicarious satisfaction over his love of Narayan, which allowed her to feel free about returning Tammy's love.

These reflections helped her put things into perspective: the tall cripple, the bullets striking the temple's surface. Sometimes she believed she'd definitely seen him in that little group upon the beach. At other times, the figure of the cripple in his various and conflicting aspects – cruel and tender, sinister and piteous – almost seemed to be a figment of her troubled imagination.

After Veerapan had left, she'd seen in the village a little girl who'd much resembled the cripple's child. Clare had been sitting at a table outside a ramshackle little roadside eating place, where a man and a woman were taking turns at feeding the child; this had surprised Clare because she'd assumed that was exclusively the woman's role. It suggested the man was particularly fatherly, the impression she'd had of the cripple when she'd seen him and his daughter together back in Madurai. Had she seen a pair of crutches lying near him on the ground? She could not be certain this was the same man, because he'd worn dark glasses and a large dilapidated hat that had partly hidden his face. She couldn't recall his wife's features all that well either; the woman had been in floods of tears the only time she'd seen her. All she could remember clearly was that she had a worn and honest face, and looked rather old to have so young a child; the same could also be said about this woman. Clare might have approached to get a closer look, but she hadn't known how to do that without seeming intrusive.

She told Tammy about it later.

'If the cripple tried to kill me to stop me witnessing against the youths, their now being dead would remove any further motive for his trying again,' he said, sounding irritated.

The deaths of the assassins had been announced on the radio and television, although this hadn't satisfied the public demand that their mastermind accomplice should be caught and punished.

The police guard continued to protect them, prowling around the premises with his bleeping headset, and seizing every opportunity for one of his formidable salutes.

'You have no rational cause to feel fear,' Tammy insisted. 'And you have no reason to feel guilt about Vijaya.'

Clare wanted to talk about Vijaya. Tammy did so reluctantly in an effort clear her troubled conscience.

'When I got engaged to Vijaya I hadn't really known what love could be. I used to suspect it was a fiction, a romantic myth to induce men and women into marrying each other. I'd never quite believed in its reality… until I fell for you.'

As soon as he had uttered those words, he reverted to their better-charted channel of discussion.

'Oh these interminable problems of the country: poverty, disease, rural dispossession and unemployment. And then there's sectarian bigotry and the spread of further prejudice and violence.'

'Come on, Tammy!' Clare objected. 'This is too much gloomy disillusionment and not enough realistic hope.'

He grinned and then talked of the growth of high technology.

'Computers, satellites and the seemingly ubiquitous mobile phones are breaking down the isolation of rural life. Mobile clinics now visit the villages. The vans contain small laboratories that test for typhus, malaria and other diseases that could otherwise be fatal.'

'You're starting to sound dangerously optimistic,' she joked. 'You'd better watch it.'

'Well, all right, I may often seem a bit of a doomster. I see many improvements but also many things that need to be made so much better. And now I feel you've come into my rather dismal life and made me feel there's enormous, vital point to it. Maybe it sounds disgustingly sentimental but, in spite of all the poverty I see, I've never felt such hope in all my life.'

The next day he received another text message from Shahpur:

'Kalyani has finally run away from her family to marry Shahpur,' he told Clare. 'They've left Kolkata and gone to Mumbai, where he hopes to get a job. It's very brave of her, since her father is thought to be in furious pursuit. Her mother's doing her best to stop him. God knows if he'll ever track them down.'

'How lucky we are by comparison.'

'Exactly. I hope to God nothing stops their getting married. That manic religious prejudice won't prevent it.' He paused before adding: 'As I hope that nothing stops my marrying you when you're divorced from Max.'

This was the first time he'd spoken of marrying her. She was amusedly delighted by his eccentrically indirect proposal, but she was also perplexed and undecided. She'd discussed with Maria the marriage she seemed about to be giving up. The nearer she got to abandoning it, the more it reasserted its gentle hold with little surges of nostalgia.

'You know, when I was very young, I was afraid I'd never fall in love. And suddenly there was Max, and within a month I wanted him so much I couldn't imagine the world without him. And now I suppose what's happened is a sort of semi-transference of that to Tammy… and my promise to myself about Vijaya…'

'Is something to be tactfully forgotten,' Maria interrupted. 'I forbid you to torment yourself about it. All is surely fair in love and war.'

Maria continued to do all she could to reassure her, but then seized the opportunity to reveal further details of her own love life and the possibility of its resumption.

'I've had another text message from The Animal. He claims he's about to leave the Innamorata, and I'm not at all displeased by this development.'

Overflowing with robust goodwill, she counselled Clare.

'Don't feel so bad about Tammy and Vijaya that you give him up yourself with some revolting gesture of self-sacrifice. You and

Max are both so impossibly high-minded. Frankly, it makes one feel like throwing up at times. Look, you resisted temptation for longer than is proper, and now it's high time you had some decent self-respecting fun.'

Maria went on to recount an especially implausible anecdote about an incident in Rome.

'The Animal got more drunk than usual and made outrageous passes towards the singer in his favourite restaurant. She had a face like an ape and a voice like an inebriated corncrake. Of course he only did this to provoke my jealousy, which he never thought sufficiently Italian and dramatic.'

Max and Narayan drove to the ashram, which was farther down the coast. It was late when they arrived. They were given a little room with two separate beds, but they managed to sleep together in one of them.

Max kept half-waking, his mind coloured with the vestiges of passing dreams. One dream was of a lingam, anointed and garlanded, in a temple sanctuary. A woman was bowing before this phallic symbol, praying for fertility. When she turned around he saw that it was Clare, and he wished it was his child she longed for. Another dream was of the sea temple, now carved with embracing figures. A man was wading out of the sea. When Max woke he recalled reading in the Shiva Purana about how the ocean assumed the form of a man and how the seed of Shiva came to rest in the holy waters of the Ganges. He'd spoken to Narayan of this particular myth, but Narayan had never heard of it.

'Look out, Max, you're in danger of knowing more about Hinduism than most Hindus!' he'd said laughingly. Still, I'm really glad about your growing knowledge and admiration.'

'I love its amazingly affirmative attitude to sex,' Max had replied. 'I really admire its veneration of the yoni as well as the lingam, the symbols of female and male genitalia. What I admire most, though, are the ideas in the Bhagavad Gita, which you and Subramaniam prompted me to read.'

'It's said to be the glory of Hindu thought.'

'I compare it to the Sermon on the Mount, with its inspiring if difficult ethical ideals. I'd love to be strong enough to be indifferent to worldly success and failure, to be all-forgiving, invulnerable to adversity and beyond despair.'

'All this is possible… if one follows the path of light and avoids that of fire, with its greed and unrest.'

'Yes, but the way of fire also includes human desire, which I'm not quite so keen to be above.'

This brought Max to think of Rick, who'd always been so wonderfully accepting of his sexuality, and he wondered when he'd hear about the tests. He felt his dread about what could happen to Rick like a shadow over his happiness with Narayan. Rick was the first of the three loves of his whole life, and Max could never forget those impassioned, if confusing, times together.

Narayan appeared to be in a disturbed mood when he woke in the morning, and Max asked him what the matter was.

'I hate myself when I get these downers,' Narayan told him. 'I suppose I'm scared.'

'Of what?'

'The future… what it holds in us. You don't know the enormous pressure to marry we Indians live under… and the prejudice against gay love.'

'The future is whatever we make of it,' said Max simply. 'We have to fight the prejudice. We've every right to be happy.'

Narayan didn't reply directly. Max put his hands to his head, squeezing it slightly as if he could impress upon the brain within something of the tenderness that nagged him. He loved their mental intimacy, which always instilled in him a desire for a physical equivalent. Narayan responded in kind to the feelings he uttered, the words infusing their kisses with a growing warmth and then a sudden release of passion. Max loved how his climax was beyond his control, and the sense of freedom that paradoxically always gave him.

Later, Max again challenged Narayan's anxieties. He laughed at them, knowing how Narayan found reassurance in the humour.

'So I'm bound by convention, am I?' Narayan replied. 'The oppressive concept of sexual normality? My God, think of all the taboos we're breaking, Max: race, religion, sexual orientation. It must be quite a record, in its way.'

'If the taboos are wrong, they should be broken.'

'Not by shouting one's defiance from the rooftops, as least not unless you want to be turned into a martyr, and I'm afraid I don't. You mustn't expect too much of me. I'm not as strong and independent as I give out, and I don't want to see you hurt.'

'I won't get hurt, whatever happens,' Max said, expressing his words with a certainty he didn't feel.

∴

Narayan had a friend at the ashram, a Bengali woman named Mohini. They'd met at the university, where she'd been a lecturer in politics. Mohini joined them at the ashram the next morning. Max reckoned she was in her late thirties. She had a pale complexion and determined eyes. She'd got permission for Max to bring his camera and, as she showed them around, he took photos of people sitting at their spinning wheels and hand looms, of cows and buffaloes being milked by hand, of the shrine of the sadhu, which was densely covered with flowers, and of the disciples prostrating themselves with a reverence Narayan seemed to share.

Max found himself thinking about Narayan's divided allegiances: to the luminous world of Western science on the one hand, and to his cherished Hindu faith on the other. Could he maintain a balance, or would the insistent, solemn demands of his deep-rooted culture reassert themselves and overcome Western influences?

Max thought that Mohini came across as a somewhat divided spirit too. She was enthusiastic about the traditional values of the ashram, but, like Vijaya, she was determined not to be perceived as old-fashioned and submissive. Unlike Vijaya, though, she allowed a certain defensiveness to colour her initial attitude towards Max.

'So you've come to have a laugh at our quaint ways? We had an English writer here last year, full of simplistic condemnations and determined to find India a catastrophe. He decided the ashram was really a bit phoney, the swami a sort of spiritual conman. When your own clever-clever book appears, I trust you won't be following his example!'

'Why the attitude?' Max asked, taken aback.

'Well,' retorted Mohini, shrugging, 'we do get quite a bad press in the West at times. It's usually something along the lines of how fascinating the ancient culture is but, with a few ultra-technical exceptions, what a corrupt old mess of a modern country.'

'No one thinks the West is so marvellous that we can't learn from both your old traditions and your modern country,' countered Max.

Mohini nodded.

'I realise the West is losing its over-confidence,' she said. 'People are worried about fossil fuels and global warming, and taking up the fibre diet of poor Asian peasants so you don't die too early from heart attacks as a result of scoffing all that rich food.'

Max continued to find her style of argument abrasive, but Narayan came to her defence.

'How annoyed we are by how Westerners overreact to our country. We don't want to be embarrassingly gushed over, but we also don't enjoy being told what an area of darkness India now is and how beyond all salvation.'

Narayan showed enthusiasm when Mohini pressed them to attend the ashram's dawn meditation, an experience she hoped they would be open to.

'The swami will appear upon his balcony. There will be no noise... just the sound of the sea. We will watch the sun rising. You stand there as the swami sings... that's all you do. And let your own inner peace come through.'

'What first brought you to the ashram,' Max asked her.

'I suppose the Gandhian belief in non-violence. I'm a widow, which probably explains why I'm so self-reliant and so independent of conventional middle-class prejudice. I've sacrificed none of my individuality in joining the ashram. Much as I admire the swami's principles, I make my own decisions in my life.'

∴

Max and Narayan had to be at the ashram for the meditation session at five o'clock the following morning. When the alarm clock went off beside the bed, Max opened his eyes and glanced at it. It was ten past four. He turned on the light and gently woke Narayan.

'It's time to get up,' he whispered to him. 'I hope you've had a good sleep,' he said, a little louder.

'I had a dream,' said Narayan, stretching. 'I still feel I'm in the middle of it.'

'What was it about?'

'There was this mountain... covered in trees that bore both fruit and blossom. The juice from the fruit was running down into the sea... and the waves were rolling in.' Narayan paused and smiled at Max. 'You were kissing me,' he said. 'And then you woke me up. All very symbolic, I've no doubt. But, please, no cold and reductive psychoanalysing, if you don't mind. Hey, let's have a swim before we go.'

'A swim?' asked Max, bemused.

'Yes!' exclaimed Narayan, getting up. 'Why not?'

He began pulling and pushing Max playfully before they leapt out of bed, got dressed and set off in the darkness.

On their way to the beach, their mood changed, and they began talking about Subramaniam's beliefs, which so fascinated both of them.

'He's a bit of a pantheist,' suggested Max, 'and he believes in eternal life. I don't think I do, though.'

'Oh yes,' answered Narayan, 'he sees eternity in the waves and clouds. He believes in forgiveness and compassion above all. He thinks Gandhi would've forgiven his murderer. He also thinks Venkataraman would've forgiven that mad boy, but I'm not so sure.'

'What was it Saint Augustine said? Something about hating the sin but loving the sinner?'

When they reached the beach, the sea was high and racing, and the air was filled with salty spray. They ran into the crashing waves. The sun trembled on the edge of the turning world, and Max was moved to hope that a new dawn was slowly breaking in his life too. When they later got dressed to go to the meditation, Max sensed a disturbance. It seemed to him that when Narayan put on his Indian clothes – the loose, hand-loomed cotton garments he'd recently come to favour – he also adopted an identity that was different to the one he possessed when naked in Max's arms, or swimming with him far out to sea, or in any other place where they were marvellously alone together.

The place of meditation was beside the sea. When they joined the group below the balcony, it was as if Max had emerged from the warm, private world he shared with Narayan and joined a public one with colder claims on him. Mohini was there, and she greeted them both with particular friendliness. She positioned herself right next to Narayan, and Max found himself separated from them by two young men with reverently expectant looks. A few metres away, a man on crutches – a woman and a young child standing next to him – glanced at Max.

People came from all directions and silently gathered near the balcony and on the windy beach. The sky was lightening. Swollen clouds, veined with threads of turquoise, were massing to the east. A shaft of sunlight broke from the horizon as if it were escaping from the unseen world beyond and threw its pale dazzle on the early-morning sea.

At last, the swami appeared on the balcony. The dawn sunlight touched his face as he began to pray. His prayers were murmured at first, but they soon swelled into a delicate, humming chant that floated across the beach as the people began to participate. A flock of wild geese were passing overhead, honking loudly, and a chorus of cockerels greeted the new day with enthusiastic crowing. These noises fused with the swami's chant, which was spreading fast among the crowd. Max noticed that the crippled man had picked up the child and was now holding her in his arms. His eyes were shut, his lips trembling with fervour. The woman was praying with equal devotion, but she had her eyes open and she was gazing at the man and the child.

Max looked at Mohini and Narayan, now standing closely side-by-side. They shared a look of quiet reverence, about which Max – thinking about all his secret jokes with Narayan, their irony and fun – felt distinctly ambivalent. He concentrated on the spreading chant and on the rapt people. He prayed for Clare's happiness with Tammy, although he found this difficult. It was easier to pray for Rick, although he wasn't at all sure who or what he was praying to. As he glanced again at Narayan and Mohini, he realised he was starting to feel excluded and even jealous.

When the chant came to an end, the swami prayed quietly for a while. A profound silence descended on the crowd. Then the swami lifted one arm in a solemn gesture of benediction before he slowly retreated and disappeared from view.

The crowd began to break up. Max was about to depart with Narayan and Mohini when the cripple, the woman and child at his side, awkwardly approached them. Narayan spoke with him in Tamil. Max had suspected it was the same cripple he'd seen once before, and the one that Clare had talked about seeing, and indeed it was. Narayan translated for the cripple, who spoke directly to Max.

'I want to say how grateful we are to your wife for saving our child from being injured. She's the light of our lives, our only child.'

'Our little girl's always been very thin and stunted,' his wife added. 'We haven't been able to feed her properly because of our poverty. I've just been praying to the Lord Shiva on her behalf. I was also praying for your good wife.'

She began to cry, wiping the tears from her cheeks quickly as if embarrassed at showing such emotion in front of Max. He was moved by her forthrightness and by the timid smile that creased her face. She glanced devotedly at her child and at her husband; they all bowed their heads and put their hands together, which Max reciprocated. They moved away and were soon lost in the dissolving crowd.

'It's strange that he's revealed himself when he's wanted by the police,' Max said to the other two. 'I suppose I should report it to Veerapan, but I feel the man has trusted me. I hate the idea of betraying his trust.'

'He should be punished, to stop him doing anything similar again,' said Mohini. 'Society needs protecting from its killers.'

'As the mastermind, he was as much a killer as the boy,' Narayan added. 'If not even more so, despite having this redeeming side – his care for his wife and daughter.'

Nodding, Max sent a text message to Veerapan, telling him where he was and who he'd seen. The Inspector texted back immediately to let Max know he was sending around two police officers. They'd be unlikely to find the man, Max supposed. By the time they arrived, the crowd would have broken up and the cripple gone back into hiding.

He turned to Narayan.

'What will they do if and when they catch him?'

'The newspapers are saying the surviving accomplices to the assassination must be caught and hanged. Death sentences are sometimes handed out in India, though they're rarely carried out.'

'I don't support capital punishment,' said Mohini. 'It contradicts the doctrine of ahimsa – no violence of any kind.'

Narayan nodded at this.

'I'm worried,' Max said quietly.

'What about, exactly?'

'I'm worried they might decide the cripple's wife is an accessory to the murder. If they do, she too might be sentenced to be hanged, which would be terrible.'

∴

Clare was with Tammy in his hotel room in Sandeha when she heard a noise. It was like someone tapping on the ground outside. A quick look out of the window showed it to be only Subramaniam's walking stick; he had wandered out to look at the night sky. He was murmuring to himself and vaguely sighing, as if at the infinite scatter of stars.

'The enormous size and age of the universe is a thing to marvel at, not feel belittled by,' he had said to Clare a day earlier. 'What does space matter? Or time? The lifeless aeons have negligible importance in the eyes of God when compared with the sentient creatures on his living earth.'

Although keen to dismiss her anxieties, Clare was fairly certain she'd seen the cripple and his wife feeding their child outside that little eating place. She was disturbed to think he could still be here in Sandeha. Had he stayed behind because he wanted to make another attempt on Tammy's life? She realised her level of anxiety could be higher because she was now so very much in love with Tammy.

She suggested they should go for a swim. It would be the first time since his accident, so they agreed they wouldn't swim out very far. They walked down to the beach, where the waves came hissing down in delicate loops and crescents. As they approached the temple, it seemed to soar above them like a haunting apparition, insubstantial and yet curiously peaceful. It was almost as if the ruined building had been suspended in the air, remote and dissociated, luminous and beautiful. As Clare gazed up at the striated stonework, she became aware of the headlamps of a car approaching.

She waded into the water with Tammy, who was hesitant at first. Clare thought this understandable, given his last experience in the sea. They began to swim together. A little way out they came to a sandy ledge under the water, where she found she could stand with the water just waist-deep. Tammy held her in his arms, kissing her mouth, fondling her breasts. He put his arms around her and lifted her upwards. She wrapped her arms around his neck and drew herself up to him. She felt the wind on her skin as he felt between her legs to stimulate her, all the while kissing her mouth. His foreplay was deep and prolonged, but he finally entered her, moving slowly. She tightened as she felt him come, such was her sense of his seed within her. She exulted in her acceptance of it and in the downward rippling that seemed to strike her lower spine and then course upwards, as in some inexorable motion that seemed to pulse almost against her skull.

Satiated, Tammy gently lowered her back down in the water, and they embraced for a while longer. Then Clare happened to glance at the shore. She could make out two figures, visible because of the whiteness of their clothes. They were standing at the sea's edge, as though confronting them.

For a moment she was immobilised with horror. They could shoot them down in the water; they could murder them!

'Oh my God,' she breathed. 'Tammy!' she shouted, then dived, hoping he would do the same.

He did. Their movements took them into deeper water. In her panic, she found herself swimming wildly against the undertow. She recalled the puffs of dust on the temple stonework. She imagined the bullets hitting him this time, cruelly piercing the flesh she'd come to love. Terrified, she broke the surface of the water, gasping and spluttering. She twisted her body, looking for Tammy.

'Clare!'

It wasn't Tammy's voice. It was Max, and he was wading out to her. The figures she'd mistaken for the assassins were Max and Narayan. She felt immense relief, like a burst of happiness. And then it dawned on her that things must now come to a head. Narayan would be appalled if he'd seen her and Tammy making love, as he surely must have. Narayan stayed on the beach, but Max was swimming out to join her.

'Clare!'

This time, it was Tammy calling. She'd been separated from him by the undertow, and was about ten metres away. Max had reached her by now. She was touched by the fact he'd come out to her. When Tammy joined them, the three swam back to shore together. It was then she noticed a third figure on the beach but assumed it was some harmless fisherman.

Narayan was standing at the very edge of the water in an attitude of extreme hostility. He glanced furiously at her as she waded out of the sea with Max, and he glared at Tammy as he walked up to him. Tammy reached out to put his hand on Narayan's shoulder, but he knocked it away in a gesture of contempt.

The third figure she'd noticed was now fast approaching. He was dressed in white and walked with a stick. She realised it was Subramaniam lurching towards them; he was trying to come between Tammy and Narayan, but they didn't seem to notice the old man's presence. Narayan and Tammy were shouting at each other. Narayan punched Tammy in the chest, at once seeming astounded at what he'd done. Subramaniam cried out, and the stick slipped from his grasp. His body shuddered, as if all the breath was drawn from it, and he collapsed. Narayan stood frozen for an instant, amazed and horrified, but then he rushed forward to kneel beside him.

Chapter Sixteen

The doctor they called for arrived within half an hour. Within a minute of arriving, this portly, bald and self-assured man had confirmed that Subramaniam had had a moderate heart attack.

'He's all right for the moment,' he said, 'but you must get him back to Chennai as soon as possible, and into hospital for tests.'

'I feel responsible for precipitating this,' Narayan told him. 'My cousin and I had a very bad argument that came to blows. Our great uncle was trying to intercede when he collapsed.'

'At his age and with his frailty, it could've happened at any time,' the doctor reassured him. Narayan wasn't all that reassured, even though the old man fell that night into a peaceful sleep.

Later that night, back in Tammy's room at the hotel, Tammy and Narayan had another argument.

'Clare and I are deeply in love, and Max knows about it.' Tammy said. 'We want to marry as soon as they're divorced.'

'I didn't know about it, though I occasionally had my vague suspicions,' Narayan answered. He hesitated for a few moments, searching for the right words. 'Look, I'm really sorry I hit you. I was desperately angry and I lost my temper. But you're supposed to be marrying Vijaya, for God's sake, and this is gross betrayal. She'll be utterly devastated.'

'So what about you and Max? Hasn't Max betrayed Clare all this time! Talk about double standards.'

'My affair with Max doesn't involve the sort of public humiliation Vijaya will now endure, having been engaged to you for so long. No, I don't forgive you, though I admit to feeling enormous guilt concerning Clare.'

The next morning Subramaniam was taken back to Chennai in an ambulance; Max and Clare were allowed to sit with him on the journey. Tammy and Narayan returned in their separate cars. They all met later to the hospital and were relieved to learn he was not in any present danger.

∴

'I wish to give up my life in Los Angeles so I can live with you in India,' Max said to Narayan once they were back at his house. 'Of course it does depend on Rick being okay. I'm waiting for an email from him about his tests.'

'I'm very touched,' Narayan answered, 'but Tammy's charge of double standards has really got at me.'

'You've a really tender conscience,' Max replied. 'That's one of the things I've always loved in you.'

Vijaya refused to see Tammy or Clare, obviously immensely hurt by the fact that Tammy had decided to leave her for Clare.

'I'm planning to leave Chennai to live with my relations in Kolkata,' Vijaya told Max. 'In the meantime, I'm going to visit a woman in the suburbs of Chennai. She's had acid thrown into her face by a manically infatuated youth whom she'd rejected.'

'How monstrous!' Max said, horrified.

'The poor woman's face has been horribly disfigured. I understand the youth has been arrested. His despicable male pride was offended, and he went off his head. The victim wants him hanged. She's extremely vengeful.'

Max thought about the possibility of the cripple being hanged if it is proven that he was an accessory to the murder.

'Have you decided what you'll be doing in Kolkata?' Max asked Vijaya.

'I'm in touch through the internet with an orphanage for abandoned girls,' she replied. 'I've sent them my application to work there. Baby girls are often abandoned; baby boys seldom are. Oh yes, we've still a lot of sexist prejudice to shift.' This led to further jokey comments about her male supremacist aunts. 'I'm escaping their suffocating prudery. I'm not exactly intending to become a scarlet woman in my spare time, but I might bathe in a swimsuit and not a sari that balloons out in the water, giving a woman the shape of a fat sea cow. You should see the ogresses when they go swimming in the sea! Seriously, I need to make a total break from the past. I've led too narrow and useless a life so far.'

∴

After a week in hospital, Subramaniam was allowed to return home. He was very frail now, but he still liked to sit and talk on the veranda of his house every evening. He spoke of Hinduism mostly but also referred to the Christian idea of an incarnate god.

'I liken him to Vishnu,' he said, 'although Christ suffered human agony, achieving immortality through pain and death.'

He often talked about Venkataraman's assassins, comparing them to Gandhi's murderer.

'They were hugely evil in what they did but not in the souls they would pass on.'

He spoke of human evil and the evil that arises from accidents of nature: earthquakes, floods, hurricanes, famine and disease.

'Death as such is not evil, though,' he suddenly affirmed to Max, who was sitting with him one evening. 'Nor is suffering an evil; not necessarily. It's something we endure on our great journey onwards, from body to body, from soul to soul. A thousand times we die so that we can be born again, travelling from life to life, until at last we achieve union with the mysterious world soul.'

The two men watched the sun as it was going down one evening. Subramaniam, holding on tightly to his much-thumbed copy of the Bhagavad Gita, turned to Max and scrutinised him.

'Tammy told me of Shahpur and Kalyani,' he said quietly. 'I greatly hope her father will relent in his pursuit of them. As a young man, I saw a wife and husband killed in the Partition riots. The husband was trying to shield his wife. They were both hacked to death. I've longed ever since, with all my heart, for reconciliation between Muslims and Hindus.'

He put his shivering hand on Max's arm and said he was feeling cold.

'The light is fading,' he said.

Max knew this was no reference to the sunset, and he felt an immeasurable sadness.

'I think I can hear the sea,' said the old man softly, 'but perhaps I imagine it. Yes, the Mahatma striding onwards… the procession nearing the shore… those gentle cries of triumph.'

Subramaniam sighed. His hand dropped down, and the book slid to the floor as his head fell forward.

'Narayan!' Max called out.

Narayan came rushing out, already knowing the reason behind Max's cry. When he saw Subramaniam, though, he let out a tiny gasp. Max and Narayan sat together, the old man's body between them, just as they had sat with the body of that young woman on the beach at Malibu. Narayan held Subramaniam's body in his arms, slightly rocking it to and fro as if it were a living child in need of being comforted. He did this for a short while before gently placing Subramaniam's hands together and closing his eyelids.

∴

Subramaniam's cremation on the riverside steps moved them all. As the fire leapt upwards around the shrouded body, Max visualised the old man's soul being carried skywards on the twisting smoke, his old voice rising in one of those prayers he used to chant. In his final days, he'd been disturbed to learn of further communal troubles among the poor and unemployed. He, like Tammy, had come to believe that the assassins were part of a wider malaise, yet a weird serenity had informed his grieved reflections.

Max found himself remembering one last conversation he'd had with the old man.

'Progress, you have asked me about, Max. Yes, I believe life is a progression, with huge significance beyond itself. The spirit progresses as the river flows; the world has meaning, although the people suffer. There will always be those who suffer, but there will also be those who are compassionate. And there will always be people who hate each other and fight, the spirit of cold vengeance and the mad assassins'

Max had swallowed hard.

'Such horrors… yes indeed,' Subramaniam had continued. 'But we must try and help the weak and frightened in their loneliness and pain. The spirit lives. The soul of the breathing world will breathe forever. When I die, think of my spirit that is within the wind, passing down the river to the open sea…'

∴

Clare often thought of the assassins and the strong affinities that had bound them, especially the older youth's affectionate protectiveness of the boy.

'The cripple approached me at the end of the meditation,' Max told her. 'His adoration of his wife and child and his evident gratitude to you are also redeeming factors for him. Seen in isolation, the assassins seem to be figures of hatred and revenge, but they had their mitigating loyalties and mutual tenderness.'

Clare confronted the break-up of her marriage with mixed feelings. She and Max had moved out of Narayan's house, out of necessity, and were living in a small antiquated hotel. A pair of lively monkeys was kept in a cage in the garden, and a parrot shifted fussily back and forth on its perch. A peacock, with its spectacular tail and dowdy mate, strutted about the grounds. These days were like a late summer for Max and Clare's marital affection. Her love for Tammy had continued to grow, yet her nostalgia for the past life with Max was akin to her feelings at Subramaniam's cremation, as he passed out of their lives, his ashes carried away along the river as wild ducks flew overhead in a sudden rush of wings.

She didn't regret that her sex life with Max had ended as all her physical desire was now reserved for Tammy. She loved Tammy more and more deeply, but she didn't like to think that the intimacy she had shared with Max was something she must now relinquish and forget. Could they not retain a little of what had grown between them and been strengthened by the trials they'd endured? Or would this threaten the marriage Tammy wanted but to which she'd not yet assented? Did she need to exorcise Max from her mind before she could agree to be engaged to Tammy? She was worried about what might happen to Max now, for she doubted Narayan's commitment.

She pondered on her present feelings for Narayan. Her former resentment and jealousy had disappeared, but she was little impressed by his attitude to Tammy: his continuing implacability. She also thought it was tactless to make so much of his friendship with Mohini when Max was there. It was obvious that her confident experience of the world would appeal to Narayan, as would her feelings for India's traditions. But why was Narayan's manner with Max strangely patient as in some form of solace?

Work on the book was going well. Thanks to Tammy's help, Max was able to expand it by incorporating a great deal of economic commentary. It gave him the opportunity to increase western awareness of India's need for realistic foreign aid that wouldn't be spent on grandiose, prestige projects or vanish into the pockets of venal government officials, something about which Tammy felt particularly strongly. The demands of the book brought a need to journey farther afield. They planned to set off northwards, provisionally for a month at a time, returning to Chennai between trips.

Maria received another text from Antonio. She showed it to Clare, so dispelling her suspicion that the so-called Animal was more myth than monster.

'You see, he now claims to have completely thrown over the dire Innamorata,' Maria said, her voice triumphant. 'He longs only to be reunited with the all-forgiving me and the darling Putto, unaware of how fierce and greedy the little darling Putto has become.'

'Have you replied?' Clare asked.

'Yes. I've told him I'd be happy to return to live with him in Rome but only if he promises there will be no more philandering. I demand exclusive adoration. He must also make an honest woman of me. My wish to marry him must sound quaintly old fashioned and not very feminist,' said Maria. 'You have to understand, though, that he's a fickle, male chauvinist pig, with those rapacious eyes that forever roam lustfully around. How else could I possibly keep him captive?'

∴

Max wanted to do something more substantial for Indian famine relief. This was partly out of his love for Narayan, although he didn't tell him this.

'I see it as showing my respect for Subramaniam,' he said instead. 'I'll go over the matter with Clare, then email my brokers and my bank.'

Unsurprisingly, Max's attitude to Mohini changed when her attitude to him changed. She may have been impressed when Narayan told her of Max's impending donation, but this wasn't in the hope he might be equally generous towards the ashram.

'It's sufficiently endowed,' she said to Max. 'What it needs is realistic hope. What it can do without are the fashionable moaners indulging in their prophecies of doom.'

She'd clearly become rather attached to Max, happily dropping round to indoctrinate him with what he called her neo-Gandhian ideology. Max responded positively to her opinions, however impractical he sometimes found them. Narayan, however, would insist on arguing, more to show he wasn't overly influenced by her views, which impressed him more than he liked to admit.

'Oh, Max,' Mohini began, 'what wouldn't we give these days for an ounce of Gandhi's courage and inspiration? Yet some people are fool enough to say that he was naïve.'

'Oh come on!' rejoined Narayan. 'He was naïve, in a way. Sublimely naïve. He was a great teacher, with a noble simplicity that set him far above the cunning that politicians usually need.'

'Why confuse simplicity with naïvety, Narayan dear?' replied Mohini. 'Oh Gandhi had simplicity all right; that's true. It's always the complicated, devious people who end up making a terrible mess of things. He had an earthy realism. It's the poor sods who talk him down these days who are naïve. Gandhi knew that it's only hope and trust that really work with people, darling, whatever our modern cynics say.'

Mohini stayed a month in Chennai. Max sometimes wondered about the endearments she used when talking to Narayan – the dears and darlings. Were they merely her way of insisting on her emancipated spirit? Indeed, she would often kiss him lightly on the lips, in amused violation of India's strict code of public manners. On their last night together, she and Narayan had a particularly lively dispute, which they both equally enjoyed.

'Instead of giving tractors and medical aid to Third World countries, the West sells them tanks and military aircraft to plunge them even further into crippling debt,' said Mohini, hardly pausing to catch her breath.

'She's off again!' exclaimed Narayan in mock alarm. 'Having another go at the exploitative, crafty West. Pretend not to hear, Max. With any luck, she'll stop.'

'Max is too open-minded to want me to stop,' said Mohini. 'Unlike some people, who are jealous because my views aren't hidebound by majority opinion.'

'Oh yes,' said Narayan, smiling. 'I'm so jealous of your political views, I'm thinking of taking a course in basic anarchism. All we need is for the military to be abolished, and then universal brotherhood would burst out overnight. No arms! No army! No police! No sectarian violence and no civil riots, either. All we'd need then, you see, would be a million ashrams with a Mohini in each and every one, ruling over them.'

'I wish you wouldn't parody my opinions, Narayan dear,' said Mohini. 'What's more, in the ashram I'm loosely attached to, I keep a very low profile.'

'Only so you can get your own way more subtly, wrapping that old swami around your little finger, then doing exactly what you want.' Narayan turned to Max. 'She's always been like that, you know. An undercover power freak; a real manipulator with far more than her fair share of nerve.'

'I'll forgive you for that,' Mohini laughed. 'I may have a touch of modest confidence, but I'm not pushy and conceited, am I, Max?'

'Of course not,' Max told her. 'Anyway, I like confident people.'

'Always so reassuring, Max dear. Unlike your friend here, with his little cracks about me. Oh well, we must pity the poor thing, I suppose. All that foreign gallivanting and scientific wizardry. When it comes to the crunch, though, he's so pathetically unthinking, he hardly knows what life in the new millennium is all about.'

Narayan opened his mouth to say something but found he couldn't and burst out laughing instead.

Chapter Seventeen

Three days after Mohini left, Max received a long email from Rick.

'The growth is Kaposi's sarcoma,' he wrote. Max's pulse raced as he read on. 'It's been excised but this means I've developed full-blown AIDS. Isn't it ironic this should happen just when I became so respectably monogamous? Well, they're making medical advances all the time. You and Clare are not to worry. Concentrate on getting your book written.'

They decided to put the book on hold for the present and to return to LA.

'I want to offer Rick support, moral and financial, when we get back,' Max said to Clare. 'We also need to set our divorce proceedings in motion so you'll be free to marry Tammy.'

'I don't want to talk about that possibility yet,' she said. 'It's a bit soon.'

'Well, I'll try to persuade Rick to come back with us to India for a while, if he's well enough, when we return to complete the research on the book. He's got no one now it seems, and you'll remember how wickedly amusing he can be. He's been such a loyal friend to me for years.'

∴

For a day or two, Max moped around in a state of dazed sorrow. This seemed to correspond to Narayan's mood; he was missing

Vijaya and Mohini. He appeared uncharacteristically remote. So it was with mixed expectations that Max went to visit Narayan on their last night in India. They kissed, but their kiss lacked the excited expectation of the past. Narayan looked very nervous.

'What's the matter?' asked Max, simply and with some dread.

'I've got to tell you something, Max,' Narayan said. 'I'm afraid it's going to hurt.'

Max said nothing. Narayan was silent for a while, as if he feared Max's reaction. When he spoke, he seemed resolved, supported by much thought-out decisiveness.

'I'm in love with Mohini,' he suddenly said, 'and I want to marry her.'

'That's ridiculous,' said Max, his voice flat.

'Why ridiculous?' Narayan didn't appear to resent Max's reaction; he was far more concerned about being believed. 'Surely you've seen this coming?'

'That you'd want to marry her? Of course not.'

Max felt his temper rising and wondered if he could control it. He wanted to sound cool and rational, but he was shaking from a jealous fury. His mouth went dry. It was difficult to speak, to even form the words in his mind.

'I knew you liked her,' he heard himself say at last. 'You enjoyed her company, the attention that she paid to you. But marrying her? That's mad! How much have you ever seen of her?'

'I've been seeing her a lot recently,' admitted Narayan. 'More than I've let on.'

'Oh,' breathed Max. Another shock. 'Really?' He gulped for air. 'I mean, wasn't that being a bit deceitful?'

'No,' answered Narayan. 'We always agreed that we weren't bound to tell each other everything.'

'We only agreed that at the start. Things change. We grew closer, didn't we? Anyway, I think you're fantasising. You pretend to yourself an emotion you just imagine... because it's socially required. You're not in any real sense in love with her. You can't be. You should have the self-honesty to see it.'

'I am being self-honest,' Narayan said quietly, again anxious to convince. 'Look, right at the start, I told you I didn't know myself. I didn't know how I'd react to you. How do we ever know we're going to end up loving someone? Deceitful I may have been, in a way, but only because I didn't want to hurt you. I've loved you, you know that, and I still think the world of you, I swear. But now... now I'm in love with Mohini. I wouldn't tell you that if it wasn't true.'

'You know it isn't,' Max blurted out, unable to stop himself. 'You're lying to yourself. You haven't got the guts to live the life you should. Well then, go ahead and marry her,' he said, his voice getting louder as he lost control. 'Just... just fuck off and marry her, damn you! You've shat enough on my life, so now go and screw up someone else's.'

Narayan reached for him.

'Don't touch me!' Max shouted. 'You make me sick. I never want to see your lousy face again.'

His eyes were blurred with tears of rage. Narayan tried again to touch him, extending a hand, but Max refused to take it. The hand hung in the air, in sad apology, before Narayan withdrew it and hesitantly left. He paused briefly to look back at Max before disappearing into the night.

Max slammed the door after him. His rage began to ebb. At first he felt foolish for the things he'd said, the coarse clichés and inflated accusations. He felt shame at his loss of self-control. Bitterness. Futility. He went upstairs to Narayan's bedroom and lay down upon the bed, where despair overcame him. His brain seemed full of violent and confusing images from the past: the rock carvings disfigured, his swimming pool drained, Narayan lying contorted on its slimy bottom, as if his neck were broken. He turned from the images, shocked by their brutality, and tried to conjure up good memories Narayan. But they shifted in his mind, dulled and impotent, and only served to darken his distress. He longed for sleep and eventually a fitful sleep came to him. He dreamt he was nursing Rick, who was lying on a bed and looking out to sea.

'Can you see them?' Max asked. 'The river… the temple… the hopeful mourners… the smoke on the river from the funeral rites?'

Rick shook his head sadly. Max saw the river was clogged with effluent, the mourners inconsolable and scared. The temple was a pile of disintegrating stones, like a dismal burden on the sand. He woke, determined to curb his depression, to dismiss the exaggerations of his dreaming mind. Dawn was breaking.

He got up and went to the window. The garden was still, the trees were motionless and there seemed to be no birds about the place. He spotted someone at the gate, looking searchingly up at the house. It wasn't Narayan, although that had been his first thought. Whoever it was had a rounder face. Max vaguely wondered what he was doing there.

Sighing, he went back to bed. A few minutes later, someone entered the room. At first, Max felt a certain trepidation, worried that it was whoever had been standing in the garden – a burglar, perhaps. But it was Narayan.

'I've been walking all night,' he said, heading straight for Max and gently kissing him. 'I've been thinking all night about us,' he said. 'Thinking about you.'

Max thought Narayan brave after the abuse he'd given him the night before and the likelihood of his kiss being rejected. Narayan seemed hugely apologetic and distressed. This caused Max to melt, and he kissed him deeply back. Narayan resisted, but only for a moment, before succumbing to his growing fervour.

They undressed and made love. Max did all he could to arouse Narayan, to keep him in that heightened state, as though he could imprint on his mind a memory that would always haunt him, that he would never, ever be able to forget in all the years to come. Narayan held Max with a slightly anguished tenacity, Max told him he loved him. Moments later, Narayan came with a spasm that seemed almost one of pain. Max let himself go at last, with a powerful release unlike any he'd experienced before. It was like a happiness that could never be removed.

But Narayan was leaving him. Leaving him. It seemed impossible.

'You're still in love with me,' Max said. 'You must be.'

'I suppose I am.'

Narayan was gazing down, taking in the conjunction of their naked bodies, marvelling at the sight, as if surprised by what had just happened, the joy and beauty of it. He frowned slightly, a puzzled expression on his face.

'It's mad, isn't it?' he said. 'Being in love, sort of, with two people… a man and a woman. Do you remember me telling you once that I didn't think it possible? But I shouldn't have done what I did just now. It's just… I wanted to say goodbye in a way that you'd remember.'

He put out his hand to touch Max's face.

'I'll remember,' Max replied. 'I understand about Mohini. I just don't get how the hell it's happened.'

He was determined not to be demanding or despairing. He wouldn't twist Narayan's arm emotionally. When all this was over he would have won him back with calm and measured words.

'You want a kind of marriage with me,' Narayan said, 'even if we don't get to use that dreaded word. But hey, you know what India is like. Everything we've been for one another… it's hardly acknowledged such experiences even happen… that such feelings exist at all. It's just a bizarre joke at best, and that's the worst form of prejudice of all. People have no idea how beautiful and deep the love between two men can be.'

'Then people should be shown it,' Max answered, slightly heated of a sudden. 'The tyranny of majority opinion… how I hate it!' He paused, reaching for his self-restraint. 'Remember what Gandhi said: one man can be right when most of the unthinking world's against him.'

Narayan smiled faintly.

'You're quoting Gandhi? Gandhi would never have approved of us. In his later years he barely approved of sex at all, and then only as the means by which we reproduce.'

'He'd have approved of standing up for what one believes in, surely?'

'Fighting for the rights of a disparaged, even criminal, minority,' mused Narayan. 'Homosexuality is still against the law here, remember, even though it's the twenty-first century. Oh, it's a just cause all right, but I've my own life to think of. I want a wife and family, Max, and I warned you that I wasn't prepared to shout out from the rooftops. Maybe, if I was completely gay, I would. I have this straight side of me, though, as you have with Clare. I haven't spoiled that for you, have I, Max?'

'You haven't spoiled anything,' Max told him, taken aback by his directness. He'd always been enchanted by Narayan's often startling candour but hadn't expected him to be this explicit. Well, he would be explicit back: he'd attempt to be as accurately truthful as he could.

'I've loved Clare very much,' he said, 'but it was as much a passion of the heart and mind as it was physical. The feeling was very strong, but I was always attracted to guys as well. So the question is, which side of you do you most want to follow?'

Narayan looked at him.

'I want to live with my heterosexual side,' he said. 'That's why I'm going to marry Mohini.'

'What about the sex? Isn't that something still in your imagination? If I thought you'd actually enjoy sex with her, I'd find it easier to take.'

As soon as he'd said that he regretted it. He forced an issue that was private out into the open. He knew it couldn't just be reduced to physical enjoyment. Light was streaming in through the window now. A mynah bird sat upon a bough outside, making a whistling noise that would normally have cheered him. A fringe of bougainvillea trailed across the window, and the light coming through it dappled Narayan's body. On his face was a strange expression, sorrowful and yet defiant.

'Look, Max,' Narayan said. 'I wouldn't make a decision of this sort unless I knew what I was doing. I'd never slept with a woman before, but Mohini and I… we have had sex. If you need to know, I enjoyed it very much. We're arranging things quickly. We hope to be married in a month.'

'A month? You must be joking.'

'I'm not. She's older than I am, and there's bound to be family opposition, so we're going to do it quickly and quietly. My one regret is you, Max. I couldn't feel worse about that. You've been everything to me, and I'll never forget you.' He paused, looking really conscience-stricken. 'I must see Mohini's father in Kolkata, which means I won't be able to see you off. I'm sorry. Mohini and I are flying there this morning.'

Max felt numb, shocked by the abruptness of this announcement. He supposed Narayan had arranged to leave immediately so he'd have no chance to change his mind. Narayan's look was one of immense contrition, although he tried to hide it. He tried to joke but the jokes died on his tongue. He pushed Max around as in a series of rough caresses, part of that old repertoire of play between them, but the play seemed joyless now, the repertoire exhausted.

Max didn't feel so angry with him now. He felt Narayan simply hadn't known himself enough. Perhaps he still didn't. People spend their entire lives failing to recognise themselves, confusing what they wished to be with what they were. Even now, just as he was about to leave, Narayan took Max in his arms. He cried out slightly, pressing Max to him, as if paradoxically it was he who feared being left; he who, with tears that began to mark his face, dreaded most this moment of their parting.

'I'm going to your hotel to leave Clare a letter of explanation... an apology for not saying goodbye,' Narayan said. 'I won't try to see her. She'll be sleeping with Tammy right now.' He looked at the clock by the side of the bed. 'It's only six-fifteen... far too early.'

It was Max who gently disengaged, shaking his head almost imperceptibly to indicate it was too much to bear just now. Appreciating this, Narayan went to the door, opened it and left. He did not look back.

The door closed and Max stood by the window, watching Narayan leave. The figure he'd seen earlier had gone. As Narayan drove away, Max heard another engine start. He saw a motorbike then, a passenger on the pillion, racing off with a squeal of tyres.

Too distressed and confused to think how odd the sight was at such an early hour, Max looked up into the sky. Clouds were racing across it, as if being hurled by some powerful wind towards the ocean. He recalled Subramaniam talking about the Atman, the Breath of Life, and he had a mental image of the old man slumped in his cane chair, his beloved Bhagavad Gita slipping from his fingers. That great poem had now come to mean so much to Max, with its vision of the divine love offered to help the human spirit in its fight against the forces of destruction, especially those attacking from within: jealousy, fear and anger. Max ached with longing for Narayan and knew he could easily succumb to jealous rage again. And he knew he feared for Rick.

The phone rang. Max rushed to reach it, thinking it might be Narayan. It wasn't. It was Inspector Veerapan.

'Max,' began the Inspector, his voice betraying exhaustion. 'We made a terrible mistake when we said we'd shot the two young men. They're still very much alive. One of the gang, tempted by the reward offered, informed against them. We raided their lodgings two hours ago. We caught the boy but not his accomplice, who escaped after making a furious attempt to save him. He shot one of my colleagues while escaping. He was my brother-in-law.'

'I'm so sorry.'

'My sister's husband... dead at twenty-one.' He took a deep breath. 'The boy fits the description well,' he continued. 'He appears to be the boy in your photo, as least as far as we can tell. The evidence is still insufficient for a prosecution, though, unless Tammy and Clare identify him. The accomplice obviously knows that's the situation we're in. He's already broken into Tammy's flat, ruthlessly prepared to eliminate all evidence against him.'

'Oh my God!'

'We want… we need Tammy and Clare to identify the boy this morning, without delay. Forgive my asking, but we need to know where they now are.'

Max gave him the address.

'The man was in the garden here this morning, watching the house,' he added. 'Narayan left about ten minutes ago, and I think he was followed on a motorbike. There were two of them on the bike. Narayan's calling in at the hotel…' Max felt his throat grow tight and dry with dread. 'He'll be leading them straight to Clare and Tammy.'

Chapter Eighteen

Clare woke suddenly, and a depressing thought immediately came to her: she and Max were flying back to Los Angeles, and she wouldn't see Tammy for weeks. She looked at her watch: it was twenty to seven. She turned to look at Tammy's face. He was asleep. She wanted to wake him to make love again, but he hadn't slept well for most of the night. Not wanting to be selfish, she let him sleep on. He'd had another text message from Shahpur, saying that Kalyani's father had tracked them down to Mumbai. He'd phoned them to say that he was determined to take his daughter home, not knowing they'd already got married.

Tammy hadn't been disturbed by this news merely out of sympathy for the couple's plight; he was also starting to worry about opposition to his marrying Clare. His parents were no longer living, but there were aunts, uncles and other relatives who were not exactly noted for their progressive attitudes when it came to inter-faith, interracial marriage.

Clare rubbed her eyes, puzzled about why she had woken so early. It might have been some noise still echoing in her head, as if she had first heard it in her sleep. She heard it again – it sounded like the tapping of a stick on the concrete path outside. Then she thought she heard the shutters creaking.

Their room was in a ground-floor annexe at the rear of the hotel. The shutters were closed to keep out the early morning light. The ceiling fan was swishing in the air, giving off the occasional plaintive creak. Tammy's own flat had modern air-conditioning, and he laughed at Max and Clare's perverse preference, as he put it, for everything old and likely to break down: the antiquated fan, the aged plumbing, with its thudding pipes and temperamental gushes of pale brown steamy water from the taps. The night before he'd jokingly apologised for parking his car directly outside their room in case it spoiled the view: the mustard-coloured walls, the bougainvillea, the monkeys in their cage, the cantankerous parrot on its stand, the self-admiring, rustling peacock. Clare did think it tactless of him to park there, for it advertised to the doubtless conventional hotel manager that it was Tammy and not Clare's husband who was spending the night there.

The manager of the hotel rarely had foreign guests to stay, so he'd booked them in with surprised delight, apologising for the lack of modern conveniences – and the existence of all the ancient inconveniences. Thin and self-deprecating, he was the polar opposite of the manager of the hotel just outside Madurai, the one with the massive belly and majestic waddle. He'd seemed bewildered by Tammy being there so often, and Max being absent, and Clare didn't want to add to his confusion.

Clare was fully awake now, and there it was, the noise again. Was it someone pushing at the shutters? That's certainly what it sounded like. As she looked over at the shutters, Clare noticed there was a gap between them, wide enough for someone to peer in. She didn't like this at all. As she got out of bed, she heard the tapping begin to move away. The creaking by the door, however, was getting louder.

'Hello?' she called out softly.

The noise stopped.

She heard a telephone ringing in the main building and wondered who could be phoning at this early hour. Shrugging, she opened the narrow window, which gave her a limited view of the garden. Tammy's car was slightly blocking the view.

A brightly coloured bird was perched on a frangipani tree, delicately preening its blue plumage. Nearby stood the monkeys' cage, around which the peacock was fastidiously strutting, rustling his tail ostentatiously. Clare had often heard his raucous scream imperiously directed towards his frumpy mate. The peahen, Clare noted with strange satisfaction, remained firmly unimpressed.

The parrot was just outside, moulting and malevolent, with a lethal-looking yellow beak, and a thin, black, pointed tongue. It cawed loudly in bilious distaste and shuffled up and down its pole with growing indignation, as if offended by some intolerable impertinence.

The monkeys were usually quite lively. They would swing from their long, prehensile tails or cling tenaciously to the bars of the cage, thrusting out sharp little paws and blinking imploring eyes at anyone who passed by. Now, though, they were darting frantically around, twisting their white faces from side to side, chattering shrilly with excited fear.

This got Clare worried. Was there a predator nearby? Was it animal or human? She drew in her breath sharply. The phone had stopped ringing; presumably, someone had answered it.

Suddenly, the peacock came running back into view, not in pursuit of his reluctant mate but more as if it was fleeing in fear. She heard someone calling out up at the house. Then, far away, above the sound of the calling voice and the shrieking of the bird, she heard the wailing of a police siren.

A crowbar was being violently thrust between the outer door and the doorjamb.

Clare screamed.

The crowbar was being levered backwards. The wood splintered, and the instrument was forced further in. There was a harsh crack, and the door was prised half-open.

'Tammy!' yelled Clare, rushing to bolt the inner door, with its metal anti-mosquito mesh.

Again the crowbar was thrust forward, and the outer door was torn wide open. Behind the mesh Clare could see the outline of a man, holding a knife. He put his shoulder to the inner door and pushed. Tammy, meanwhile, had sat up in bed. He quickly realised they were under attack when he saw Clare's frightened face, sweat breaking out upon her forehead.

Tammy leapt out of bed just as the intruder threw his weight against the inner door and it burst open. A man half fell and half stumbled into the room. He had a stocking over his head, covering his face and flattening his features.

Tammy reached for the nearest object he could find to defend them. He picked a chair and held it out in front of himself and Clare. The man leapt forward with his knife. Clare felt sick with terror but she also felt extreme anger. She seized a stone ashtray from a table and threw it at the man, striking him hard in the chest. The knife fell from his grip, clattering to the floor as he cried out in surprise and pain. Tammy darted forward and kicked the weapon beneath the bed.

That voice, the one that had been calling, was getting closer – as was the sound of the siren. The intruder pulled a handgun from his pocket and fired. The bullet hit Tammy in the shoulder, sending him staggering backwards, his blood spraying.

The voice was right outside.

It was the hotel manager. He was in the doorway now, resolutely gripping a revolver in his shaking hand.

'Stop!' he shouted. 'Or I'll fire!'

The siren was howling. The man ran from the room. He pushed past the hotel manager just as Clare heard a car swing fast into the drive.

Tammy, clutching his shoulder, stumbled to the door with Clare just behind him. Kneeling there, they watched their attacker race for his motorbike. The police car stopped with a shriek of brakes and three police officers leapt out, Veerapan among them. The assassin rushed towards the wall surrounding the compound. He turned as he ran, firing at the police before diving behind a bamboo clump.

The policemen knelt for cover, one of them behind the monkeys' cage. They fired repeatedly, and the man fired back. A tiny howl came from the cage. Silence followed, broken only by a little plangent wail that grew to a shrill pitch and then ceased.

The silence intensified. Clare remembered there was a ditch at the edge of the garden. She presumed the man was trying to make his escape by squirming his way along it.

Then, with a sudden rustling of leaves, the peahen broke from cover, her wings beating. She scuttled with harsh cries across the grass. At that moment, Clare saw the attacker's head, his arm. He was in the ditch, wriggling towards the gate at the far end of the compound, which was covered in a mass of bougainvillea. He had almost reached it.

'Inspector!' she shouted out, signalling the man's position.

The Inspector saw her signal and barked an order to his men.

The assassin attempted to leap up the wall, but the police opened fire again. His body jerked as the bullets struck him. He reached out, grasping desperately at the bougainvillea, before slumping to the ground. The police ran up to him and fired shots into his body at point-blank range; Clare thought this a senseless act.

Tammy, meanwhile, had sunk to the ground, blood pouring from his shoulder. As Clare bent to help him she saw alarm in his eyes. Tammy put a hand on her arm, urging her to look behind her. She turned and saw the cripple lurching towards her on his crutches, his shoulders rising and dipping.

He came right up to her. Her heart was beating fast, although she saw he was unarmed. His face was ravaged by grief as he glanced at the body of the assassin, bloody and still. With tears pouring down his face, the cripple turned back to stare at Clare, his eyes full of fury. Why? Because of her signal to the police? Without that they wouldn't have seen his accomplice trying to escape. Or was it because he'd seen his body jerking horribly from the bullets being fired by the police, whom she had aided.

Clare froze. The cripple made a decision, opening a lid in the top of one of his crutches and pulling out a small knife from inside. He grabbed Clare by the arm.

'No!' she screamed, struggling to break free. He held her fast with surprising strength.

Tammy struggled to get to his feet to defend her, but was too weak now from the loss of so much blood. Clare turned to see where Veerapan and his officers were; they were at least twenty metres away, engrossed in taking off the assassin's stocking and examining his face.

Clare stared directly into the cripple's eyes. She saw desperation in them, and he saw her terror. Perhaps remembering how she'd saved his daughter and how he'd later promised not to harm her, his hold on her arm loosened.

He let her go.

With a gesture of futility, he slid the knife back into its hiding place. Mere seconds later, Veerapan was there, slapping handcuffs on his wrists and leading him, without protest, to the police car.

Max arrived only five minutes later and found Clare attending to Tammy's shoulder. Despite his injury, Tammy seemed weirdly cheerful, perhaps from sheer relief. Clare was not in the same spirits. She'd hated seeing the body of the gunman. It had turned out to be the older of the two young men. The body bled profusely but the face remained unscathed. In one hand was a sprig of bougainvillea, which had torn away as he'd grasped at it. Clare had been saddened by the sight of one of the monkeys, its chest shattered by a bullet; she cried as she watched its mate utter lonely little whimpers over its lifeless body.

The parrot shrieked its disapproval of anyone who came near, flicking its tongue and irritably scattering its seed.

∴

Tammy was taken to hospital. Later that morning Clare had to go alone to identify the body of the boy assassin. Veerapan was there, acutely embarrassed at having told them the two youths had been killed. He apologised profusely.

'The cripple's wife has been to see me,' Veerapan said. 'She heard on the radio what happened. It's all over the news. I said you would be expected to identify her husband in a line-up, and she desperately wants to speak with you. She has no English, of course, but I can translate. You see… their daughter has died.'

'No!' Clare exclaimed, knowing how much she'd meant to them.

'Yes, from typhus,' Veerapan went on. 'There's been an outbreak of it in the shantytown where they live; it was brought on by crowded, insanitary conditions. The medical facilities are inadequate to deal with the spread of the infection.'

Clare agreed to see her and they met at the police station. The woman's eyes were red from weeping and her hair was dishevelled. She looked exhausted. She spoke with restraint at first, Veerapan translating.

'Our daughter has never been strong and succumbed to the disease. Her father's off his head from grief. This made him react insanely to the shooting of his nephew. He's been like a father to him ever since his parents died.'

She began to weep.

'Please forgive him,' she asked Clare. 'He's never forgotten how you saved our daughter. In his right mind, he'd mean no harm to you. There's good in him as well as bad.'

'I do forgive him, Clare replied, 'but I have to do my duty as a witness.'

Veerapan hesitated before translating what the cripple's wife said next.

'You see, I fear the police might torture him to get information on who has been employing the assassins. They've worked out he's been paid certain sums, but it was in cash that had been left in various hiding places. I knew nothing about this.'

Veerapan spoke to the woman, trying to reassure her.

'A confession extracted under torture is totally unreliable. I promise they'll not resort to anything so wrong as well as so ineffective.'

Clare was horrified to think this was even a possibility, but she could not deny her obligation to testify correctly.

After the woman left, Clare was alone for a time while Veerapan arranged the two identification parades. She longed to have Tammy with her, to give her moral support and let her escape the burden of sole responsibility.

'I've told the boy of the death of his accomplice,' Veerapan said as soon as he returned.

He informed Clare of this before they entered the room, she thought this unfair, since it was now obvious which one was him – only one of the young men in that line-up seemed on the point of breaking down. She looked into his tearful eyes, trying to avoid feeling pity.

When she came to the cripple in his line-up, she thought of her promise to forgive him and of the possibility of his being tortured if Veerapan's scruples were ignored. But she also thought of the bullets striking the temple walls, and of Tammy being almost drowned. And she thought of the cripple's appalling look of triumph as Venkataraman was knifed to death.

She turned back to the boy, who fell to his knees. They ordered him to his feet. He didn't move so someone forced him to stand up. He seized her hand, crying out as they prised him from her. He stood still, his arms being held behind him. She hardened herself, recalling that lethal cruel embrace.

'This is Venkataraman's assassin,' she said, 'but he seemed extremely reluctant to do the deed.' She turned back to the cripple. 'This man spoke twice to this boy just before the killing. He obviously put great pressure on him.'

She was torn between compassion for the cripple over his daughter's death and abhorrence of the murder he'd incited and the murder he'd attempted at Sandeha. He appeared to stand in dignified withdrawal, as if the world around him held no further claims upon him.

Afterwards, Veerapan told her all they'd been able to discover; some of the information had come from the informant and some from the cripple's wife.

'The dead man was the boy's elder brother,' he said, 'and the cripple was their uncle. It seems their parents were killed in a sectarian clash between Muslims and Hindus, and the brothers were led by their uncle to join a terrorist group.'

'Have you any idea who hired them?' Clare asked.

'We think it was an alliance of industrialists and politicians that had felt threatened by Venkataraman's anti-corruption campaign, although we've no hard proof who they are.'

'The boy was too naïve and confused not to have been dominated by the other two,' Clare insisted. 'They gave him the security he'd so violently lost. A ferocious loyalty seems to have bound them together. It was all they had.'

∴

Next morning Veerapan came to see Clare at the hotel to tell her about cripple.

'They found him at dawn, lying in a pool of blood. His wrists had been cut and his crutches lay on the floor beside him.'

In the rush of events, Clare had omitted to tell them of the knife hidden in one of the crutches, and was saddened to learn that he'd used it in this horrendous way.

'Did he think he was going to be tortured?' Clare asked. 'Or was he driven to suicide because of his nephew's death and his grief over his child?

'Certainly he might've feared he'd be tortured,' Veerapan conceded. 'So now both he and his nephew are dead. The boy was just a catspaw. It's going to be difficult finding out who hired them.'

'The boy won't be tortured? Can you be sure of that?'

'Fairly sure. He's obviously too simple-minded. He'd know nothing.'

Clare remembered the first time she'd seen the boy. She recalled his beautiful face lit up by the roving spotlight as he followed Max, trying to snatch his camera. And she remembered the first time she'd seen the cripple – coming out of the dark at that election meeting in Madurai. She imagined the long years of imprisonment he might have had to face. Then she thought about his widow and was in two minds about the deliverance he'd sought.

'My superior's raised the question of her being an accessory to the crime,' Veerapan told her. 'He thinks she must've known of her husband's assassination plot.'

Clare thought, with horror, about the possibility of this poor woman being hanged. She could see the woman was loyal to her husband, but believed she could have been ignorant of what her husband was involved in.

∴

Max and Clare were in the departure lounge of the airport, waiting to board the plane that would take them back to Los Angeles. Tammy had insisted on coming to see them off, despite his heavily bandaged shoulder. The lounge looked so anonymous and bleak, but the women in their brightly coloured saris and the excited, jostling children provided some relief. A sudden shaft of sunlight burst through the window, dazzling Max.

All too soon for Clare, the departure of their plane was announced. While Max was seeing to the tickets, he caught a glimpse of Tammy kissing Clare goodbye behind a screen. They both looked as bit abashed when they joined Max again, perhaps suspecting Max had seen them and not wanting him to feel humiliated. Tammy embraced Max warmly, as if to make up for what he had just done. Max and Clare walked out of the departure lounge and across the tarmac towards the plane, leaving Tammy feeling somewhat lost.

Max reflected on recent events: Veerapan phoning him, his racing to the hotel to find the crisis over, the cripple handcuffed and led into the police car. Clare had been very brave, according to Tammy, and Max was proud of her defiance. These reflections filled his mind, blocking out thoughts of Narayan. It was as well Narayan was by now in Kolkata and wasn't coming to see them off. Tammy had phoned Narayan to tell his what had happened, and he had been understandably horrified. He'd passed on his deep commiserations to Clare, for neither she nor Max had wished to speak to him directly. Clare could not forgive him for leaving Max to marry Mohini, and Max knew he could not have stood it.

As they approached the plane, the sun blazed down on its aluminium wings, shimmering in the afternoon light and heat, reminding Max of the shimmering rock face carvings at Sandeha that had seemed so insubstantial in the dazzle of the sun. It was as if even with their physical solidity, and their great age, they were just a fleeting mirage dissolving in the shadow of a lonely cloud.

As he neared the steps to the plane, he looked back and saw someone standing on the roof of the airport building, looking forlorn. The way he stood reminded Max of Narayan, although of course it could not possibly be. Max tried to believe that what had happened the previous morning had been Narayan's form of valediction and his way of saying sorry. He didn't want to see

Narayan ever again, but he was determined not to feel hard done by or to entertain, even in his unspoken thoughts, useless and embittering resentments.

As he began to climb the steps, he turned to peer again at the distant figure. It could just conceivably have been Narayan, he thought: his stance, his shape, the lonely waving of his hand but, in the heat and dust and at that deceptive distance, it was obviously Max's wishful thinking. But then he had a sudden memory of Narayan running out of the haze of the afternoon sun, with the great beach behind him. He thought of his body lying on the beach: the wide masculine shoulders, the powerful legs. He knew it was now most unlikely he'd ever get Narayan back or preserve his marriage save as a continuing good friendship, based on a hard-won, unsentimental knowledge of each other. He took one last look at the distant figure but he'd stopped waving. He turned and entered the aircraft, Clare just behind him.

They took their seats, Max closest to the window. He looked out at the airport roof, but the figure had disappeared.

'You okay?' Clare asked.

'Just thinking some strange thoughts.'

'Share them?' Clare invited, smiling faintly.

Shiva was the Lord of the Dance, Max thought, and the dance was everlasting. Despite that, he wasn't sure the Hindu religion had reconciled him yet to the existence of evil in the world, whether it came from the murderous will of man, or the effect of economic circumstances, or something purely arbitrary. But he did believe in the strength and courage Krishna gave to

Arjuna in the Bhagavad Gita: the freedom from egotistic pride and anger.

'I'm thinking about Subramaniam,' he said at last. 'I'm thinking about his death… and his cremation. We talked a lot.'

Clare nodded, a little sad.

'Yes,' she said, 'I don't think I'll ever forget that. I can see the flowers… scattered on the water with the ashes.'

'The smoke in the sky… dissolving in the wind as it blew down the river,' said Max. 'He believed so deeply in the human spirit.'

'He certainly did. We're going to miss him.'

'Tammy and Narayan will miss him too,' Max said, then added decisively, 'I'm going to do more with my life. I want to make it count for something.'

'For Subramaniam… or Narayan?' Clare asked tentatively. She paused. 'Or Rick?'

Max shook his head, almost imperceptibly.

'For all of them,' he said, smiling faintly. 'And for ourselves… for everyone.'

Chapter Nineteen

A year later, Clare and Tammy were back in Chennai. In the early hours of 26 December 2004, they were woken by earth tremors. Their apartment shook but was largely unaffected by the giant wave that was to mark that day as cataclysmic.

At first there was a huge sucking back of the ocean. The fishermen on the beach were astonished to see such a vast extent of the seabed, with its sands and clumps of seaweed, its rocks and coral, the protruding ribs of a wrecked fishing boat. Then, astoundingly, they saw the eroded remains of an ancient temple being revealed by the retreating sea. Several children gleefully scampered out to catch some of the scuttling crabs and the fish that wriggled in the sand pools. The tsunami itself at first appeared as a white fringe of water in the distance, but then it began to advance ominously.

The fishermen and children gazed in awe, not comprehending what was happening. Then the children began to turn back as the tsunami surged towards them with a mounting roar. Some fishermen rushed towards them, shouting in bewilderment. The enormous wave came on, swallowing the temple remnants in a rage of spume. The children were running now, screaming in terror. A fisherman scooped two of them up in his arms, while two more raced to the temple on the shore, clambering in panic up its stonework. A colossal wall of water, the height of a coconut palm, hurtled towards it. One of the boys was dashed from its surface, but the other boy managed to hang on, despite the water swirling up around him. A woman shot forward to save her child, holding out her arms and screaming, but the wave crashed down, and she was swept away, her sari inflating in the churning water. The water careered more than a kilometre inland. It shattered the flimsy shacks and sheds, scooping up the fear-struck fishing people, their boats and catamarans, their sails and nets. It overturned trucks and cars, adding them to the swirling flood of broken roofs and furniture, struggling dogs and cattle, and countless battered, drowning human beings.

∴

Max was by Rick's bedside in Los Angeles; he was watching the news on TV, horrified. He was thinking about Clare and Tammy and, of course, Narayan. He knew they lived some way from the beach and up a little hill, but he was extremely worried.

He squeezed Rick's arm in the vain hope of communicating with him. He wiped the dying man's emaciated face and then tucked the sheet around his exhausted body. He watched Rick in his coma before his gaze reverted to the appalling scenes of havoc being broadcast.

He was struck by the comparison: the slow destruction of a body by a lurking virus and the quick ravage of a coastline by an undersea convulsion of the earth. Max was shocked by the estimated numbers of the dead and missing and by news of other devastated shores around the Indian Ocean. The scope of the disaster was so huge that he felt numbed. There was some film of the coast of Tamil Nadu, which the wave had hit several hours previously. The waters had subsided into a muddy flood of floating wreckage and dead bodies, human and animal. The sight caused him to lean over and press Rick's hand, instinctively seeking the solace of his company, but there was no returning pressure, no reassurance; he had sunk too deeply into unconsciousness.

Rick had been on combination therapy for quite some time before the virus reached his brain. His illness had intensified Max's feeling for him, and he'd become determined to nurse him until the very end, which he now believed could be at any moment. As he stroked Rick's hair and held his hand, he was also determined to do something to help the victims of the dreadful disaster unfolding before his eyes.

He rang Clare with a certain difficulty, since communications with Chennai had been affected. Eventually he managed to get through to her.

'Are you all right?' he asked. 'You and Tammy?'

'We're fine,' said Clare.

'And Narayan?'

'He's okay too. There's been massive damage down by the sea front, though. The wave swept away the joggers and destroyed the huts of the poor around the railway station. It was terrible when the sea retreated. There were bodies all over the shore… one was hurled up by the wave into the branches of a tree. There are over a hundred dead in Chennai, Max… a thousand more in the suburbs. Tell me, though, what news of Rick?'

'He's in a deep coma,' Max replied. 'He won't last more than a day or two. It'll be a merciful release when it comes.' He paused. 'Look, I must fly out when he's gone. I want to write an article about the tsunami victims. I want to do something to raise funds here in the USA to help them.' He paused again. 'So... Narayan's okay?'

Yes, he is,' she answered.

'I'm so relieved,' Max said. Another pause. 'So he didn't go through with his marriage to Mohini?'

'No. There was a lot of opposition from Narayan's uncles and aunts.'

'On what grounds?' Max asked.

'Mainly because Mohini is ten years older,' Clare told him. 'Her parents weren't pleased either, to put it mildly. Narayan and Mohini are just good friends now... I wonder if that's really all they ever were.'

∴

Tammy had resisted family objections to his marriage with Clare. They had once worried him but now he was determined to see them as rather comical.

'I routed the Sergeant Majorette in combat, man to man,' he claimed, as he and Clare lay in each other's arms in bed one night. 'And The Battleaxe, whose steely cries of protest I ignored! This provoked her to stomp around, directing a Medusa glare at me in the vain hope of turning me to stone.'

'I suppose the aunts principally object to your marrying a European divorcee,' suggested Clare, snuggling up to him. 'They doubtless see me as a femme fatale who'll lead you even further into decadent Western ways.'

'And divorce me when she inevitably tires of me,' he replied, kissing her gently on the face. 'The uncles provide less stubborn opposition. I can soften their disapproval with the whiskies with which I ply them, much to the chagrin of both teetotal harpies.'

∴

While Clare was in Los Angeles, Tammy had visited Shahpur and Kalyani in Mumbai. When Clare got back, he was keen to tell her about what he'd learned. They walked hand-in-hand around the garden.

'Apparently there was an appalling row when her father discovered they were already married. He furiously disowned his daughter, as he'd threatened to. He'd said her name must never again be mentioned in his house.'

'How monstrous of him.'

'She wept bitterly but was consoled by her mother's continued devotion to her. She doesn't hide this from her tyrant husband, despite the marital friction this gives rise to. Well, Kalyani and Shahpur have been married for six months now.'

'Has she stayed a Hindu?' Clare asked Tammy, plucking a frangipani flower from the branch of a tree.

'Yes, and he's remained a Muslim. She sometimes goes to the mosque with him, but she says it's with the figures of Shiva and Vishnu uppermost in her mind.'

'Obviously he opposes her being veiled,' Clare said, admiring the pale, waxen-looking petals of the flower in her hand.

'Of course. He claims that's an imported custom that is not in the original spirit of the Koran.'

'Does he visit her Hindu temple?'

'Yes, he sometimes prays to his monotheistic God within her temple. He claims to see the various images as expressions of God's universal compassion and divinity. And now there's some very good news.'

'She's pregnant?' Clare asked, putting the flower behind his ear and laughing.

'Yes,' he answered smiling. 'And they intend to bring up their child in a spirit of veneration for both religions.'

∴

Clare was extremely relieved to hear that the cripple's widow had been found innocent of any knowledge of the assassination plot. Tammy had kept in contact with her.

'She was severely interrogated but not tortured,' he told Clare. 'She didn't break down in the courtroom but spoke out with dignity and clarity. She admitted she'd known her husband was very close to his nephews, but she herself was kept strictly out of their affairs.

'He was obviously an old fashioned husband.'

'She said she now knew of the crimes he'd committed, but she couldn't hate him. She thinks mainly of the good parts of him, and prays to Shiva for his soul.'

Although reassured about the cripple's widow, Clare was horrified to hear that the boy assassin had been sentenced to be hanged.

'I know such sentences are seldom carried out,' Clare said to Tammy, 'but to live with the possibility would be a continuous nightmare for him. It'd destroy all hope for improvement in his life. Max and I have always opposed capital punishment.'

She now put in a plea for clemency through his lawyer.

'He's so young,' she said, 'and he was pressured by his uncle and older brother, as I personally witnessed. Is there any chance I might visit him in prison?'

His lawyer said it wasn't likely but advised her to persevere. She intended to as she waited apprehensively for a final verdict.

∴

Rick died the day after the tsunami struck. He managed to communicate with Max briefly before he sank into a coma.

'Remember me as I used to be,' he said, lifting up his wasted hand.

Max knew he'd never forget the extraordinarily vital man he had been as well as the man with the pitifully ravaged body. At the end, Rick's face was very thin but strangely beautiful; his cheekbones were now so prominent that his eyes seeming larger and startlingly brilliant.

'I dreamt you'd died when it should've been me,' Rick said, smiling faintly. 'I dreamt you'd died and I was totally alone.'

'You'll never be alone,' Max answered, kissing Rick's head, hoping to lend courage to the frightened brain within, as if he might briefly touch the invulnerable soul Max wanted to believe in, the soul that soon would be escaping its ruined body. 'You'll never be alone, I'll be always with you.'

'Does that mean you'll be following me?' Rick joked, as usual not wanting to appear sentimental. 'But maybe I'll be coming back… just when you thought you'd finally got rid of me.'

Then, thinking his joke a bit harsh, he grinned ironically and reached for Max's hand. He died twelve hours later. Max kissed his face, whispering his name over and over as if Rick could miraculously hear him still, intently hoping for some form of immortality or at the least some other lasting, personal significance.

Max approached his old friend Jimmy, who'd once inadvertently precipitated the trouble over Narayan's present. He asked him to arrange Rick's funeral.

'I want to get out to Tamil Nadu to try to help the surviving victims as soon as possible. I feel I could do more good to the living than the dead. I think Rick would approve.'

Max caught a plane next day. On the flight to Chennai, he thought about his donation to the tsunami appeal that had already been quickly organised. He recalled Christ's advice to the rich man – go and sell all that thou hast and give to the poor – and it seemed less reproachful than once he'd been. The advance they'd received for their book on India had encouraged him to think he could now rely on what he earned. As a result, he'd put his house on the market, intending to give most of the money it would yield to help the tsunami victims and to support an institute for AIDS research. Subramaniam's enduring influence, the ideals of Gandhi and the Bhagavad Gita, the simple life he'd witnessed in the ashram, even Narayan's joshing about his decadent materialist lifestyle had all helped to turn those words of Christ from a nagging message into positive inspiration.

As the plane flew in, Max had a view of the Coromandel coastline, with its sprawl of shattered villages, and he thought how especially cruel the disaster was in striking at an area of the world where the people were so vulnerable already. And he thought about how the AIDS that had killed Rick had now become the scourge of Africa, the earth's poorest continent.

Clare and Tammy met Max at the airport. He wasn't sure how he would take to seeing them as a married couple. There was an awkwardness between them at first, but they soon got over it.

'Rick's end was peaceful,' he told them. 'He was put onto a morphine pump and he just slipped away after a few hours.'

'You're going to miss him horribly,' said Clare.

'I want to do something to commemorate him. That's one of my motives in wanting to help the tsunami victims. I'd sort of feel I was still helping Rick. I hope my paramedic training can be of use.'

'They're desperately in need of any medical assistance,' Tammy said.

Tammy drove them to Sandeha in a four-wheel truck that managed to negotiate the ravaged roads. He had arranged for Max to meet the chief medical officer.

'Do you know enough to dress minor wounds?' the man asked him. 'And inoculate survivors against the diseases that now threaten them?'

'Yes, I've been trained to do those things,' Max replied, believing that in this work he'd find a purpose that would help to take his mind away from the grief he felt. The practical urgency of it would lessen the spiritual despair that so heavily oppressed him. He shared this with Tammy and Clare.

'The tsunami... why has this terrible phenomenon occurred? And why this merciless pandemic of AIDS that's now devastating Africa especially? Is there any ultimate moral intention in the world, or is everything a matter of unmeaning accident?'

'Remember what Narayan said on the subject of the physical world,' Clare answered. 'Don't the laws of physics imply there must be some purpose in the universe? How could nature evolve such a complicated thing as a living body, as a human brain, without some designing intelligence.'

'An idea most modern biologists furiously object to,' interpolated Tammy.

'But if there is this intelligence and it's supposedly benevolent,' said Max, 'why such pointless, arbitrary destruction?'

The single good thing the tsunami had done was to scour away the accumulated sands of many centuries to reveal the ruins of another ancient temple and a rock covered with animal carvings, but this sole happy accident did nothing to stop the questions that troubled Max more urgently than ever.

∴

Clare wondered why Max didn't wish to contact Narayan, even though he knew he was no longer with Mohini. It was mainly because of Rick, she supposed. Perhaps the sense of his own survival after Rick's death also connected with his resolve to give even more of his inheritance away. In their divorce settlement,

Max had already provided more than adequately for Clare, but she worried lest he would later on regret his more extreme generosity.

Clare knew how long Max's resolve had been quietly developing and how he always avoided sounding at all self-righteous. He hadn't made her feel obliged to follow his example: she was grateful for the settlement, which she would use responsibly. But she wondered about Narayan's reaction: he'd teasingly disparaged Max's riches but hadn't he been attracted to them too, even if he didn't admit it to himself? But she must now resist being cynical about him.

She'd phoned Narayan.

'Why not came out to Sandeha to meet Max,' she asked.

'Do you think he'd want to meet me?'

'I'm sure he would. You made him happy once. To be perfectly honest, I once loathed you for it. But now I'm happy myself I want to see him happy too. I really hope you could make him so again.'

'I don't know that I can now, but I'll certainly come to see him if you think that wise.'

Maria had finally decided to risk flying back to Rome to see The Animal, and she'd left a month ago. Clare had seen her off at the airport. Maria had been in quite a fluster, searching desperately for the passport she'd temporarily mislaid, dragging along the infant as it bawled its disapproval.

'I'm going with extremely cautious expectations,' she'd said as she was about to leave. 'I'm going to miss you all terribly, and I really hate leaving my beloved India.'

The day after her arrival she'd phoned Clare to say.

'The Animal forgot the time of my arrival, of course. He finally put in an appearance an hour late, finding me very cross and The Putto even crosser. He seized The Putto in his loving, hairy arms, but it didn't entirely reciprocate. It's been used to having a whole mother to itself, so it's taken against its father with alarming animosity.'

'Oh no!' Clare exclaimed.

'Narcissistic as The Animal is, he hasn't found this at all endearing. At present, an erratic civil war rages between the two of them, with me as mediator and unenviable victim.'

'Poor you,' commiserated Clare.

'You can say that again. What am I to do, torn between the bonds of motherhood and the even more dubious bonds of marriage with The Animal? I wonder now if I was wise to abandon the prospect of a gentle, faithful Indian husband.'

'Only you can answer that,' said Clare guardedly.

'I know, darling. Of course. This is no sentimental fantasy. In affairs of the heart, I'm an iron realist'.

∴

Max was going through the photos he'd taken of the tsunami victims, but at times his mind was elsewhere. Clare had told him that she'd contacted Narayan, but Max still wondered if he really wished to see him. He recognised it was partly owing to his pride, which had been more sorely injured than he'd at first acknowledged. But he also suspected that the cruel contrast between Narayan's healthy and strong body and Rick's diseased and weakened one had possibly, paradoxically, dulled his once vibrant memories of Narayan. Rick had crucially needed Max, and his dependence had made Max feel disloyal in recalling an attraction that had once been so potent and exclusive.

Max recalled a conversation during one of Rick's more lucid moments towards the end.

'I've had a dream, Max.'

'Tell me about it.'

'I dreamt I was sprinting along a shore… vigorously splashing through the sand pools. I woke with this frail body and such heavy disappointment.'

'Don't think of that,' Max had said, feeling his compassion so piercingly that he'd almost wished he could be more detached from Rick, with a firmer – but not a colder – heart. 'Think of our love instead,' he'd added, knowing he must be strong if he were to do any good, nursing him as his condition relentlessly got worse.

He now forced his concentration back to the photos of the tsunami victims: shrouded corpses on a communal pyre, the flames leaping up and the smoke billowing, the faces of grieving women, a howling father, an old man praying before a muddied shrine. But then Max turned to some photos he'd taken to provide some notes of hope: a woman dug out alive from a pile of debris, a child born amid the devastation, medical supplies dropped by helicopter, a stone pillar bearing the eroded image of Shiva the Preserver that had been revealed by the tsunami.

Some archaeologists had come to investigate, having been excited by claims that a temple had been glimpsed when the water had retreated before the tsunami struck. There was an old Tamil legend of a city lost beneath the sea, a city so beautiful that the gods had sent a flood to cover it and hide it from view. And now, with strange irony, this ferocious buckling of the tectonic plates beneath the ocean had brought this temple briefly into view again.

Despairing of ever hearing from Max, Narayan decided to drive out to see him. Max was surprised but not unwelcoming. At first they spoke of the possible discoveries, a subject behind which they could hide their initial shyness with each other. They went to talk to the archaeologists, who told them about underwater photographs that showed a ghostly structure covered in barnacles and algae, the remains of the unknown temple now submerged once again. Max and Narayan walked across the sand, which was covered in strange whirling traces and piles of tumbled seaweed.

'I'm desperately sorry about Rick,' Narayan said. 'It's good that you've come out here, though. It really is. All this work will help you to forget.'

'I don't want to forget him,' said Max. 'I never could.'

'You forgot me, didn't you?' Narayan blurted out but then paused for a moment, thinking he was being self-centred. He continued, though, his voice quieter. 'Well, I deserved it. I behaved very badly towards you. I didn't behave too well with Mohini either.'

'Neither of us behaved that well,' admitted Max. 'So what did you do to her that was so terrible?'

'I resented her parents' endless subtle criticisms. Mohini accused me of being touchy, and I'm afraid I lost my temper. A bit later, I told her how I loved you once. I…' Narayan paused, obviously finding the telling difficult. 'I thought her more broad-minded than she turned out to be. All her bright, progressive talk had given me the wrong impression. She was really upset when I told her we'd been lovers.'

'Did she never realise?' Max asked. 'Before, I mean?'

'It never entered her mind. She described you as so masculine and tough! She had the usual stereotypical preconceptions, basically. I told her that what I loved about you was your masculine exterior and the feminine sensitivity within. It wasn't marvellously tactful of me, but you know I've never been too good on tact.'

'But weren't you stereotyping people too?' Max couldn't help chiding him. 'Why must masculinity be seen as tough and femininity as sensitive?'

'You have a point there,' Narayan conceded.

Max spoke frankly of Rick's suffering

'He had these bad dreams. I slept beside him so I could hold him in my arms when he awoke.'

'That's really sad… but I'm worried you're still so troubled by it.'

To divert Max, he went on to tell him about Vijaya

'I've been to stay with her,' Narayan said. 'She's over Tammy, quite amazingly. She's even formed a mild attachment to one of her co-workers. He's short, bald and spectacularly fat. Hardly a reed shaken by the wind, as Vijaya puts it. She treats him with a jokey condescension, which he rather seems to like. He's a widower of a certain age. She tells him she's glad he's not exactly in the bloom of youth. In fact, she treats him like a piece from her collection: the more antique, the better.'

'How is she getting on at the orphanage for abandoned little girls?' Max asked.

'She loves it. She also works on a helpline for distressed women. She's befriended a woman who's had female twins. When a scan revealed she was carrying them, her husband and his relatives demanded she illicitly abort them.'

'Should you be telling people about this? Isn't it confidential?'

'The woman actively wants it known. They virtually imprisoned her at home and were very hostile. Her husband actually threw her down the stairs to bring on a miscarriage. That didn't work, thank God, and now she's taking him to court. There are special women's courts now, so there is some progress. Vijaya's helping her to publicise the case. I'm glad Vijaya's happily fulfilled, but I miss her very much.'

Narayan and Max met twice again. Although their old familiarity was returning, it lacked the excessive attraction that had once so excited Max. He told Narayan about his plans to travel.

'I've proposed to my publishers that I put together a short book on the tsunami. It will include photos of the coasts that have been severely damaged. So I'm making a journey of some weeks.

'Where to?'

'Sri Lanka, Indonesia and Thailand initially, then possibly the Maldives and the Andaman Islands. I hope the suffering I'll doubtless witness will put my memories of Rick's suffering at the end into some sort of perspective. I want to recall the figure Rick cut in his days of strength and confidence and fun.'

He felt sure he couldn't avoid thinking of Narayan, but he hoped he wouldn't think of him too much.

Chapter Twenty

Max's first flight was to Sri Lanka, where thousands of mango and banana plantations, and almost seventy per cent of the fishing fleet, had been destroyed. He imagined the tsunami approaching the coast at five hundred miles an hour, swelling and moving silently along. It rose only three feet above the surface here because of the great depth of the Indian Ocean. It was only as it neared the continental shelf that the wave had reared up to its fatal thirty feet. It made him think of the AIDS virus travelling stealthily through countries and continents, its symptoms equally unnoticeable at first.

While working as a paramedic, he met a Buddhist monk who'd officiated at communal cremations of both Buddhist and Hindu victims. This elderly Sinhalese with a shaven head just happened to be a published poet in English, and spoke with soft eloquence and equanimity.

'Buddhists or Hindus, Sinhalese or Tamil, death makes no distinctions. For all of us, life is fleeting. The Diamond Sutra says that life is like a flash of lightning… a guttering lamp… a phantom or a dream.'

'Do you think life is that brief and meaningless?' Max asked.

'No,' the monk replied, earnestly shaking his head. 'All things in life are but the seeds of sorrow, but there is hidden meaning in our sorrows. They give us compassion for all living beings, but we mustn't cling to them. We should be free of all attachments, all passions and possessions.'

'Can't we take detachment a bit too far?'

'Detachment is very difficult,' the monk acknowledged. 'I hate to see all these dead and dying people, the mothers weeping, the babies and children crushed or drowned. At first, I wept as well, but the words of the Buddha's Fire Sermon came to help me: our minds are burning, not just with the quick flames of greed and anger but with the slow fires of despair and grief. If we don't cling to the world, the darkness of our lives is vanished, and death itself is gently burnt away.'

Narayan phoned Max on his mobile that evening. It surprised Max that he should do so soon after their parting; he hadn't thought he was that keen to keep in touch. Max told him what the poet monk had said.

'You're not intending to become a Buddhist as well as a Hindu now, are you?' Narayan gently teased. 'Wouldn't that be rather overdoing things?'

'Well, the two religions have much in common,' answered Max, wanting to stay serious. 'They both teach detachment from strong feelings and the world.'

'I don't want to be too detached from my feelings, Max. The world's a horrifying place at times all right, but there are bits of it I like being attached to.' Narayan paused. 'I'd quite like to hold onto my feelings for you, for instance.'

'That so?' Max asked after a thoughtful pause.

'Yes. I wish I could come with you to these disaster areas. I feel so useless. I'd like to help. I suppose it's all very harrowing?'

'It's just about endurable,' Max told him, 'as long as I don't stop to think too much and stay very active.' He paused briefly. 'Frankly, I'd rather do this on my own.'

Afterwards Max wondered why he'd snubbed Narayan so perfunctorily; perhaps he felt Narayan was pushing him too fast. He was quite glad their relationship was opening up again, yet he still felt a piercing grief for Rick and wished to experience it alone. He'd been surprised by his lack of desire for other men when Rick had become critically ill, especially his lack of desire for Narayan, which had once been so consuming and resistless. On reflection, he was touched by Narayan's offer to help him. The idea of resuming their love affair did occur to him yet it appeared so unlikely. His deepest feelings were still attached to Rick; by contrast, others seemed remote and inaccessible. But he felt slightly remorseful over what he'd said and vowed to ring Narayan when he flew on to Thailand. He spoke of some elephants that had seemed to anticipate the wave.

'They stamped the ground and waved their heads before lumbering up into the hills.'

'How could they have known it was coming?' Narayan asked.

'Their feet can sense the seismic vibrations. It's strange how so few wild animals were caught by the wave, while man, with all his high-tech instruments, had no idea what was coming.'

'They've dug up another granite elephant at Sandeha,' Narayan told him. 'It's wonderful to think of this lost Tamil city being uncovered. It's believed to have been a great port under the Pallava kings, used for trading in silks and spices throughout East Asia.'

'I'd like to see that when I get back,' Max said, 'but I've a lot more travelling to do before then.'

The following day, Max flew on to Phuket, on the coast of Thailand. This area had been badly ravaged by the tsunami, and the medical authorities welcomed Max's skills as a paramedic to help the survivors. The day he started work he met a Thai aid worker, a lecturer in English from a university in Bangkok. She spoke of the proximity of extreme wealth and extreme poverty in Thailand.

'Skyscrapers and hovels, luxury resorts and run-down shantytowns, billionaires and beggars. And yet this country is supposed to be a Buddhist one. Remember that Buddha was a prince who renounced his worldly riches.'

'Like Saint Francis,' said Max. 'He left his wealthy father's house, casting off his clothes.'

'And taking up the begging bowl,' she said, nodding in agreement. 'Yes, I know... following Christ's example. Well, Saint Francis may have believed in my Lady Poverty; for us weaker spirits, though, there's surely nothing wrong with a moderate number of possessions. Don't we all want to make poverty history now, even though it seems a bit unrealistic at present?'

Max rang Narayan, feeling a need for his supportive humour in the midst of the destitution. He was starting to realise that he missed his lively presence more than he'd foreseen. He had some difficulty reaching him, and this frustrated him. When he eventually heard his voice it was with distinct relief. He told him what the Thai woman had said.

'You surely don't expect me to take up the begging bowl?' Narayan replied. 'Or sail out of my father's house, clad only in my birthday suit?'

'Not really,' said Max. 'As much as I admire your birthday suit, that is!' he adding wryly. 'But no, I wish to see my Lady Poverty put into voluntary retirement.'

'Is there any hope she's willing to retire?'

'There'd be more hope if we had more redistribution between nations. I studied *King Lear* at college, and I was struck by what Shakespeare had him say about the poor: "so distribution may undo excess and each country have enough".'

'Who'll judge what is excessive and who'll say what is enough?' Narayan asked. 'Still, let's hope we may one day live to see it.'

Max flew on to the Andaman Islands, which in British times had housed a penal colony where some political dissidents agitating for independence had be incarcerated. Max was told that numerous snakes and crocodiles had rushed inland in an effort escape the tsunami, terrifying the already-frightened people. Max met an old, retired teacher who'd lost his entire family. In a cruel twist, his granddaughter had died from a snakebite after the wave had struck.

'What have we done?' he asked, the tears trickling down his withered cheeks. 'First this horrible wave, and then the snakes and crocodiles. Why does God want us punished twice?'

'Don't think you're being punished,' Max told him. 'It was just a terrible accident of nature.'

'I've always tried to be a good Hindu. I've followed my dharma, my duty, without thought of a reward. God is all-powerful, all-knowing. I've called on the Lord Krishna and made him offerings. I've given him devotion from the depths of my old heart, so why does God let nature be this cruel?' The man gestured hopelessly at the ocean. 'Why didn't the sea take me as well?'

When Narayan rang again, Max could barely hear him at first, and he desperately wanted to. Eventually the line cleared and Max told him what the old man had said.

'Yes, but perhaps he asks too much of both God and nature,' Narayan replied. 'Nature is pitiless and life ruthlessly unfair, but if God had made them perfect, what kind of moral challenge would he be setting for us? What spiritual progress could we make?'

'Is life all about moral challenge and spiritual progress?' Max asked. 'What that old man most wanted from it was happiness. Just to be happy. Like most of us, I think.'

Max was pleased by Narayan's persistence in keeping in contact. He felt lonely without him and had come to rely on these phone calls.

'Next week I'm flying on to the town of Banda Aceh in Indonesia,' he said. 'That's where the tsunami did its worst, I gather, being so close to the epicentre of the shock.'

When he arrived at Banda Aceh he learnt that the wave here had been eighty feet high and had swept a mile inland. Tens of thousands of people had died; freighters had capsized and boats had been smashed and tossed into the trees. Half-a-million people had been made homeless, and there were fears of outbreaks of typhoid, dysentery and hepatitis. Max took some photos but spent most of his time inoculating people against infection in the medical tents that had been pitched among the ruins. He'd just finished a fourteen-hour stint and was sweaty and exhausted when Narayan rang.

'Is it as bad there as you'd been told?'

'Worse, I think. There are some cases of cholera, and that's such a horrible disease. We're trying to control the water supply. I've inoculated about a hundred people already.'

'I really admire you for what you're doing.'

'Please don't admire me. I've got feet of clay, as you once said to me about yourself. Do you remember?'

'I've still got mine. If anything, they're worse.' He paused. 'Max, I can't stop thinking of you. Be honest with me: is that rather pointless?'

'What do you mean?'

'I think I've fallen in love with you again. Does that embarrass you?'

Max looked around and wondered if it was wrong to feel joy in the middle of such misery. An excavator was clawing its way through the chaos of ruined houses, while sniffer dogs searched for the bodies crushed under the rubble. Four-fifths of the dead were women and children. Less able to escape the wave, their bodies were found buried in the mud, in piteous jumbles of limbs and torsos.

Max found an unexpected gladness in what Narayan had said, even in these appalling circumstances. His openness had that old familiar appeal: it showed extraordinary trust. He exposed himself so unguardedly, not knowing whether Max would return his feelings.

'I used to be so conditioned and conventional,' Narayan went on. 'I was always worrying what other people thought. I know myself much better now and feel freed by that.' He seemed to screw up his courage before continuing. 'Max, I want to live with you. You wanted to live with me, once. Is it too late for that now?'

Max was relieved he could still feel exultant. An almost shocking surge of hope invaded him, almost against his will. As he took in his surroundings, he wondered if the people here could ever hope again, if happiness could revisit their ruined lives.

Eventually he said, 'If your aunts and uncles objected to Mohini, how will they react to me?'

'I'm not that feeble now. I can stand up to them, pathetic as their prejudices are.'

'And what about the part of you that's so very hetero?'

'I love you as a person, not a body. How often in life does anyone really fall in love?'

Max found it ironic that Narayan was taking the initiative. Last time it was Max who had started the affair and loved the more; now the situation was astoundingly reversed. If it had to be unequal, was it better to be more the lover or the loved?

'Very seldom,' Max answered him. 'I've fallen in love only three times in my life. Sometimes I wonder if I ever will again.'

He thought he'd once felt too much in Narayan's power, and he'd occasionally resented it. But now it was he who had the power and he knew he must not abuse this dubious advantage. He was touched by Narayan's feeling, of course. However, recalling his previous changes of emotional direction, he didn't now entirely trust it.

'I hope I'm one of the three,' Narayan answered. 'And I hope that in time you will fall in love again.'

'Of course you're one of the three,' Max said, laughing with some embarrassment. 'But who in the world knows what the future holds for us?'

∴

Max was working hard while he was travelling, writing up his notes for the new book. He wished to emphasise the enormous amount of aid that would be needed to repair the damage. When he returned to Chennai he stayed with Clare and Tammy and initially avoided contacting Narayan. He tried to resist thinking of him too much, fearing it might affect the concentration he needed to write. He asked Tammy to come up with some conjectural figure for the losses in the fishing community.

'About eighty per cent of the dead in Tamil Nadu were fishermen,' Tammy said. 'Almost forty thousand boats, plus miles of netting, have been destroyed. The remaining fishermen are already horribly in debt to the shark money lenders, as most of India's poor have always been.'

In his book, Max decided to put the need to help the tsunami victims into the context of aid in general. He set the promises of Western governments against what they'd actually got around to donating. Tammy provided him with more figures to substantiate his argument, stressing that the West spent about eighty billion dollars on aid to the Third World in 2004, compared with a thousand billion dollars on munitions. Almost half of that was spent by the USA, whose foreign aid amounted to four per cent of its arms bill; in the UK it was one-sixth. Galvanised by these figures and the priorities they represented, Max decided to write more about the need for medical aid.

'Yes, it's health that divides the rich and the poor worlds most of all,' Tammy said when Max told him this. 'Western countries should be subsidising Third World medical care, providing hospital equipment and drugs India can't afford for more than a privileged minority. Our so-called economic boom gives the wrong impression. So much attention is focused on poverty in Africa, but there are more poor in India than in that entire continent.'

'India seems to be two nations now,' said Clare, 'as England was in the nineteenth century.'

'There are a few MRI scanners for the prospering middle class,' Tammy said. 'But that obscures what happens among the disadvantaged. There's a terrible lack of organised public health care. The poor have to rely on private doctors many can't afford, and a lot of those medics have limited training. The immunisation of children is totally inadequate. Their under-nourishment leads to them being underweight and stunted, like that cripple's daughter. The only hope for seeing any improvement is by publicising the facts more widely.'

∴

Clare was intensely relieved to hear that the boy assassin had finally had his death sentence commuted on appeal. She was now allowed to visit him in prison, and she asked Tammy to accompany her. They were vetted for drugs, sniffed at by dogs, and even required to have their mouths inspected. They were then led to the visiting room, which was beyond the bleak prison yard, its high walls surmounted by huge coils of barbed wire.

Clare was having lessons in Tamil but Tammy helped to translate for them. A warder led the boy in, shackled and at first extremely shy. He glanced nervously at Clare and Tammy, as if puzzled why they wished to visit him or suspicious of their motives. He looked thinner; his hair had been closely cropped and he had a small bruise upon his forehead.

He spoke eventually of his sorrow for the crime he had committed.

'What I did was horrible. I remember it now like a dream. A kind of madness entered me. I was very frightened. I didn't really know what I was doing.'

He didn't lay responsibility on his uncle and his brother for pressurising him. He said nothing about the fact they were now dead, as if mention of them would disturb him too much to go on. He didn't speak of his parents, who had been killed in that communal riot, although he did talk about the village he'd been brought up in

'I long again to climb the coconut palms… to hear the cocks crowing… to hear the jangling of goat bells and the lowing of the cows. I hope one day I'll be free to go back.'

'Do you have any relatives there still?' Clare asked.

'I have some aunts and cousins but they're not allowed to visit me. One of them can write but I'm only allowed a letter once a month. I can't read myself but I have an older friend who can.'

'Were you ever tortured?' Clare asked quietly.

Tammy murmured the question because a guard stood nearby, although he looked rather bored and inattentive. To her inexpressible relief, the boy said no.

'Are you were ever bullied by the other prisoners?'

'Just a bit,' he answered, 'but I stand up for myself. And I have this older friend who helps defend me.'

'Will they give you some training in technical work for when you're released?'

'I don't know, but I hope so,' he replied. 'There are classes in plumbing and electricity. These things are much needed in my village.'

'The prison service speaks of training of this sort but seldom manages to put it into action because of the crowded conditions and lack of money.' Tammy told Clare. 'The prisoners tend to fall into three categories: mad or sad or bad. This one's a combination of all three, I think.'

After half an hour, the warder fairly amiably said their time was up.

'We'll visit you again,' Clare said. 'I promise.'

The boy smiled as he raised his shackled wrists to shake their hands. As Tammy and Clare walked out past the high security walls, she wondered how long his imprisonment would last. It was obvious he must be punished for the murder he had committed, and society must be protected, but she hoped he wouldn't lose all hope in life in the harsh years that lay ahead of him. These thoughts made her more acutely aware of her own easy, privileged existence.

∴

A couple of days later, Clare went with Tammy to visit the cripple's widow, whose name they now learnt was Kamila. She lived in a sprawling shantytown in the inland suburbs of Chennai, which had been spared the onslaught of the tsunami. Kamila lived alone in a ramshackle hut that had been patched with flattened kerosene tins and sacking. In the street outside was a malodorous, open drain. Rain was drumming on the corrugated iron roof when they arrived. Again, Tammy translated from Tamil.

'I was married for fifteen years,' Kamila said. 'I miss my husband terribly, though I now know he did great wrong. I told the magistrate I didn't know at the time what he was up to. He told me nothing. He wished me to stay innocent in case I was interrogated. I loved him very much. I was terrified appearing in the courtroom and answering all those questions. But in the end the magistrate was kind to me. He was like my father with his white hair and beard.'

'You must also miss your daughter terribly,' Clare said to her.

'I do,' Kamila answered. 'The loss gets no better. Every morning I wake up to this weight upon my heart... this pain. I worry that I didn't do enough for her. I took her to the mobile clinic but it was too late to stop the typhus. She had this purple rash and bad headaches. We put her to bed, where she soon became delirious. Her father was frantic about her. We tried to get a doctor to visit but there aren't enough doctors. There aren't enough drugs and medicines. She died in her fever, shaking and crying out.'

'Tell her how deeply I sympathise,' Clare said to Tammy, remembering Violet fighting for breath but then being put into an oxygen tent to relieve her suffering.

'Is there any chance Kamila might marry again and have another child?' Clare asked Tammy.

'I think I'm unlikely to find another husband,' Kamila replied when Tammy had posed Clare's question. 'There's prejudice against men marrying widows. I can't provide a dowry and I'm probably too old to conceive again.'

'How old are you? Clare asked.

'I don't really know… perhaps forty.' She smiled timidly. 'Also I'm a Dalit and many village people look down on us.' Clare felt she was quite unused to telling people this. 'Also I can't read or write. I'm trying to learn but I find it very difficult.'

She said she was helping to look after the daughter of a neighbour, who was an Adavasi. The little girl eventually appeared, overcoming her embarrassment in front of these strangers. Kamila stroked the girl's cheek and kissed her, and the little girl buried her face in the embroidered sari Kamila had specially put on for their visit.

'Adavasi?' Clare asked.

'The Adavasis are tribal people who make up eight per cent of the population,' Tammy explained. 'The Dalits have become a fairly vocal political force, but the Adavasis, who suffer even worse social discrimination, are not yet this organised.'

Kamila offered them tea. The water was boiled on a smoky primus stove, and the tea was the usual thick, milky and very sweet concoction that Clare had come to like. When they left, Kamila bowed her head and put her hands together. Clare stepped impulsively forward to kiss her on the cheek. Kamila looked embarrassed but also moved, so Clare didn't think her impulse out of place.

'Let's provide the money for a dowry for her,' Tammy suggested later. 'It might help her marry one of the widowed fishermen who lost their wives and children in the tsunami.'

Clare jumped at the idea and suggested something else. 'If needed, let's also pay for IVF treatment so that she might conceive again.'

'That's very rare in India,' answered Tammy. 'Only the extremely affluent could afford it. It's a good idea, though, so let's ask when we see her next, but she might be too shy and modest to accept such an offer.'

∴

Clare was starting to conciliate Tammy's relatives. She invited The Battleaxe aunt to a meal she'd prepared, having studied a Tamil cookery book, and managed to avoid making too many disastrous errors. As Tammy was seen as practically an alcoholic, The Battleaxe was impressed that Clare should drink only mango juice, unaware that such temperance had been briefly assumed for her benefit. A few days later, The Sergeant Majorette asked Clare around for a modest cup of camomile tea. At last she was prepared to overlook the disreputable fact that Clare was a divorcee, deciding she might even be sufficiently in love with Tammy not to capriciously get rid of him after a year or two in what she saw as the Western manner. She was also pleased to hear how much Clare wanted children, although disappointed when Tammy said they planned to have only two.

The elephantine uncles relented far more quickly. They were delighted to discover that Clare now cooked Tamil dishes, and didn't stint in the amount she fed them, which they consumed with joyous appetite and the occasional appraising belch. They guzzled formidable amounts of whisky too, and laughed at Tammy's jokes about the aunts, even when they were subtly scabrous. They overflowed their chairs, quaffing and interminably smoking, shaking with raucous laughter, triple chins wobbling and bellies quaking.

∴

Clare had resigned her job as a charity fundraiser in Los Angeles, and applied to teach media studies in the university in Chennai, having gained a degree in that. If she succeeded, Tammy and Narayan would be her colleagues there. Maria would not be in Chennai, though, unless her Roman plans failed. Maria had phoned Clare recently.

'The combat between Antonio and Sam, which is not always unarmed, seems to be drawing to a merciful conclusion. The

Animal's decided The Putto takes after him in looks, apart from his designer stubble and mane of greasy hair, which he mistakenly imagines to be so sexy. Certainly, they both favour the same malevolent expression when not having their own way, but they also share the same sweetie smile when they fondly imagine that they are. To tell the truth, I'm rather enjoying having two males in my affections. I'd only return to find a pacific, soulful Indian if a lethal civil war again breaks out between them.

Clare now had even more of a soft spot for Maria. She relished hearing of the extravagant drama of her life, which she knew she partly created for Clare's entertainment, and hoped she'd hear more of it through her impressively inventive exaggerations.

∴

After a fortnight, Max, now confident his work was progressing well, went to see Narayan, who seemed hurt that he'd not done so earlier.

'I was starting to wonder if I'd scared you off,' Narayan said, taking Max's hand and holding it for several seconds, as had been his wont. 'With what I said on the phone, I mean, when you were in Banda Aceh. You didn't think I was flinging myself at you, did you? If you did, I could always take it back.'

'I flung myself at you once,' Max reminded him, 'but then I started to worry in case I'd scared you off! So, no… please don't take it back.'

'Here I am in love with you again, I think. Do you love me back or are you playing hard to get? Are you just trying to lead me on?'

'These embarrassing leading questions,' said Max. 'I won't answer them, thanks, if it's all the same to you.'

'Why not? Because you like to keep me in suspense or pay me back? You're really horrible, Max.' Narayan laughed. 'I think I may go off you once again... if I still can.'

Max found his directness as appealing as ever. He wasn't yet sure if he was in love with Narayan again, but he was certainly beguiled by his amusing, unsentimental frankness.

∴

One morning, Clare divulged that she was pregnant. She and Tammy were both delighted. Max was delighted too, though a twinge of regret mingled with his joy, and he had a sense of wasted opportunity. For a while he regretted losing her, but he knew he must stop these backward-looking hankerings and exult in her being pregnant by a man he much respected. He should now concentrate on the possible revival of his affair with Narayan, about which he ought to be more open with himself – more self-aware and so less unforgiving.

Tammy and Clare were friendly with Narayan and invited him and Max to supper several times. Tammy stimulated Max with his opinions, and lent him his computer to carry out research.

'Much of this financial aid will doubtless disappear into the wrong pockets,' said Tammy, although Max thought he had lost some of his cynicism. 'What does get through will be frustrated by the usual, bumbling officialdom. What's more, people in the West will forget about the issue as soon as they've slaked their short-lived consciences.'

'You miserable old pessimist,' Clare said. 'The tsunami's revolutionised the situation. Individuals are giving to the destitute as they never have before.'

'Bully for the bleeding-heart Western individuals. What about their stingy, dawdling governments?'

'Their stingy governments are waking up to the problem,' Max answered. 'They're now cancelling some national debts in Africa.'

'Not before time,' said Tammy, 'even though some debts were incurred by monstrously corrupt dictators who salted the loot away in foreign bank accounts.'

'Let's hope that's not used as an excuse to be less generous,' Max replied. 'Further aid needs to given, but I agree it needs greater control so it's spent wisely and where it's needed.'

Prompted by these discussions, Max arranged to sell most of his securities and real estate, intending to donate the proceeds to the tsunami survivors. 'One day I'll probably have no capital at all, apart from what I can earn as a writer,' he told Narayan.

'You've always wanted that, and I love your wacky idealism,' Narayan said. 'I want us to live together, and I do have a salary of my own, you know.'

Narayan's airy carelessness about the matter of money charmed Max. He wanted to talk only about this plan to live together, and Max found himself responding with a keenness that surprised him. The next time they met, Narayan brought up the idea again, becoming more urgent the more Max opposed it.

'You're far wackier than I am,' Max teased him. 'You decide on things with such crazy suddenness. You change your mind and your affections, as you did with Mohini. You burn out your feelings by acting on them too fervently and too fast.'

'Maybe I did once,' Narayan conceded. 'I was attracted to Mohini, but I didn't love her as much as I should have… not enough to marry. I feel guilty about that, although she wasn't as much in love with me as she'd imagined. I think she wanted to remarry to please her over-demanding parents, not anticipating how choosy they would prove to be. Look, my feelings for you won't burn out, I promise.'

'They did once before, remember?'

'Why remind me, Max?'

'I was horribly in love with you… certifiably insane!'

'And don't you think for my sake you could go insane again?'

Max paused. For an instant he remembered Rick with all his old vitality and fun, diving clowningly into the swimming pool, twisting in the air and pulling loony faces. This led to his recalling Narayan strenuously climbing the temple a year ago, laughing at Max below for being so slow and tentative. Rick and Narayan: his memories of them seemed to briefly intermingle, and he was surprised by the exhilaration suddenly welling up within him. At last he answered with a certainty he didn't know he had, in an attempt to match Narayan's humour.

'Yes, for your sake, I do think I could go insane again.'

'Enough to want to marry me?'

'Yes.'

His answer came out so suddenly that Max couldn't quite believe he'd actually said it. He leant forward to kiss Narayan on the mouth.

'So you love me again?' Narayan asked, kissing him back, and holding him. 'Why did you take so long?' His body was shaking in Max's arms, shaking with the laughter of his intense euphoria. 'Look, India's light years away from gay marriages, I know. But let's do something special, even if Tammy thinks it embarrassingly schmaltzy.'

'He married Clare by exchanging rings,' Max pointed out. 'He refused to follow the Hindu custom. What's the Hindu equivalent of a ring, incidentally?'

'The man gives the woman a thali, a reddened cord. He puts it around her neck and ties it with a knot.'

For a day they deliberated before telling Clare and Tammy.

'We're planning a kind of personal symbolic marriage. We want our close friends to know about 'our love'.

'I'll be telling a few 'select relations', Narayan said, 'and if they don't like it, they can bloody well lump it. I won't flaunt it in their faces, but I refuse to be furtive about my gayness any longer. I hope they'll at least acknowledge it and not treat it as some shameful secret… or some rare, unmentionable disease.'

Clare was really pleased.

'I'll certainly stand by you,' she said.

'I'll do so too,' Tammy promised, 'whatever the ignorance and bigotry you're bound to meet, especially among the middle-aged and elderly.' He laughed. 'Just when straight people start to give up marriage, gay people decide to take it up. I thought you gays were so independent, yet here you are aping us benighted straights.'

'Tammy, if you go on being so cynical,' Clare said, 'Narayan may not ask you to be his best man.'

'I don't want Tammy as my best man,' Narayan said. 'He's far too sarky and phlegmatic. Anyhow, we're each other's best men, Max and I. We want it to be just the two of us.'

'So that's my reputation, is it?' Tammy protested. 'Cynical, sarky and phlegmatic.'

'You're still such an ersatz Englishman,' Narayan said. 'You're terrified of showing emotion of any kind.'

'The result of your education at that frigid English school,' Clare added, 'where the warmth of human feeling is so suspect. Thank God I've managed to cure you just a bit.'

∴

As Max and Narayan approached the sea temple in the dusk, they had to make their way past the new discoveries. Another granite elephant had been revealed; someone had hung a string of marigolds around its head. The archaeologists were digging down around another piece of sunken stone, and the couple wondered what image would eventually emerge. Possibly Vishnu and Lakshmi, symbols of married love. Possibly Hanuman, a symbol of human loyalty. Just possibly a holy serpent.

Holy? Max recalled the old man on the Andaman Islands, whose daughter had been bitten by a snake from out of the sea, and how he'd thought of the inexplicable cruelty of the world of nature. It was believed the tsunami had caused over a quarter of a million deaths altogether, and had left five million homeless. About fifty thousand had died on the coast of Tamil Nadu alone, and the cold anonymity of their deaths appalled Max. Their destruction seemed so arbitrary and final. He thought of Subramaniam's words: 'The souls of the departed are beyond destruction. They migrate into other earthly forms or merge at last into the Atman.'

Max longed to accept this difficult belief, as he'd longed to do when Rick had died. He had set up a trust fund to help the surviving fishing community in Sandeha. He'd named the trust after Rick, wanting to commemorate him as well as all those whose names would soon be lost, especially the unknown children swept out to sea, drifting for a while with the silent undercurrents or lying among the coral ridges. He was determined that Rick's life should not to be forgotten, that he shouldn't fade into the oblivion that had seemed to quietly haunt him as he lay dying.

They'd reached the sea temple and up they climbed, he and Narayan. The also time they did this was in the intense heat of the day, but now night was falling. As Max reached up for the handholds, some of the scenes of destruction he'd witnessed came to mind, but the memory, like the memory of Rick's death, seemed to be losing something of its pain. He remembered Rick's last ironic smile, the sudden laughter of some children among the horrors of Banda Aceh, the laughter of the archaeological divers as they put to sea to film the nameless underwater temple.

He wished for laughter for himself as well, believing it went with the detachment the Bhagavad Gita taught: the release from pain and grief as well as from fear and anger. He'd taken that little book on his travels, reading it repeatedly so as not to be overwhelmed by the suffering he'd seen. He recalled a passage about the terrors of Arjuna, which ended with the face of Krishna bending down upon him, bringing him peace of spirit at last. More than ever, Max longed to love one god, ultimately benevolent in some mysterious way. Krishna's claim to be both the father and the mother of the universe, an intelligent light in its fathomless obscurity, made Max long for it to be true, if only as a metaphor to give some transcendent meaning to our precarious existence on this lonely little planet.

He thought of Kamila and how she had found light and meaning in the existence of her stunted little girl. It was a sadness that much haunted him. But Tammy, true to his word, had provided her with a dowry and she had indeed married a widowed fisherman; and Clare was looking into the possibility of Kamila having IVF.

As Max and Narayan climbed, they placed their feet gently on the stonework. Max turned to look at the immensity of the ocean, the beauty and the peace of which seemed ruthlessly ironic when he thought of the recent destruction it had caused. As he thought of the survivors, he hoped that his book would make some contribution, however modest, to growing world opinion in favour of far more foreign aid. Yesterday he'd watched the many Live 8 rock concerts being broadcast across the globe, and he felt cautiously optimistic about their ideal of reducing poverty in Africa. He'd already decided that his next book would be about AIDS in Africa: he'd focus on the hospitals and drugs that were so urgently required and the widespread need to educate people about prevention through the use of condoms, which he believed should be free. He also wanted to learn the cost of arms sold by the West to African governments, relative to what they spent on health. He'd already discussed this with Narayan, who had offered to help with his research and to come with him on his travels when his job allowed. Narayan hoped as much as Max did that this challenging shared enterprise would bond them together even closer.

Max suddenly became aware of the risk of falling so far to the beach, which intensified the excitement of feeling Narayan so physically close, breathing fast and sweating. Soon they neared the finial of the temple. At the prospect of holding Narayan tightly in his arms, Max felt the blood pulse in his veins. Narayan was the first to reach the top and he stretched down a hand to help Max up.

They stood there in solitude, the sun gone down. Narayan took the thali from his pocket, hung it around Max's neck and then tied a knot in it. Then Max put the ring he held on Narayan's finger. After they'd embraced and kissed, a long lingering kiss, they stood in silence to watch the moonlight glisten on the emerging buried carvings far below and the gently rolling and withdrawing waves.

SB

TOGETHER : DISCOVER

For more on our authors and titles, visit our website
spellbindingmedia.co.uk

Follow us on Twitter
@SBMediaUK

Join the conversation
facebook.com/spellbindingmedia

Subscribe to our free newsletter
spellbindingmedia.co.uk/subscribe

For interviews and audio excerpts
youtube/spellbindingmedia